LEABHARLANNA CHONTAE NA GAILLIMHE
(GALWAY COUNTY LIBRARIES)

BS

Acc. No. F. 123,528....   Class No......................

Date of Return	Date of Return	Date of Return

Books are on loan for 21 days from date of issue.

Fines for overdue books: 10c for each week or portion of a week plus cost of postage incurred in recovery.

Joyce Holms was born and educated in Glasgow. The victim of a low boredom threshold, she has held a variety of jobs, from teaching window dressing and managing a hotel on the Isle of Arran to working for an Edinburgh detective agency and running a B&B in the Highlands. Married with two grown up children, she lives in Edinburgh and her interests include hill-walking and garden design.

HOT POTATO

Solicitor Tam Buchanan and his friend
and colleague Fizz Fitzgerald arrange to
get away from it all on a hill-walking
holiday in the Scottish Highlands. Unfortunately, their idyllic break is ruined
somewhat when they witness an horrific
car crash. Fizz and Buchanan hear the
dying wish of the crash victim — a plea to
protect the second passenger in the car, an
elderly gentleman with a price on his
head. Taking a pit-stop to decide what to
do, they are amazed to witness the police
make a murderous attempt on the old
man's life. Getting away from it all now
includes getting as far away from the long
arm of the law as possible!

JOYCE HOLMS

HOT POTATO

Complete and Unabridged

ULVERSCROFT
Leicester

First published in Great Britain in 2002 by
Allison & Busby Limited, London

First Large Print Edition
published 2004
by arrangement with
Allison & Busby Limited, London

British Library CIP Data

Holms, Joyce
   Hot potato.—Large print ed.—
Ulverscroft large print series: mystery
1. Fizz (Fictitious character: Holms)—Fiction
2. Buchanan, Tam (Fictitious character)—Fiction
3. Law students—Scotland—Fiction 4. Lawyers—Scotland
—Fiction 5. Detective and mystery stories
6. Large type books
I. Title
823.9′14 [F]

ISBN 1–84395–507–5

Published by
F. A. Thorpe (Publishing)
Anstey, Leicestershire

Set by Words & Graphics Ltd.
Anstey, Leicestershire
Printed and bound in Great Britain by
T. J. International Ltd., Padstow, Cornwall

This book is printed on acid-free paper

F 123, 528

£ 28 . 00

1

'You'd better believe me, Buchanan,' Fizz said, hitching round in her seat to spear him with her eyes. 'This is a matter of life or death.'

'No it isn't.'

'Yes it is — well, *virtually*. You have about thirty seconds to stop this car or I won't answer for the consequences.'

Buchanan waved a hand at the terrain beyond the windscreen. 'What's the point of stopping here? There isn't a blade of grass you could hide behind for a hundred yards on either side. You'd have to do a ten minute hike across peat bog before you came to a scrap of cover.'

'Frankly, I'm beyond caring about privacy. If you'd stopped back at that bridge where I first asked you to stop I wouldn't be in this state now.'

Buchanan had suspected for the last five minutes that it would all turn out to be his fault. He himself had taken the opportunity, as they descended the track from the summit of Stac Pollaidh, to wander off into the trees, and he couldn't imagine why Fizz hadn't thought to do the same. She knew as well as he did that the next part of their journey would be through the most uninhabited part of the UK, indeed she probably knew the topography like the back of her hand, having climbed here before.

He searched ahead for a patch of greenery or at least some fallen rocks but the floor of the glen was flat and featureless from the road to the sharp rise of the mountains on either side.

'You can hang on for a couple of minutes, surely,' he said. 'I can see a loch in the distance. There's bound to be a better spot around there.'

'Look, Buchanan,' Fizz said, pointing. 'Watch my lips. Right here is just fine. Stop this bloody car and let me out. Now.'

'What if someone comes along?'

'Dammit, what if they do? There are no public toilets between here and Ullapool. If I gotta go, I gotta go! Besides, we've passed only a tractor, two hikers and a sheep since we left Stac Pollaidh and that was all in the first two miles.'

Buchanan glanced in the rear view mirror, his foot hovering over the brake. 'Okay, if you're that desperate. No wait! There's something coming.'

The speck of black that had just swung into

view around a distant bend took only seconds to expand into a dirty Mitsubishi people carrier. Seeing a set of bull bars approaching his back bumper at a speed which was suicidal on a single-track road, Buchanan swung into the nearest passing place and let it flash by.

'Bloody hell,' Fizz commented. 'He's in a hurry!'

'She,' said Buchanan, watching the erratic course of the vehicle as it dwindled into the distance. He had seen only a flash of blonde hair and a bare arm behind the wheel but he had the impression that there had been someone else slouched in the passenger seat.

Fizz seemed to have forgotten her crisis situation for the moment. She was sitting half in and half out of the doorway with her eyes on the road ahead as if she were in momentary expectation of witnessing a horrendous accident. And, in a moment, she did.

Just as the Mitsubishi was about to pass out of their line of sight it swerved into the nearside verge, over-corrected in a wide arc that swung it violently sideways and, in a blur of movement, started rolling boot-over-bull-bars, along the road.

Half a mile away, Buchanan could hear the grating clangour as it hit the tarmac again and again, glass and debris bursting from it at every impact. Finally it left the road and ploughed into the peat, and the silence of the summer afternoon settled over the scene like a shroud.

'Oh, my God!' Fizz whipped in her feet and slammed the door as Buchanan gunned the engine and took off in a spurt of gravel. 'Nobody's going to step out of that one without a scratch. Sure you want to look, Buchanan?'

Buchanan had been acting on autopilot, dashing to the rescue like you were supposed to do in this sort of situation. Fizz's rhetorical question didn't slow his knee-jerk response but it did remind him to steel himself in case he was about to witness something he wouldn't forget in a hurry.

A deep trench scored across the peat from the roadway to the upside-down vehicle. The blonde woman had been thrown clear and now lay some twenty metres away, her long hair glued to her face with blood. More blood was pumping at an alarming rate out of a huge gash in her thigh and as Buchanan dropped to his knees beside her he could see she was struggling to breathe.

He hadn't a clue what to do. Mouth to mouth resuscitation? A tourniquet? Treat her for shock?

'You're okay,' he lied helplessly. 'You're going to be fine . . . '

Fizz's knee took him in the small of the back, shoving him aside, and he felt her hand grabbing his shoulder for balance as she put a foot on the gash and stood on it, lifting the other foot off the ground for added pressure.

'Femoral artery,' she muttered. 'It's the only way you can stop it spouting.'

That didn't sound too good to Buchanan. He lacked the experience Fizz had garnered as a member of a Mountain Rescue team but he had a feeling that they'd have trouble keeping up that amount of pressure till they got this woman to a doctor. She'd already lost a huge amount of blood and could hardly travel upwards of twenty-five miles with Fizz standing on her thigh.

He used his hanky to smooth the bloody hair away from her face and found two half-focused grey eyes staring up at him. A two-inch cut above one of them had opened her forehead like a little gaping mouth and blood was spilling from it and running across her temples into her ears. He wiped it away, knowing it was futile, knowing beyond doubt that the woman was already too far gone to save.

She opened bone white lips and started to say something but a bout of painful choking shook her into silence.

'Don't try to speak,' Buchanan said. 'We'll look after you. You're going to be all right.'

She moved a hand. 'Help him . . . '

Buchanan, suddenly remembering the other passenger, glanced quickly around but saw no one. 'Your passenger? Yes, don't worry. We'll look after you both.'

He started to get to his knees but hesitated, seeing by the woman's agitation that she had more she needed to say.

'Please . . . ' She choked again and a good deal of blood spilled from the corner of her mouth. Buchanan cringed to see how much it hurt her, but she was determined to speak. Again and again she struggled for enough breath to get the words out, managing only the merest puffs of sound and getting visibly weaker with every attempt.

Finally, and in fragments, she whispered what Buchanan understood to be: ' . . . trying to kill him. They're coming.'

He twisted round to look up at Fizz's face and she lifted her brows at him.

'Somebody's trying to kill your passenger?' she asked the woman and waited several seconds before she got any response. Then the woman managed a feeble nod.

'Police . . . kill . . . '

'Police? The police are trying to kill him?'

Fizz tightened her grip on Buchanan's shoulder, but he couldn't imagine what she was trying to communicate, other than perhaps that they were dealing with a madwoman.

He said, 'Well, don't worry about that right now . . .'

'White car . . .' The woman's eyes widened with the intensity of a final effort and Buchanan had to bring his ear close to her mouth to catch the words. 'Chasing . . . Please . . .'

'They were chasing you just now?' said Fizz's voice close to Buchanan's ear. 'Is that why you were speeding?'

The woman's eyes closed, then opened to show a line of white between her lashes. 'Quick . . . save him.'

'Yes, yes, of course we will,' Buchanan murmured, anxious only to make her stop talking and rest. 'We won't let any harm come to him I promise you.'

The grey eyes focused suddenly on his with such unblinking intensity that it was a moment or two before he realised that they weren't ever going to blink again.

Fizz crouched down and dug her fingers into the base of the woman's neck. 'Dead,' she said, expressionlessly and ran a hand over the still eyelids to close them. 'I don't think we could have got her to hospital alive whatever we'd done.'

Buchanan got to his feet and found his knees wobbling. This was the first time he'd actually witnessed someone's passing and he felt as if his guts had been stirred with a wooden spoon. It was also, as far as he knew, the first time Fizz had been present at a death — although she had certainly seen more than one corpse and at least one of them a pretty gruesome one — but showed very little sign of distress. Profound empathy with her fellow creatures had never been her long suit.

She glanced over at the upturned car. 'We'd better find casualty number two,' she said, 'and if this lady knew what she was talking about, we'd better find him real soon. Like, before the baddies arrive.'

'You think we should take her seriously?' Buchanan followed her, at a jog, towards the people carrier. 'She may have been hallucinating. It doesn't seem likely, does it?'

When Fizz didn't answer he followed her gaze and saw a pair of feet sticking out from the buckled rear door of the Mitzubishi. The vehicle had landed on the forward edge of its roof, embedding itself a couple of feet deep in the soft earth. This meant that the rear end stuck up at a sharp angle beneath which, in a pool of petrol, lay an elderly man.

Fizz, beating Buchanan to the scene by a short head, crawled under the overhanging metal and felt the man's pulse.

'He's alive,' she said, and prised open an eyelid. 'Unconscious . . . but I can't find any broken bones. If I'm right he's one lucky bastard. I think we have to take a chance and move him. Let me try to raise him a little, then you grab his ankles and slide him out.'

Buchanan did as he was told, sweating nervously, and a long thin body slid forth into the sunlight, virtually unmarked and smelling strongly of petrol. 'You sure we should be moving him?'

'No,' said Fizz with more than her customary honesty. 'But we don't have a lot of choice, do we? We can't leave him here, the nearest phone is God only knows how many miles away, and for all we know the police are hot on his trail and ready to shoot on sight.'

'I suspect we can disregard the last bit, Fizz. Look at him. He looks like a vicar.'

Even Fizz couldn't have denied that. The guy was well into his seventies with a halo of white fluffy curls and he lay on his back in an attitude of such placid repose that he needed only someone to cross his hands upon his breast to be the very picture of a departed saint. Ignore the grass and mud that was stuck to him and you'd put him down as a respectable well-to-do landowner. The tweed suit was a trifle old-fashioned but it hadn't come from Marks & Spencers and neither had the Omega watch showing beneath his cuff.

It did occur to Buchanan that one could not always go by looks (witness the diminutive, angel-faced and golden-ringleted harpy at his elbow) but no way could he bring himself to imagine this guy as a dangerous criminal.

'It's academic,' Fizz decided. 'We have to get him to a hospital anyway, and we won't be doing him any favours by hanging around to see if his lady friend was kidding or not. I don't want him dying on me, do you?'

There was only one answer to that so Buchanan took the chap's shoulders and Fizz took his feet and, with much swearing from Fizz and sweating from Buchanan, they folded him into the back seat of the Saab and covered him with a traveling rug.

'Which way is the nearest outpost of civilization?' Buchanan said. 'Back the way we've come or forward to Achiltibuie?'

'Back the way we've come. Achiltibuie is nearer but I'm pretty sure there isn't a doctor around there and Lucky Jim here is going to need more than a district nurse. There's bound to be at least a telephone at Ledmore junction.'

Buchanan swung the Saab in an arc and started back along the single-track road as fast as he dared. From time to time there came a soft groan from Lucky Jim in the back seat but Fizz kept a close eye on him and reported no sign of his return to consciousness.

She had apparently forgotten her urgent need for toilet facilities — indeed only ten minutes had passed since she had first complained — but the sight of the conveniently wooded bridge she'd spotted earlier brought her discomfort smartly back to the front of her mind.

'Stop! I can't wait another minute!'

Buchanan slowed down and pulled over into the opening of a rough track that meandered over the bridge. Fizz had the door open before he had the hand brake on and lost no time in scrambling down the bank of the river below. There being plenty of bushes around, Buchanan took the opportunity to make use of them while he had the chance and was standing there in the thicket, zipping up his fly, when a white car suddenly appeared over a sharp incline in front of them and sped past without checking its considerable speed. Inside, in caps and short-sleeved shirts, sat two policemen, both of whom gave the Saab a hard scrutiny in passing.

Buchanan knew better than to leap to conclusions. Just because there were two policemen in the vicinity it didn't necessarily follow that they were intent on killing the person currently under his travelling rug. However, he was curious enough to scramble to the top of a nearby hillock from where he could catch intermittent glimpses of the police car heading towards the crash site. During the periods when it was out of sight he tried to pick out the corner where the Mitsubishi had left the road but the terrain was too confusing and the road too twisting for him to be sure of the exact spot. It took him by surprise, therefore, when he spotted the white car again and realised it was not getting further away but racing back towards him at an appalling speed.

He hadn't a clue what was happening. Had the woman been hallucinating? Lying? Were these genuine policemen or masquerading assassins?

Cursing with dismay he sprang up off the rock he'd been sitting on, lost his balance on the slope and took a header into a patch of brambles. He didn't particularly register the pain, although judging from the depth of the scratches he discovered later it must have been considerable, but it seemed to take forever to claw himself free from the thorns and start plunging down the hill to his car.

He couldn't see the Saab for the trees till he was quite close to it but when he did he was just in time to see Lucky Jim emerge from the rear door and start off, staggering, across the bridge.

'Get back!' he started to yell, intent only on gaining time to think, but then grabbed a handy branch and dragged himself to a halt. He could already hear the approaching police car. It was too late to do anything before it arrived. Maybe the best thing for him to do was to let the man wander into the woods and stay hidden till the situation clarified itself. And Fizz? Only a couple of minutes had passed. If she'd heard the car approach would she have the sense to keep out of sight?

He hesitated, willing the stumbling figure to keep heading for the trees, but to his horror, the man stopped on the bridge, leaning his thigh against the low parapet and staring over into the river below.

'They're coming!' Buchanan shouted. 'Get out of sight!'

Nothing stirred. It was like one of those nightmares where you can hear the approach of the THING but can't move a muscle.

Then the white car burst into view and, instead of braking, dropped a gear with a roar and drove straight at the man on the bridge.

2

Although the urgency of Fizz's need had faded somewhat while her mind had been on other things, she was on borrowed time before she made it down the riverbank. The river wasn't all that wide but it was hellish deep and as fast flowing as all-get-out so she wasn't taking any chances.

There was fairly firm standing under the ancient stone arch which was just as well because if she'd felt less than safe she'd have done it where she stood and to hell with Buchanan's sensibilities. A widdle was only a widdle, for God's sake, and he wasn't going to peek.

The noise of the torrent was so magnified beneath the bridge that the first she realised that something was going on was when she heard the fast revving of a car. She was washing her hands at that moment and it took her a couple of seconds to realise that it wasn't the Saab she was hearing.

'What the hell?' she was thinking, still standing there frozen like a meerkat when, with a splash like a tidal wave, a body plunged into the water on the upstream side of the bridge and came swirling down past her feet.

She wasn't stupid enough to make a grab for it. She'd once seen a shepherd go into the river Dochart after grabbing at a ewe and he'd never come up again, so she wasn't likely to make that mistake. However, the body itself was still very much alive and not going down without a fight. An arm whipped up in a spray of sparkling droplets and hooked, for barely a second, around the rock Fizz was standing on. She was already scrabbling for a secure grip with her left hand and found it just in time to snatch a good handful of clothing with her right. Using the force of the current, plus every iota of muscle from the toes up, she managed to swing the dead-weight a matter of inches further up the rock from where, in a whirl of limbs and several gallons of white water, it completed its own salvation. Only then did it become identifiable as the seriously ill-starred survivor of two life-threatening experiences in the one afternoon.

'Christ!' he said between retches. 'That was refreshing!'

Fizz could hear voices shouting above the thundering of the river. 'What happened?' she found herself asking, unable to believe what she already suspected.

15

'Bloody police car . . . damn near killed me!'

A bout of choking cut him off but Fizz had heard enough. If someone had deliberately tipped this guy over the bridge they'd be down here at any minute to make sure he hadn't come up. Policemen or not, questions would have to be asked. But not now.

'We've got to get the hell out of here.' She hooked an elbow under the man's arm and hauled him, still coughing, to his feet. 'Quick, before they see you. Upstream. They won't look for you there.'

'Extr'ordnally kind . . . ' began the guy, in a plummy voice, but Fizz hissed him into silence and drove him bodily away from the voices which had now moved to the downstream bank.

He was hampered by the weight of his saturated clothing and none too steady on his pins but it was only a few paces to the side of the bridge where they could crouch behind the buttress. It was only a temporary solution but there was no other cover within reach. A scrubby patch of gorse screened them a little, but not enough to hide them from a close inspection.

Fizz took a quick recce along the river and its banks. It was far too turbulent to make an attempt to cross it an option. Upstream, there

16

was nothing but patches of brushwood for at least fifty yards, none of them dense enough to conceal a cat. She was too low down on the bank to see either the Saab or the police car but, a flash of colour up on the hillside beyond caught her eye and she realised that it was Buchanan. He was hurtling down through a thicket of gorse and birch in a series of suicidal leaps, not looking where he was going, his attention fully on what was happening at the bridge.

He saw Fizz at the second she saw him and halted on the spot, his chest heaving and the whites of his eyes gleaming as he stared at her. She could see he was in one of his mother-hen panics which was amusing and insulting in about equal measures. One of those days he'd accept that she was just as resourceful as he, and usually twice as ferocious.

She lifted a hand, palm forward, to warn him off and indicated, in a general way, that whatever danger they could expect was presently downstream.

He nodded as though he approved of her tactics — which was comforting — and, drawing back into the trees where he was a lot less obvious, he worked his way down to the parked cars and started edging round behind the Saab. Just what he intended to do if the policemen returned, Fizz could not imagine. There was little concealment within dodging distance so if the worst came to the worst and the cops spotted him he'd have to try to brazen it out, which would be disastrous because Buchanan couldn't lie to save his life.

At the moment he was safe enough because the two policemen were now under the bridge. She could hear them shouting to each other although the words themselves were indistinguishable above the din. For one heart-stopping second a curve of shoulder appeared at the edge of the buttress, a yard away, but it emerged no further and presently she heard footsteps retreating back under the bridge.

'I say,' said a loud voice in her ear. 'Do I know you?'

Fizz clapped one hand to the back of the fugitive's head and the other across his mouth and made furious faces at him, but it was too late. A bareheaded man, tall and thick set, stepped out in front of her, but for the moment his eyes were on the river. If she hadn't been afraid that his mate was close behind him and would see her do it she could have stretched forth a leg and booted him into the current with no difficulty at all.

And his mate *was* there, stepping out of the

shadows with a hand up to shade his eyes from the glare off the water. He was as beefy as the other copper but shorter and from what Fizz could see of his face behind his hand he looked a good bit older. Had he moved that hand while he was standing as he was he couldn't have avoided seeing two pairs of horribly distended and terrified eyes staring back at him.

'Bastard's gone,' said his chum. 'Either snagged on something down deep or carried down with the current. Don't see him getting out of that alive anyway. Not the state he was in. What d'you reckon?'

'I'm not takin' no chances, Malkie. We better have a look further downstream just in case he — *where'd that bugger come from?*'

Everyone's head went up as though on the same puppet string and there was Buchanan leaning on the parapet at the far side of the bridge, grinning down at them.

'Caught anything?' he said as the two coppers swung round to face him, their backs now reassuringly towards their prey.

'Just looking,' said the older copper. 'A bit too bright the day, probably. Been fishing yoursel'?'

'No, just doing a bit of hillwalking, but I had a look at the water before I went up and wondered if it would be worth a cast later,

19

when the sun goes down a bit.'

'Just back, are you?'

'Just this minute.'

'The Saab's yours, then?'

'Aye. It's okay if I leave it there a bit longer?' Buchanan straightened from the parapet. 'Desperate for a cuppa. Maybe I'll brew up and then hang around for a while and see if anything shows.'

The policemen glanced at each other, then both turned towards the bridge without glancing behind them. 'Aye well,' said the older one, raising a hand. 'Tight lines, then.'

The gorse was applying quite painful acupuncture to Fizz's rear and an incipient cramp in her arm abruptly reminded her that she still had her hand across her new acquaintance's mouth. He didn't appear to object too strongly to being taken advantage of in this manner, indeed, on loosening her grip she found a placid smile underneath.

'Dashed decent of you . . . '

'Shush!' A choice expletive or two would have carried more weight but she had made a firm decision to clean up her act before graduating and in any case brevity was definitely called for.

They had to wait there for ages before she heard the car drive away. Buchanan had disappeared again and there was nothing to be heard above the river but the occasional drone of an insect as it settled on the yellow blooms around them. The air felt thick with sunshine, heavy with the tang of myrtle and the coconut-oil smell of gorse.

Taking her first good look at the man beside her she was, at first, pleasantly surprised. Given that his hair was sopping wet and streaked with weed and his clothes were nothing but bags of river water, he retained a distinct air of good breeding and charm quite — almost amusingly — out of keeping with his situation. He rested at his leisure with his strangely round head against a mossy stone and appeared to be quite happy to remain there, regarding Fizz with benevolent appro-bation, for as long as she required it of him. She could see no sign that he had been at all traumatised by his recent experiences nor did he evidence any great interest in where his pursuers might have gone or what they were up to.

At least his dip in the river had rinsed off both the smell of petrol and the mud that had enveloped him after the crash but in their place there now appeared two different clues to his persona which they had previously masked. Firstly, without the petrol there now emerged from his person a fainter but just as familiar perfume easily identifiable as whisky.

F 123,528

And secondly, his freshly laundered condition revealed a badly executed tattoo in the shape of a heart enclosing the word 'Survive' on his right wrist. A type of adornment, Fizz couldn't help thinking, that didn't quite fit with his otherwise upper class appearance.

If he saw her face flicker with uncertainty he gave no sign of it, just continued to lounge there smiling up at her with rather attractive clear grey eyes. He was obviously keen to chat but even more disposed to do whatever she told him to.

Buchanan slid down the bank a couple of minutes after they heard the car pull away. He was bleeding from a dozen or so deep scratches on his hands and arms and you could tell from his face that he was in one of his tizzies or, as he would phrase it, taking matters seriously.

'I thought they'd killed you,' he said to the man in the grass. 'Are you hurt?'

'Decent of you to ask, laddie.' He slid an amused glance down the long, elegant length of him. 'Apparently not. Thanks to this angel of mercy.'

Fizz was still finding it difficult to accept the fact that she had just witnessed a genuine attempted murder. 'They pushed you over?'

'Drove the car at him,' Buchanan answered her. 'Definitely tried to put him out of commission. If he hadn't fallen over the parapet he'd be seriously injured at the very least. What on earth is going on here?'

They both turned to stare at Lucky Jim who was engaged in reassembling himself in a vertical position.

'D'you know, I don't have the faintest idea,' he said mildly, and raised his eyebrows at each of them in turn as though he hoped somebody would enlighten him. 'You think those chaps were actually aiming for me? I thought their motor had gone out of control. Surely it was an accident?'

'No more an accident than the car crash,' said Buchanan, twisting his eyebrows in a baffled sort of way.

Lucky Jim leaned his head a little towards him and tipped it to one side. 'The car crash?'

'You were in a car crash,' Fizz told him. 'Don't you remember?'

'Aaah . . . ' He thought deeply for quite a while and then said, 'Recently?'

Fizz blinked at him. 'About half an hour ago. Don't you remember? You were in a big Mitsubishi people carrier — black — with a blonde woman?'

A faint frown creased his brow. 'Dear me, was I? D'you know, my dear young lady, I have not the slightest recollection of ever being in such a vehicle. Now isn't that strange?'

'Nothing to worry about,' Buchanan said, reaching out to steady the old man as he wobbled a little on the mossy slope. 'Post traumatic amnesia. It's quite common after a bang on the head. It'll clear in no time but right now I think we'd better get you back to the car. There should still be some coffee in our flask.'

'How very kind,' murmured Lucky Jim as Buchanan helped him back to level ground. 'A cup of coffee would be most acceptable. Um ... I don't suppose you'd have something stronger in the car for medicinal purposes?'

'I have,' Buchanan admitted, squinting at the guy's face. 'I'm not sure that whisky is what the doctor would order, though.'

'My dear boy, there's not a thing wrong with me, I assure you.' He stumbled gamely forward with his sopping trousers clinging like supplicants to his knees. 'Just a trifle shaken, that's all, and the possibility of pneumonia if I don't get these wet clothes off rather quickly. A small nip of firewater will do the trick.'

Back at the Saab he downed the last of the coffee while Fizz found the whisky flask and Buchanan sorted him out some dry clothes.

There was nothing in the car to choose from but the old socks, slacks and sweaters they each kept in reserve in case they were caught in a downpour halfway up a mountain but fortunately both Buchanan and Lucky Jim were the long, lanky type.

'Wonderful. Wonderful. How very fortunate that you happened along when you did, dear people. I can't thank you enough.'

He crawled into the back of the Saab with an armful of clothes and the hip flask. Fizz got Buchanan by the sleeve and drew him out of earshot.

'We've got a right one here, Kimosabe.'

Buchanan nodded, turning his back to the Saab. 'I think you're right. Did you notice his tattoo?'

'You bet. And also, I don't think his loss of memory has anything to do with a knock on the head. For my money, he wasn't concussed, he was blind drunk. Even after his dousing, the alcohol on his breath was a fire hazard.'

'Really? I hadn't noticed, but I never got as close to him as you did.' Buchanan eyed the road the policemen had taken, and jittered about a bit from foot to foot. 'You think he's a drunk?'

Fizz snorted at the term. 'A drunk? Dear me, no. Poor people are drunks: people like

Lucky Jim are alcoholics.'

'Well, drunk or alcoholic, he's certainly a bit of an oddball, but I don't think he's dangerous. Dangerous to be standing next to, maybe, considering his friends, but I can't imagine him personally being much of a threat, can you?'

'He's still pissed,' Fizz pointed out. 'We don't know what he'll be like when he's sober.'

'I'll tell you what he'll be like: he'll be seriously hung over and in no fit state to cause trouble.'

Fizz glanced back towards the car where Lucky Jim was getting rapidly outside the contents of the hip flask.

'So what are we going to do with him? We can't just turn him loose to wander back into the arms of the boys in blue.'

'Not *those* boys in blue, no. I can't believe they were really constables. Can you? That's not the way they operate, no matter how dangerous a criminal they're dealing with. Those two had to be fakes.'

'Or bent,' Fizz suggested.

Buchanan wasn't even going to think about that. 'He must have some inkling of what's up. When he gets his head together we'll get the whole story out of him and hand him in to the nearest police headquarters.'

Fizz had to smile. She'd no idea where the nearest police headquarters might be but if it was closer than Inverness, on the opposite side of the country, they'd be lucky. There might be a copper or two in Ullapool but the chances were that they'd be the two oddities they'd just met.

'We'd better be on our way,' Buchanan said. 'There's no telling whether those guys might come back.'

'Right.' Fizz scanned the two or three miles of road that followed the river downstream but nothing moved on it but a couple of crows pecking at a scrap of roadkill. 'I'll have to change my trousers but I can do it as we go.'

Lucky Jim was in good spirits when they got back to the car, and some thirty-five centilitres of good spirits were in him.

'Tell you what, chaps,' he said, lacing up Buchanan's old trainers with deep concentration and the manual dexterity of a snake. 'First decent restaurant we come to we'll have a damn good dinner. My treat. Least I can do.'

They wouldn't be passing a decent restaurant or even an indecent one in this neck of the woods but it seemed impolite to mention that.

'Shouldn't you be heading for home?'

Buchanan suggested. 'Won't someone be worried about you?'

'Not a bit of it. Free as a bird.' He waved a illustrative hand and then stuck it over Fizz's shoulder. 'Should've introduced m'self earlier. The name's Scott McKenzie.'

'Fizz Fitzpatrick. And this,' she added, just to clarify matters, 'is my boss, Tam Buchanan.'

'Ah . . . your boss. I was wondering. I thought you were a bit on the young side to be his girlfriend.'

Fizz didn't bother to reply. Everybody took her for a teenager at first sight and, though it never failed to amuse Buchanan, she'd long ago learned to let it go.

'And what line are you in, Tam, if I may ask?'

'I'm a solicitor,' said Buchanan shortly, not bothering to elaborate on his current status as embryo advocate. He was constantly checking his rear view mirror and keeping his foot down as much as he dared as they sped back along the road towards Achiltibuie.

By the time they got there, Fizz reflected, there wouldn't be much time for the walk they'd planned along the beach. Even though they'd left Edinburgh at lunch time they'd wasted an hour on the summit of Stac Pollaidh, photographing the stunning view of the Summer Isles, and now the light would be going by the time they reached journey's end. At this time of year it would only be properly dark for a couple of hours but the shoreline was too dangerous to traverse without being able to see where you were putting your feet.

'And you, er . . . Fizz,' McKenzie leaned over the back of Fizz's seat, subjecting her to secondary intoxication with Glenmorangie fumes. 'What part do you play in Tam's business?'

Obviously he was expecting her to say she was on some sort of Job Experience scheme for school leavers so there was some satisfaction in being able to tell him, with almost total truth, 'I'm a solicitor too.'

There was the small matter of her final exams still to be satisfactorily surmounted but she felt confident enough to extrapolate.

There was a short silence while McKenzie absorbed this information. Presently he found an apple on the back seat and started chomping off bits and chewing juicily. Then Buchanan braked and said, 'Take a look at this, Scott. That's the vehicle you were travelling in when it left the road. We found you underneath. Now do you remember?'

'Never saw it before in my life,' Scott stated with what sounded like certainty. 'Can't stand those things with their bloody bull bars. What sort of an idiot needs bull bars? How many bulls are they likely to meet in a day's work, h'mm? People carriers? People killers, more like!'

'It was driven by a woman,' Buchanan persisted. 'Long blonde hair. Maybe early thirties. Maybe thirty-five. Does that ring a bell?'

McKenzie froze for a second, his teeth embedded in the apple, then he completed the bite and shook his head. 'To be honest, my young friend, it's all a bit hazy. There was a blonde young lady — I'm damn sure there was, but who she was . . . No. Can't help you there, I'm afraid.'

He didn't look to Fizz as though this loss of memory was giving him any cause for concern. His guileless, china blue gaze was politely apologetic, as though he was sorry to disoblige such charming people but, clearly, a certain amount of amnesia was nothing new to him.

Buchanan was hesitating, looking in his rear view mirror and clearly swithering about getting McKenzie out to look at the corpse. Fizz was against the idea: mainly because she wasn't keen on getting into a car chase with the two cops, should they return, but also because it wouldn't help matters. McKenzie already remembered the woman, and the rest of the story would probably come back to him when he sobered up.

She was starting to say as much to Buchanan when a series of soft snores interrupted her. The effects of his stressful afternoon, not to mention his intake of Glenmorangie, had caught up with McKenzie and he had passed out, the half-eaten apple still cupped in his open palm.

'He'll be fine in the morning,' Fizz told Buchanan as he drove off. 'We'll have to take him to the B&B with us. You always get a twin room anyway, don't you? And the girls will be glad enough to get another guest for the spare bed.'

That idea didn't really grab him, Fizz could tell. He didn't say anything but he was grinding his teeth.

3

Buchanan knew perfectly well that he was being paranoiac. It was totally illogical to blame this debacle on Fizz but the facts were irrefutable.

When, for instance, in the thirty halcyon years before Fizz exploded into his life, had he had anyone die in his arms? How many times had he witnessed attempted murder? How often had he been forced to share overnight accommodation with a total stranger in the advanced stages of alcoholic poisoning? That sort of thing did not happen to normal, clean-living, respectable people like Buchanan but it happened with astonishing regularity to Fizz — and inevitably to those around her — and if her occasional reminiscences were to be believed, it had done so all her adult life.

Her anecdotes about strippers, pig smugglers and, more understandably, suicidal flatmates beggared belief — or *had* done before their shared experiences over the last few years had dulled Buchanan's sensibilities. Now they ranked as barely remarkable. She didn't appear deliberately to put herself in the way of such experiences although, admittedly, working one's way around the world for seven years, as she had done, might not be considered the best way to avoid them. Nonetheless, you could be reasonably sure, even in a virtually uninhabited wilderness like this, that every weirdo within twenty miles would be drawn to her like pilgrims to Mecca. Coincidentally, it was rarely she who suffered for it.

And now, here they were, lumbered with a guy whose life was in imminent danger. Obviously, he'd have to be protected until he could be handed over to the authorities or at least until he sobered up and took over responsibility for his own safety. If they were lucky, that obligation could be discharged in a matter of hours but Buchanan regarded himself as a seriously unlucky sort of person. He had hoped to enjoy his evening in Achiltibuie, not spend it babysitting a drunk.

Furthermore, they hadn't a clue who this guy was. He looked perfectly angelic but, as Fizz was fond of reminding him, the Boston Strangler had a lovely smile. For all anybody could tell, McKenzie could be a dangerous psychopath or an escaped criminal whom the police had orders to incapacitate on sight.

This, Buchanan felt, was absolutely not the time to get himself involved in anything that could be professionally embarrassing. He had only just taken an important step forward in his career and if he was ever going to be called to the bar it wouldn't be with any sort of public blunder hanging over his head. Larry, his 'devil master' who was probably the most venerated advocate in Edinburgh and an evil tempered bastard to boot, would kick him out the door at the least breath of scandal.

'You're grinding your teeth again, Buchanan,' said Fizz's voice.

'No I'm not.'

She batted her eyes at him like a pert schoolgirl, the low evening sun glinting on her Shirley Temple curls. 'You bloody are.'

Buchanan took a slow breath. 'What the blue blazes are we doing here, Fizz? We're hiding a guy who's obviously a wanted man. Are we crazy or something?'

'Suggest an alternative,' Fizz invited. 'We should have left the guy under the Mitsubishi? We should have watched the coppers mow him down? We should have handed him over and gone on our merry way? Hardly what you promised a dying woman, right?'

'I didn't promise to protect him for the rest of my life, dammit!' Buchanan raged, exaggerating a bit in case she realised how deep that shaft had gone. 'There are agencies for that. We get shot of him one way or

34

another first thing in the morning. Okay?'

'Absolutely, mon capitaine. This is the last weekend I can afford to take off before my exams and I want to get some decent walking done. When we find out what Lucky Jim's been up to we can decide who'd be best to deal with him — we could even phone somebody and pass him on tonight. Anyway, we'll have plenty of time to do Cul Beag in the morning and Cul Mor in the afternoon and that'll leave all day Sunday for Suilven.' She leaned an elbow out the open window and tilted her head to let the draught ruffle her hair. 'Nothing to start gritting your teeth about.'

Buchanan felt his jaw muscles tightening again and forced himself to relax. He was only now beginning to register the full horror of the car crash and it was giving him the creeps. Fizz looked calm enough on the exterior but she was never one to share her woes so you couldn't be sure.

He said, 'We should take this guy straight to the nearest police station. We should report the accident as soon as we get to a telephone. But we're not going to do either of those things, are we? So if McKenzie turns out to be on the wrong side of the law we're up the creek.'

Fizz regarded him through a thrashing

thicket of hair. 'Buchanan, if you have no other options you have to take the one open to you. Why waste time agonising over it? It's not up to us to report the crash: the police were already at the scene. And, as far as McKenzie's concerned, what's the hurry? He's not going to pull a gun on us, is he? I mean, look at him.'

Buchanan adjusted the rear view mirror till it framed a somnolent McKenzie, his mouth a little open and an out-for-lunch expression on his face. Buchanan's once superb cashmere sweater and faded chinos hung on his spare frame so loosely that any gun-shaped bulges would have been instantly apparent. It was possible that he had a weapon of some sort underneath him and, of course, he could be faking both intoxication and sleep, but if that were the case, he deserved an Oscar.

The worst that could happen, Buchanan decided, was that he'd turn out to have no money on him and it would be he himself who'd have to fork out for his overnight accommodation. A few months ago that would not have caused him any great degree of angst but right now he was facing a year's devilling to Larry without a penny coming in and thereafter he'd be living off his fat till he started getting some briefs of his own. He had to think twice about spending every penny, even on an occasional hillwalking weekend.

As they neared Achiltibuie the western sky was just beginning to darken into the bluish haze that preceded sunset. On their two previous visits to the area the weather had been less than perfect but that hadn't prevented Buchanan from falling in love with the atmosphere of the village. Whatever the weather, he cherished the sense of being at the edge of the universe and even now the sight of the low sun shining on turquoise breakers went a long way towards gladdening his heart.

The 'girls', as Fizz referred to them, were out on the step to greet them before he had parked the car. They were both in their sixties: Jeannie, the short tubby one, was probably sixty-five-ish and Isa, the even shorter but thinner one, a few years younger.

'Here you are at last!' Jeannie marched forward with her mannish stride and Isa followed, half hidden by her sister, with her elbows clamped to her sides and her chin ducked in painful shyness.

'We got held up a bit,' said Fizz.

'Och, we weren't worried. We knew you'd try to climb something on your way up, like you did the last time, and I said to Isa we'd

37

likely not see you till the sun went down 'cause you'd want to make the most of the good weather.'

Isa nodded and smiled behind her shoulder, speechless but showing willing.

'Actually,' Buchanan said, we've brought someone with us. I hope it won't be an inconvenience.'

'Och no. How would that be an inconvenience? But we've only the two rooms, mind. One of you will have to share.'

'Yes, of course,' Fizz responded with an airy wave of her hand. 'It's a guy, so he can share with Buchanan. Wake him up, Buchanan and I'll get the cases out.'

McKenzie didn't want to waken up but fortunately the girls chose to help Fizz unpack the boot so they didn't witness Buchanan's increasingly extreme resuscitation techniques. Finally McKenzie opened his eyes wide, blinked at Buchanan's face, and muttered,

'Ah . . . we've met before, I think.'

Buchanan frowned at him. 'Buchanan. Tam Buchanan and Fizz. Remember? We fished you out of the river.'

'Unquestionably, dear chap. Clear as crystal now, I assure you. Delightful little thing. Curly hair. Face of an angel.'

'Right. We've fixed you up with a room for

the night. You'll have to share with me but it's either that or drive to Ullapool.'

McKenzie struggled to a sitting position and smoothed his hair which had now dried to a creamy white. Bubbly curls clustered on his forehead like those on a Friesian bull. He peered out of the window at the lime-washed croft house.

'You seem to have brought me to a safe haven. Bloody marvellous! Lead on, my young friend.'

Buchanan helped him forth and, suppressing his qualms, introduced him to the girls who were much taken with him. Indeed, Isa was so overcome by the accent and by the elegant civility of his opening remarks that she ducked her head in what was probably a truncated curtsey.

'Have you had your dinner?' Jeannie asked him.

'Actually not. We had intended to stop en route, I seem to recall, but somehow or other that plan fell by the wayside.'

'Dear me, you'll be starving, the three of you. Come away in and we'll see what we can put together for you.'

They proceeded indoors, the girls ushering McKenzie between them in a manner reminiscent of two curlers sweeping a path for the stone, with Fizz and Buchanan bringing up the rear with their overnight bags.

The room, although it lacked the sea view Fizz had commandeered on their first visit, pleased McKenzie inordinately. In truth it was pretty cramped for two people but he brushed that detail aside, preferring to dwell on the little extras the girls provided: face cloths, towelling robes and mules, nail brushes, etc.. All evidence, as he needlessly informed his room mate, of an innate kindness and consideration on the part of their hostesses.

Buchanan had not yet showered, having given McKenzie priority, when Fizz came in looking, for her, quite spic and span in a fleece gilet over a T-shirt and the combat pants she'd bought off her last wages. She'd brought a cup with her in the expectation that they would already have a pot of tea on the go and, finding herself ahead of the game, set about rectifying matters.

'We won't get our dinner for at least an hour,' she said, plugging in the kettle, 'and I'm parched right down to my belly button. If you tell McKenzie to get a move on in that shower we could take a walk down the beach while we're waiting.'

Buchanan was in full agreement. He wanted to see the sunset and he also wanted a talk with McKenzie where they wouldn't be overheard. He stuck his head into the en suite shower room to relay this new itinerary and five minutes later McKenzie appeared in a white towelling robe, looking uncannily like an elderly David Gower and smelling of Buchanan's aftershave.

'Ah. Tea.' He seated himself on his bed, folding his robe decorously over his knees. 'Do we have a little something to take the taste away?'

'No, we don't, actually,' said angel face pleasantly. 'You drank it all. How about a chockie bikkie?'

He waved away the biscuits and the implied criticism with the same graceful gesture. 'Easily remedied. I imagine there's a hotel or other licensed premises in the vicinity. We can pick up a bottle of malt on our way back from our walk. I'll just get dressed.'

'You're all right for cash, then?' Fizz asked with her usual reticence.

McKenzie paused in his retreat to the shower room and his eyes widened momentarily. 'God, I bloody hope so!'

Putting his cup and saucer on the dressing table he made for the tweed suit which he had, somewhat optimistically, hung on the back of a chair to dry. After feeling in both inside jacket pockets he transferred his search

41

to the trousers and eventually pulled out a large handful of notes and small change.

'Well, that's all right,' he said with an audible breath of relief and threw the money onto the bedspread.

Buchanan was still trying to accept what he was looking at when Fizz extended a finger and prodded tentatively at the fat roll of notes as though it were something contagious in a Petri dish.

'What the hell's that?'

Nobody answered her.

After a moment McKenzie picked it up, tore off the band of paper which encircled it and unrolled a half-inch thick wad of twenties. 'Well, bugger me,' he murmured, shoving it into the pocket of his robe and beating a strategic retreat to the shower room. 'I must have been to the bank.'

Buchanan closed his eyes and allowed himself to fall back across the bed. 'What next?' he groaned. 'There must be two or three thousand pounds in that roll. What is he doing, carrying that sort of money around with him?'

He heard Fizz snigger. 'Stop finding things to complain about, Buchanan. At least you're not going to have to foot his bill.'

As far as Buchanan was able to judge, there didn't appear to be much else on the credit side of the ledger. McKenzie was a seriously scary character. He certainly gave the impression of being reasonably well-heeled, indeed he had to be to own a watch like the one he was wearing, however nobody but a nutter or a millionaire would view a couple of thousand pounds as pocket money. One had to ask oneself if he'd come by it honestly. Buchanan couldn't imagine McKenzie holding up a bank but the sight of the paper wrapper made him slightly uneasy.

He sat up and pieced together the torn pieces of paper finding nothing of interest on them other than some meaningless letters, probably someone's initials. He showed them to Fizz but her self-acclaimed intuition contributed nothing so he shoved them in his pocket for future reference and put on his boots.

Down on the beach it was so still they could hear voles nibbling in the bent grass. The Summer Isles were silhouetted against a sky that was four shades of blue and the puffs of low lying cirrus were made of rose pink swan's-down lined with gold lamé. They found a place to sit on the rocks where they were low down enough to look through the backlit breakers at the sunset and watch the seals turning over and over in the undercurrents.

It was the sort of moment that occurred

but rarely in Buchanan's life and he would have been utterly enraptured had not the picture of a dying woman occupied the forefront of his mind. He wanted to ask Fizz if she had been as deeply shocked by the experience as he had but she hadn't referred to it herself and if she had managed to blot it from her memory there was no point in dragging it up. She certainly wasn't dwelling on the incident right now because she was intent on debriefing McKenzie.

'So, how are you feeling now, Scott?' she was saying.

'Fit as a fiddle, my sweet. Could do with a dram, but other than that I'm feeling pretty damn good, all things considered.'

'Have you remembered anything more about how you came to be in the Mitsubishi with the blonde woman?'

McKenzie stared out to sea, a faintly bemused look in his eyes. 'Been thinking about that. She was a dashed nice girl. Name began with an M. Margaret? Maureen, perhaps. That sound of word, if you know what I mean. It'll come back to me.'

'Is that all?'

'The old memory's not what it was, my angel. When you get to my age things get a bit fuzzy.'

He patted her knee in an avuncular

44

manner, leaving his hand resting there as though he had forgotten it. Buchanan stirred irritably but Fizz merely picked it up by the thumb and swung it in front of McKenzie's eyes.

'What about the tattoo? When did you have this done? It's fairly new, isn't it?'

McKenzie's expression was that of a naughty schoolboy caught out by an endlessly forgiving mother: a neat balance between contrition and impudence. 'Yes, that was rather silly. All down to the demon drink, I fear. There was a wager involved, I recollect. A litre of 10-year-old Macallan.' He gave his head a totally impenitent shake. 'Shocking. Time I grew up.'

Fizz flicked a glance at Buchanan, inviting his comment, but he felt inclined, for the moment, to leave her to it. Two of them conducting an interrogation would only complicate matters.

She drew a breath and returned to the fray.

'D'you remember where you'd set off from today? Anyone else you were with earlier? What about the two policemen?'

'Ah . . . the policemen — no. Heaven only knows how I came to fall foul of those two. There were some other people, though.' His face clenched with concentration as he continued to stare at the horizon. 'Can't place them precisely, just at the moment, but I can tell you they were dashed good fellows. Generous. Never slow at putting a hand in their pocket when it was their turn for a round. Fergie? Fergie?' He tried out the name several times. 'Yes. That sounds right.'

He reached for a smooth pebble and sat rubbing it between his palms and frowning at the waves. Fizz started to nag him again but when Buchanan nudged her she took the hint, broke off, and gave him time to think.

The tide was on the ebb, leaving a stretch of shiny sand behind for the oyster catchers to pick over. Away round the coast in the direction of Polbain a dog was barking and the sound was as clear as though it were only a few yards away.

'There was some sort of a factory,' McKenzie said suddenly, stilling the rubbing of his hands on the pebble. 'No, not a factory. Maybe a warehouse . . . ? No . . . not a warehouse but something like that. They were both there — Fergie and the other one, and an ugly sort of bloke with teeth like tombstones.'

'Uh-huh?' prompted Fizz with great self-control.

'Then Marianne and the bloke with the teeth were dragging me down a lane . . . Marianne!' His face lit with delight. 'I

46

told you it would come back to me! Marianne! That was it . . . but who was she? Some friend of Fergie's? Yes, she must have been a friend of Fergie's.'

Buchanan waited for a while in the hope that something further would emerge from the alcoholic quagmire that was evidently McKenzie's mind but that, for the moment at least, appeared to be all they were going to get. He allowed Fizz to suggest various prospective lines of exploration but, although McKenzie looked as if he were cudgelling his brains, he was clearly doing so for her benefit and not because he was deeply concerned.

It was very likely that he'd been suffering memory lapses for some time and was past caring. It appeared to Buchanan that on this occasion he'd been on a binge with a couple of chance acquaintances and wandered into some place he'd no right to be. The fact that he was still in possession of an Omega watch would indicate that at least he had not fallen among thieves.

Buchanan was just about to remark that their dinner would be waiting for them when McKenzie murmured, half to himself,

'And God knows who it was that got shot.'

4

It wasn't often that Fizz had trouble sleeping. She had learned the art in a hard school where the classrooms ranged from station waiting rooms and airport lounges to bivvie bags under the stars. But when she left Buchanan and McKenzie drinking cocoa in the lounge and sought the comfort of her duvet her mind was still buzzing like a wasp's nest; haunted not just by memories of the dying woman but by real concern for her career.

Although McKenzie had refrained from hitting them with any further unsettling disclosures during the course of the evening, the essence of what he had already divulged was enough to give anyone insomnia.

It looked inescapably as though he and his two drinking buddies — Fergie and the other one — had become embroiled in some violent illegal activity or other. Somebody had definitely been shot, but McKenzie had no idea who did the shooting, who was shot or, indeed, whether the victim was alive or dead. Evidently he had been hustled away from the scene of the crime by the blonde and yet another boon companion, which seemed to indicate that, whether he deserved it or not, he had all the luck in the world. Considerably more than Buchanan or Fizz herself, who were now faced with the problem of how to get him off their hands without seriously endangering his health. And theirs.

Ullapool, Buchanan had eventually agreed, appeared to offer the best prospect of a satisfactory solution. Even if the fishing port turned out to be policed only by the two coppers they'd met yesterday there were bound to be other worthy bodies who could come to the rescue: a Social Work department, maybe, or the Salvation Army. Anybody, for God's sake, who would take over responsibility and let them get on with their weekend break.

She fell asleep at last, some time after two, and woke at seven as usual, with an hour to wait for her breakfast. She filled some of the time with making and drinking a cup of coffee, packed all her gear ready for a quick start, and then went to wake Buchanan.

She could hear through the door that he was already up and about but tapped politely and waited to be admitted. She could see at once from Buchanan's face that he was not in the sunniest of moods. He returned her 'good morning' somewhat brusquely and waved her in.

The first thing she noticed was the smell of whisky and the second was McKenzie who was lying on top of his bed in the white bathrobe with an empty bottle of Vat69 on his chest.

'Where the hell did he get that?'

She turned to stare at Buchanan who was stomping around in nothing but his jeans searching for something in a disorganised welter of gear. He found his hairbrush and straddled down in front of a too-low mirror to brush his hair.

'You tell me,' he said bitterly. 'There isn't a pub or a hotel or a licensed grocers within walking distance.'

'He must have nicked it from the girls,' Fizz surmised, starting to get angry. 'How come you didn't hear him getting up?'

'He was up and down all night, dammit. In and out of the toilet like a piston. I suppose I must have got used to the noise.'

Fizz looked at the inert figure on the bed. It looked as if it had been filleted by an amateur taxidermist and abandoned half stuffed. 'What are we going to do with him?'

Buchanan's head popped out of a T-shirt. 'He can stay there till we've had our breakfast. If he's not awake by the time we've finished we'll fill him full of black coffee and get him in the car. I can't wait to get shot of him.'

'Me neither.'

The girls always gave them a choice of breakfast: either the full bacon-egg-sausage-tomatoes job or a Scottish breakfast of scrambled eggs and smoked salmon, which was one of the things that had brought them back three times. Isa was the waitress this morning which meant that she had, over-night, overcome her shyness sufficiently to leave the cooking to Jeannie.

'Is Mr McKenzie not feeling any better, then?' she asked as she served their porridge. 'He'll be wanting his breakfast in bed, I suppose.'

Buchanan caught Fizz's eye and cleared his throat. 'He was still asleep when we came down,' he said. 'In fact, I wasn't aware there was anything wrong with him. Was he up in the night?'

Isa fidgeted with her hair, half hiding behind her hand and looking as if she'd rather not get into a conversation about it.

'No, it was first thing this morning. Very early. Jeannie was just going out to feed the hens when he came down in his bathrobe saying he was starting a cold and had we anything for it. The poor soul was fair miserable with it so I made him a hot toddy

51

and he took the bottle up with him in case he needed another. Will I tell Jeannie to put his breakfast on a tray?'

'That's very kind of you, Isa, but I wouldn't bother.' Buchanan smiled at her encouragingly. 'If he wants something before we leave I'll make him a cup of tea. I doubt if he'll be hungry.'

Isa demurred as much as her shyness would allow and then withdrew to relay the decision to the cook.

'What's that man like?' Fizz demanded as the door closed behind her. 'No wonder there's nobody worried about him at home. Who could live with someone like that? You couldn't turn your back on him for a minute.'

'Plenty of people have to live with someone like that day in, day out.' Buchanan said gloomily, passing her the salt. 'But at least he's the amiable variety of drunk. He's not going to start a punch-up on the way to Ullapool.'

Fizz was inclined to agree with that assessment. Poor old McKenzie was unmistakably a nice guy, drunk or sober — quite a sweetie actually — which was probably why so many people were disposed, even in the face of personal liability, to save him from the consequences of his peccadilloes.

She said, 'Now that we know what to

expect . . . ' and then noticed that Buchanan wasn't listening to her.

Just beyond the bay window, outlined against the glitter of the sea, McKenzie was hurrying down the garden path, making for the gate. Even in Buchanan's old clothes, he looked like the monarch of all he surveyed and the only sign of any residual intoxication was the merest hint of unsteadiness in his stride.

Buchanan lurched to his feet and swung open the window.

'Scott!'

Scott executed a three point turn, staggering a little, and retraced his steps.

'There you are, Tam! Good morning, Fizz, my angel. How are you this glorious morning?'

Fizz was about to ask where he'd been heading off to but decided there was no point in forcing him to lie. 'Come in and have some breakfast, Scott. You'll be starving before we get to Ullapool if you don't.'

'Breakfast. Ah,' he murmured as though it were an alien concept and climbed over the low windowsill with an unexpected access of speed which landed him in Buchanan's lap. 'Oh, sod it, old chap. Did I spill your coffee?'

This incident more or less set the tone for the rest of the morning. Although Buchanan managed to keep a tight grip on his temper, he had patently gone off McKenzie and wasn't too worried about hiding it. Not that McKenzie noticed anything amiss. He was just as urbane and cheerful as he had been the day before and kept up a stream of inconsequential chatter as far as Ledmore, where he fell asleep.

He was still in the arms of Morpheus when they reached Ullapool and Buchanan was all for keeping him that way till he had made arrangements for his welfare. They drove around for a while looking for inspiration. There was a decent sized police station but it seemed wiser to take advice from someone who knew the local bobbies personally before taking the chance of making matters worse than they already were.

There was a Seamen's Mission and a Free Church of Scotland and a Citizens' Advice Bureau but in the end Buchanan plumped for the Roman Catholic Chapel.

'Priests are good at keeping secrets,' he claimed, casting a last look at their unconscious passenger, 'and we don't want to confide in someone who might take matters into their own hands. I'll be as quick as I can. Don't, whatever you do, let him out of the car.'

Fizz made a teach-your-granny-to-suck-eggs face at him and settled down for a long wait. Minutes later McKenzie woke up, bubbly as a bottle of Bolly, and said he was going for a stiffener.

'Let's wait for Buchanan,' Fizz said firmly, knowing he'd be as stiff as the Eiffel Tower if she took her eyes off him. 'He'll be back in a couple of minutes.'

'So will I, girlie.' He had the door open and a leg out before she'd finished speaking. 'I'll just wet my whistle and be back in two shakes.'

Fizz cursed fluently and caught up with him before he melted into the tide of pedestrians. 'I'll come with you, then, Scott,' she told him, slipping an arm through his.

He looked at her doubtfully. 'They're tough on under-age drinking these days but I suppose you could have a lemonade.'

'I'm twenty-nine,' Fizz said, a bit snappily because he was beginning to get up her nose. 'I told you yesterday I was a solicitor, remember? Anyway, it's not me they'll refuse to serve, it's you. Look at you. You should have asked the girls to press your suit last night. You can't go into a hotel looking like a scarecrow.'

McKenzie frowned down at Buchanan's old sweater and tried to pull it into shape.

'Look.' Fizz pointed at a display of casual jackets in a shop window beside them. 'You could at least get one of those. You can't go around dressed like a tramp.'

McKenzie was clearly undecided. He hovered for a moment, sending quick glances up the street as though to check the proximity of the nearest oasis, then his innate fastidiousness won.

It was pure luck that it turned out to be a department store that they found themselves in. That meant that Fizz could not only slow down his choice of jacket by insisting he try on several alternatives but persuade him that he needed a complete new wardrobe from underwear to smart cavalry twill trousers. Every time she had him cornered in a fitting room she dashed to the door to watch for Buchanan's return and when she eventually spotted him coming she was able to signal him to join her before he flew into a panic at their disappearance.

'What's happening?' he said to her in the doorway.

Fizz jerked her head towards McKenzie who was trying on shoes. 'He was determined to get to a pub so I sidetracked him in here. He needs some decent clothes anyway and the more he spends in here the less he'll have to buy drink with. How did you get on?'

'So-so. Good news and bad news. The man I want to see is Father Goodwin. He's the elder of the two priests. I had a long talk with a woman who was scrubbing the steps and I suspect, from what she said, that young Father Bain tries too hard to be perceived as one of the boys. One of the beer drinking, guitar playing, Jesus-is-cool types. He's probably no worse than the other one but I ... I don't know. I just got the feeling the older guy might be more confident, more willing to delay taking the matter to the police. At least till McKenzie sobers up a bit and starts to remember why they're after him.'

'But, you haven't spoken to either of the priests?'

'No. Father Bain is at someone's bedside — otherwise I'd probably have settled for him anyway to save time — and Father Goodwin won't be around till this afternoon. I'm afraid we're stuck with McKenzie for a couple of hours.'

Fizz had half expected something like this. It meant that they'd either have to rush their ascent of Cul Mor and Cul Beag or think about switching their objective, perhaps to Ben More Assynt, which was nearer.

'Can't be helped,' she said, watching McKenzie charming the pants off the mature saleslady while he paid for his purchases. 'There are plenty of other good climbs to choose from around here. There'll be something worth doing whatever time we're left with. Our main problem will be how to keep McKenzie sober while we wait for your religious adviser to turn up.'

Fortunately McKenzie had chosen to wear most of his purchases, including a frightful orange, long-skipped cap to keep the sun out of his eyes, so they were able to pack the remainder into the boot beside their ruck-sacks and the raft of fishing gear that Buchanan always brought with him on the off chance of a cast or two. There was a spirited discussion about where lunch should be eaten and whether it should be liquid or solid but McKenzie was nothing if not civilized and was ultimately persuaded to accede to a picnic.

The girls had provided them only with the two packed lunches that had been requested but there was more than enough in those for the three of them. They ate on the shore, a little way along the coast from the harbour so that they could watch the fishing boats maneuvering in and out.

By the time they had eaten and lounged around in the sun for a while McKenzie was probably as sober as he was likely to get so they both had another go at jogging his memory. All that transpired, however, was the fact that it wasn't only the previous day that had failed to imprint itself on his mind, he could give no cohesive account of the previous week or so. Fergie and Marianne remained the only participants he could put a name to but he seemed confident that he'd had a great time, wherever it was, right up to the final scene when someone had stopped a bullet.

At two o'clock Buchanan decided it was time to get back to the chapel.

'We'll stick together this time,' he said to McKenzie, giving him a look which brooked no argument. 'We'll just have to take a chance that the priest won't feel obliged to give your description to the police.'

McKenzie looked mildly distressed. 'No need to put yourself to this trouble, dear chap. I can book into an hotel. Really. I'm sure it's all some bloody misunderstanding.'

It amused Fizz no end to observe him emerging from his long-term inebriation. He was no longer entirely happy to leave the management of his safekeeping in the hands of two total strangers but his innate civility was preventing him from saying so. His sole priority was to address the problem of his current sobriety and he was impatient to make his farewells. Which made three of them.

'We'll just see what this chap advises,' Buchanan said, with only a touch of gravel in his voice. 'I promised Marianne that I wouldn't let any harm come to you so I want to see you in good hands before I abandon you.'

McKenzie took that on the chin, his expression verging on the truculent, adjusted his flashy new cap and got back into the Saab without further argument.

The town centre had filled up considerably since their first visit, Saturday afternoon shoppers and summer visitors clogging up the pavements and parking places. They had to park the Saab some distance away from the chapel and walk back.

Because they couldn't walk three abreast through the press of people, Fizz had overtaken the other two and was three or four paces ahead when she realised that something was happening up ahead of her and across the road. It didn't occur to her right away that it might be anything to do with her so she kept marching towards the fuss with only the most indifferent curiosity.

Even when she realised that the rushing and jostling she had noticed was caused by two unfamiliar policemen heading in her direction it took valuable seconds for her to register that the object of their zeal was, not merely in her uncomfortably close vicinity, but almost certainly *herself*. By the time she reacted they were dodging through the traffic, looking horribly determined, and less than fifty paces away.

'Run for it!' was all she had time to say, spinning round with her hands out to halt McKenzie. Buchanan, ever the gentleman, had stepped aside to allow a woman with a shopping trolley to pass him, but he wasted less than a heartbeat looking over her shoulder then grabbed McKenzie by the arm and legged it back towards the car.

Fizz caught up with him in a couple of strides and between them they propelled McKenzie onto the roadway and took their place in the stream of traffic. The pace, at this stretch, was slow but it was as fast as they could run and if they couldn't overtake, neither could the coppers so when they arrived back at the Saab the pursuit was still at least a dozen cars behind.

'Christ!' McKenzie had breath for nothing further as he was thrown into the car and pressed hard against the seat back as Buchanan accelerated away.

'Bloody hell!' muttered Buchanan, black-browed and grinding his teeth.

'Shite!' said Fizz, between gasps.

Everything had happened too quickly to allow the full hideousness of the situation to penetrate, but suddenly there it was — they were actually evading arrest and that was something even she would have a hard time talking herself out of.

'Those buggers were after the three of us,' she panted. 'I'll lay money on it. It wasn't just McKenzie they were looking at. One of them looked right into my eyes. How'd he know I was with McKenzie? He was walking alone at that point.'

Buchanan groaned and overtook the two cars in front to scoot through the lights on amber. Blaring horns and V-signs followed them across the junction.

'Those were real coppers,' he said grimly. 'Different ones from yesterday's. Not masquerading. And probably not bent either. Why are they after us?'

Fizz had to pass on that one.

'Where are we going?' she asked, thinking that she ought to have some input in the matter since she was more familiar with the area than was Buchanan.

'We're just going,' Buchanan snapped back in a fury. 'Away. That's where we're going, dammit! Didn't you see the police car parked on the corner? If it's not on our tail right now it's because a spaceship landed in front of it.'

Fizz twisted round to look out the rear window. There were one or two cars behind them but no sign of a flashing blue light. McKenzie gave her a pleading look but still hadn't the breath to say anything.

'We're clear for the moment,' she told Buchanan, 'but we'll have to get off the main drag or hide the Saab somewhere. The trouble is, I can't think of a turn-off between here and Strath More.' She indicated the shore of Loch Broom, which bordered the road on their left. 'Keep your eyes open for a boat. We may have to hide the car somewhere and take to the water.'

Buchanan groaned, rolling his eyes a bit. 'What the hell am I doing here? How did this happen? Why did we make a run for it?'

There were no answers to any of those questions. Fizz concentrated on looking out for pursuit and, only a few minutes later, started catching sporadic flashes of a sparkling blue light behind them. Because of the curve of the loch and the inning-and-outing of the shoreline it was hard to estimate how much of a lead they had on the police car but it was probably not much more than a couple of minutes.

She relayed this information to Buchanan who put his foot down and set about pulverising his molars. There was nothing practical they could do but keep their eyes open for some means of escape, stay ahead of the police, and pray for a miracle.

5

'Without wishing wish to appear ungrateful,' McKenzie said in a voice barely audible above the roar of the engine, 'one has to ask oneself if a closer observation of road safety might not be advisable.'

Buchanan denied himself the luxury of giving way to a tantrum. 'You may not have noticed, Scott,' he said with forced calm, 'but we are being pursued by the police, some or all of whom have your immediate demise at the top of their wish list. Coincidentally, they have now identified Fizz and I as accessories and our careers are in jeopardy so I'd like to avoid them if at all possible.'

'I see,' said Scott. 'Yes, yes. I quite see. Ah . . . So I suppose a hi-diddle-diddle is out of the question?'

'What?' Buchanan noticed Fizz's quick, smiling glance at his face and accepted that this was God punishing him for not stopping yesterday when she'd asked him to. The Saab was under a year old and the last thing he needed was some drunk pissing all over the back seat. 'You'll just have to hang on, Scott.

I'll stop the minute I can, I promise you.'

The road had straightened out slightly by the time they came to the end of Loch Broom but it was still twisty and lined with trees so their view of their pursuers — and, more importantly, their pursuers' view of them — comprised only a series of brief glimpses. There were other cars on the road and, since the Saab was a commonplace dark grey, it might be assumed that the police were having difficulty in picking them out.

Fizz's head swished incessantly from windscreen to rear window, searching for side roads and reporting on the state of play. Buchanan was aware of the second she saw the tractor ahead.

'Oh God! Look!' she yelled, clutching at her head. 'Look at the width of that load! We'll never get past it!'

Buchanan had perhaps a minute before he caught up with it, maybe five minutes before the police caught up with him. On one side of him he had an impenetrable forest, on the other a four foot stone wall with a drop beyond. Defeat slackened his pressure on the accelerator.

'That's the Lael Forest,' Fizz was saying excitedly. 'There's a track around here where climbers park their cars to walk in to the Deargs. It's our one chance.'

'Are you crazy, Fizz? We can't outdistance them on foot — '

'We won't have to,' she said, stammering with urgency. 'You and McKenzie can hide and I'll lead them up the hill. I know a fast way down. Quick! I know I can do it!'

She didn't have a hope in hell, Buchanan was fairly convinced of that, but he knew that Fizz would be on her feet fighting at the final bell and he had to go along with her. There was no time to elucidate precisely what she had in mind but he could see in her face that she was perfectly confident she could accomplish what she proposed. One thing was certain: she knew a hell of a lot more about hills and mountains than he did and she appeared to know this one in particular pretty well. Part of his mind urged him to rely on the due processes of the law and give himself up but Fizz would never settle for that while there was a chance of getting off scot-free. And maybe she was right.

However, he wasn't happy about leaving the car. There was still a good chance that the police had, as yet, been unable to spot the number plate but if they saw it now they'd be able to trace it and they'd be there waiting for him when he got back to Edinburgh.

For the next half mile or so, while Fizz cursed the tractor — though, surprisingly, not in the horrific terms she normally used — and watched out for the track, he searched for a place where he could run the car into the bushes, but nothing showed. The only break in the stone wall facing the forest edge was the short strip of gravel Fizz had remembered. All he could think to do was to park the car with the front hidden in the long grass and jam a handful of bracken across the rear number plate. It was scarcely worth the few seconds it cost him to do it but one could dream.

Fizz, meanwhile had snatched McKenzie's ghastly orange cap, with what excuse one could only conjecture, and was arming herself with a bin bag out of the boot.

'Get as far away as you can,' she said, waving an arm at the woods. 'I'll be back about five minutes after the police get here so make sure you're ready for a swift exit.'

Buchanan had no time to watch her go. He got a grip of McKenzie and took a chance on trundling him a hundred yards further along the roadway before turning into the forest. Two paces from the roadway the undergrowth was so compact that he had to settle for leaving McKenzie in a base camp behind a clump of something jagged while he tried to hack his way further into the dark interior.

McKenzie was little help but he seemed to

have grasped the necessity of remaining hidden and whiled away the next minute or two by relieving his bladder and by relaying a commentary on Fizz's ascent of the hill. In the few sightings Buchanan was able to take for himself she seemed to be making excellent time.

The track ran steeply up from the car parking area, mounting the rougher face of what was, to Fizz, little more than a knoll. On one side, the hill was colonised by shoulder high bracken, through which the path zig-zagged up to a densely forested summit, but on the other side was a gentler slope clothed in a long pelt of shiny grass.

Already Fizz was well up through the bracken and going like a steam engine. Buchanan wasn't sure that he himself could have covered the distance in just a few minutes but he comforted himself with the fact that she had been born to it, whereas he had only recently converted to her hobby to compensate for those he could no longer afford.

The police arrived in a squeal of tyres, shouting indecipherable comments to each other, whipping out extendable batons — batons, for God's sake! — and staring up the hill. Following their eyes, Buchanan could pick out the glint of Fizz's golden mane and, occasionally, the flash of McKenzie's orange cap. Seen in short glimpses, together with the flash of the plastic bin liner behind her, she was managing to give the impression that there were three people up there.

One of the coppers, a fit looking bloke who probably ran up hills like this every day of his working week, immediately made a dash for the path, but the other took a quick look at the interior — but, thank God, only the interior — of the Saab before following him.

They were both fast. Much faster than Fizz. Buchanan, who couldn't bear to look away, couldn't be sure whether Fizz was beginning to flag or whether she was deliberately allowing them to catch up, but the distance between them was rapidly shortening. The leading policeman shouted something and waved his arm at her but she didn't miss a step, just put on a sudden spurt and melted into the forest.

'Where's she going?' McKenzie asked, much as though no answer would surprise him, but Buchanan did not feel himself competent enough to answer. He hoped very much that Fizz was not going but coming, but he could see no way she could be sure of giving the coppers the slip, even in the forest, and they looked quite nimble enough to catch up with her on her descent. Had there been three of them up there instead of just one, the smart money would have been on the coppers.

The two pursuers split up, disappearing into the forest at different points, and for what seemed like several minutes nothing moved except a couple of buzzards wheeling in the sky above. Buchanan's eyes were fixed on the path but Fizz did not appear at the edge of the trees. Presently, he spotted both the policemen crossing a fire break quite a bit further up, still moving fast and, surely, very close on Fizz's heels.

Then a streak of colour caught his eye, well down on the lower slopes and there came Fizz, tobogganing down the grassy slope on the black bin liner at a speed worthy of the Cresta run. In less time than it took Buchanan to react she was at the bottom and sprinting for the car park, beating the other two to the finish by rather longer than she'd planned. A benign providence rendered her speechless with asphyxia, however, so the latecomers were spared the lash of her tongue and they were well on their way before she recovered.

Although they had gained at least fifteen minutes, Buchanan didn't dare slow down. Whatever it was that had antagonised the local police force he now felt safe in assuming that it was something radically more heinous than a traffic offence and there had to be at least a strong possibility that reinforcements might already be galloping into the breach. If batons were being drawn one was at liberty to assume that even roadblocks were not beyond the realms of possibility. After the events of the last twenty-four hours, he was inclined to wonder if anything was.

'I don't know how you got away with that,' he said to Fizz when she sat up and stopped rubbing a stitch in her side. 'If anyone else had tried it they'd have ended up without a car at the very least. We're very lucky that one of them didn't stay at the parking strip.'

She gave a modest smirk. 'The secret is in not giving a sucker time to think,' she said. 'They thought they saw us all going up the path and they couldn't imagine the three of us getting past them on the way down, so why bother about the car? What were they going to do to it anyway? Clamp it?'

She leaned forward suddenly, one finger pointing ahead. 'There's the turn-off to Poolewe.'

Buchanan swung into the left turn without taking his foot off the gas. It felt real good. Two bobbies in a police car couldn't check out both roads at once and they'd almost certainly decide to stick to the main drag. The

Poolewe road led only to the scattered villages and small townships along the coast whereas the one they'd just left headed straight for Inverness and all points south.

'First B&B we come to,' Fizz said, 'I'm out of this car. It's not likely that anyone will come looking for us but there's no point in taking chances. We'll have to split up.'

Buchanan didn't like the sound of that at all. He didn't like the idea of being out of touch with Fizz nor was he exactly gagging to be in sole charge of McKenzie. Fizz's logic was, however, inescapable. There had to be a possibility, however remote, that the police could check out all the overnight accommodation and, together, they would paint an immediately recognisable picture. Fizz, with her mass of golden curls and cherubic face, would stand out a mile anywhere but she was adept at making herself look unobtrusive, and two men with rucksacks were ten-a-penny in this popular hillwalking area.

They passed a petrol station and a reasonable looking snack bar with a worn-blank notice swinging above the door. Facing it across the road they saw a B&B, a big stone house like an old manse, but there was a 'no vacancies' card stuck to its sign so Buchanan ground his teeth and pressed on.

He let Fizz out a couple of miles further

down the road, at a farmhouse B&B set well back from the road, and watched glumly as she grappled with her hair, twisting it up into a woolly hat.

'We can meet later, at that snack bar back there, for a bite to eat,' she said briskly, shoving a few overnight necessities into a day pack. 'I'm starving so don't take forever getting booked in somewhere.'

'There might be a nicer restaurant further on,' McKenzie submitted with just a touch of pique. 'Frankly, chaps, I'm a little on the thirsty side. Bloody thirsty, in fact.'

'Good idea, Scott,' Buchanan said, being fairly sure that any nice restaurant within twenty miles would be closed for lack of custom. 'We'll keep our eyes open. But whether we find one or not, Fizz, we'll meet you at the snack bar as soon as we can.'

'Roger.' She strode up the driveway of the B&B with her Doc's crunching in the gravel. In her sawn-off jeans and naff hat she always looked to Buchanan like a fourteen-year-old boy: only her walk and the shape of her behind belied the depiction.

'What a little angel,' McKenzie murmured from the back seat. 'I'll tell you this, Tam old chap, if I were your age I wouldn't be wasting my time hillwalking. Not interested?'

'If she were a little angel . . . just possibly,

Scott. Unfortunately . . . well, just wait till you know her as well as I do. Believe me, she's no Barbie doll.'

Having lurked behind a hedge long enough to see Fizz admitted, Buchanan let in the clutch and left her to it, already anxious to get back to her. She was easily as self-sufficient as he was, he knew that, but given her propensity for attracting mayhem, who could tell what might happen in the next half hour or so?

They drove a couple of miles down the road without passing another B&B. Buchanan was getting edgy, McKenzie was getting peevish, the day was getting late and they were getting further and further away from Fizz. Two B&B's appeared, close together and both fully booked, then a small triangular sign announced the proximity of a Youth Hostel.

'That'll do,' Buchanan decided. 'Ever been in a Youth Hostel, Scott?'

'I don't believe I've had that pleasure, no.' McKenzie's face in the rear view mirror didn't match the complaisance of his voice. 'One rather imagined there might be a slight age difficulty.'

'I don't believe they care much these days, if they ever did,' Buchanan grinned. 'Fizz tells me they're happy to accommodate virtually any weary traveller.'

'I wouldn't class myself as particularly choosy,' Scott sighed, 'but in the normal way of things my absolute minimum requirement is a room more or less to myself.'

'We could be lucky. Some of them have four-person or even two-person rooms.'

They weren't lucky. This one was a Class C hostel with only ten beds, four of them in the women's dormitory and six in the men's. They were just in time to get the last two bunks but whether that was lucky or not remained to be seen.

The other eight hostellers were a mixed bunch. Four were experienced ramblers, two men and two women in their thirties who were there for a week's Munro bashing. Fizz had climbed most of the Munros and would doubtless have liked to pick their brains, particularly about the Inaccessible Pinnacle which was one of the dozen or so high peaks she had yet to scale.

Of their other four boon companions, two were middle-aged male bird watchers and two were girls in their early twenties who were content to explore the less challenging collection of Corbetts and Grahams between here and Torridon.

Buchanan left McKenzie being sociable in the kitchen and went to see the warden about booking in. There was a good deal of form filling to be done, since neither was a member of the Youth Hostels Association, but it was at least cheap and the atmosphere was quiet and friendly which was all one could ask.

When he got back to the kitchen their fellow sojourners were starting to cook themselves a meal. McKenzie had absented himself to visit the toilet but he reappeared in a few minutes and allowed Buchanan to hasten him back to the car.

Buchanan noticed the smell of whisky before he had time to fasten his safety belt.

'Goddammit, Scott! Where did you get it?'

He lifted both hands in a gesture of mild perplexity. 'A small teaspoonful to keep out the cold. The tiniest — the most homeopathic of doses.'

'Where did you get it?' Buchanan repeated. 'You know that alcohol isn't permitted in Youth Hostels.'

'Ah, but it's a wicked world, Tam. There's always someone willing to break the rules and everyone knows that bird watchers always carry a hip flask.'

'Not in my experience, they don't.'

'Well, this one did,' Scott asserted virtuously. 'Not merely the type of anarchist who'd flout Youth Hostel regulations, you know, but he made me pay through the sodding nose for it.'

'In your present situation, Scott, you really need a clear head. Don't you think you should try to stay sober? Whisky is your worst enemy right now.'

'Whisky, dear boy, is God's way of showing He loves us and wants us to be happy. Did nobody ever tell you that?'

Buchanan gave up. He doubted that McKenzie could have scrounged enough booze to make him disorderly and, in fact, a certain degree of intoxication would probably keep him amenable to whatever steps it became necessary to take for his protection. It appeared that he had already imbibed sufficient for his immediate requirements and, if he was carrying an emergency supply he had the sense to keep it hidden in Buchanan's company.

They met Fizz on the road, less than halfway back to where they had left her.

'I needed to stretch my legs,' she said, signalling McKenzie to stay where he was in the passenger seat and sliding into the back. 'You got fixed up all right, then?'

'Eventually. We had to settle for the Youth Hostel but it's quite pleasant.'

She caught his eye in the mirror and wriggled her nose at him, her eyes commenting on the whisky fumes. He nodded and shrugged his shoulders but she made no comment other than the remonstrance implied by letting down the window.

The snack bar was of the cheap-and-cheerful variety with a fairly restricted choice but generous portions. It was busy with outdoor types who, Buchanan had discovered, invariably eat early, but they found themselves a recently vacated table by the window and self-served themselves from the counter.

'I heard an interesting news item on the local radio station,' Fizz said when they got settled. 'The landlady had it on in the lounge when I went in.'

'Dammit, we should have thought to monitor the news broadcasts,' Buchanan said.

'Well, let's face it, we haven't exactly had much quality time to waste,' Fizz told him.

'What was it you heard? Something to do with Scott?'

'The car crash.' She finished buttering a roll and wiped her fingers on her serviette. 'The Mitsubishi was found — burned out — yesterday evening, it didn't say by whom, and the police are still trying to identify the incinerated body inside it. Inside it, you'll notice, not yards away as we left it. The report says that the vehicle was stolen from outside a doctor's surgery in Huntly Street, Inverness.'

'Not nice,' said McKenzie, looking aghast. 'Bloody poor show — saving your presence, m'dear — but that was Marianne. Why'd somebody have to cremate that lovely girl?'

'Well, she was dead, Scott,' Fizz pointed out. She hadn't enjoyed the experience of watching somebody die but she wasn't going to get maudlin about someone she didn't even know. 'Somebody wanted to get rid of the evidence. Whoever did it — presumably your two police buddies — they didn't want anything to lead back to you and Marianne. Was it she who stole the car from the doctor's surgery?'

'My darling, your guess is as good as mine. I have certainly no recollection of being in Inverness recently, that I can tell you. Damn draughty place, Inverness.'

'Where do you come from, Scott?' Buchanan asked.

'Edinburgh. Only place to live. Always something going on.'

'Do you have a wife? Family? A circle of friends?'

'Absolutely. All three.' He tasted a mouthful of soup and appended, as an afterthought, 'On and off.'

'How do you mean, 'on and off'?' Fizz asked.

'We have an on-and-off relationship, that's

all. Corinne moved into a flat of her own, couple of years back, and the kids are both off our hands. Perfect arrangement. Still see each other most weeks. The odd cosy dinner. Suits us all.'

Buchanan, sensing hidden heartache behind McKenzie's determined buoyancy, nudged the conversation onto more pressing matters. 'I think we have to find out how you came to be in Inverness. Do you have any acquaintances there? Do you know anyone at all who has connections with the city?'

McKenzie shook his head. 'No. 'fraid not.'

'What's the last thing you remember? Back in Edinburgh. Were you drinking?'

'Very likely, dear boy,' said McKenzie with great dignity. 'No point of bein' sober if y'don't have to.'

Buchanan sighed and glanced at Fizz who said,

'Think about being back in Edinburgh. Was anything interesting happening? Any good news or bad news? Were you planning a trip? Was your wife around?'

McKenzie answered each question with an apologetic negative, faintly amused at her persistence. 'Tell you the truth, one day of my life is much like another: get myself up and dressed, down to the golf clubhouse for lunch, few drinks in the afternoon, few more in the evening, the odd dinner with friends, occasional visit from the wife or the brat pack. Just about got things organised the way I like them.'

Fizz looked at him with frustration and reapplied herself to her food, leaving Buchanan to think up a new approach, but a few seconds later McKenzie laid down his spoon. 'You know, I do believe I was drinking somewhere different recently.'

'How recently?' Fizz demanded.

'Well now, that's the question, isn't it?' he said, smiling at her with great affection. 'Could have been last week, could have been the day before yesterday, could have been a month ago.'

'What sort of place?' said Buchanan.

He closed his eyes, looking instantly ten years older, and applied his mind to the enigma. 'Not the clubhouse. The clubhouse is modern, all glass and pine, but this place was dark . . . traditional. Comfy chairs. Fancy satin shades on the table lamps.'

'But it was in Edinburgh?' Fizz asked, her face showing her chagrin at the thought of distinguishing it from several thousand similar establishments.

'Could've been,' McKenzie answered, optimism opening his eyes. 'Rather think it was. A gentlemen's club, maybe. That sort of thing.'

'Or someone's house?' Buchanan hazarded and saw by Scott's face that he really didn't have a clue. Despondency settled over the table and they ate the remainder of their meal in virtual silence. As they were dawdling over their coffee the police showed up.

'Oh shite!' said Fizz loud enough to draw stunned looks from diners at the next table who doubtless couldn't quite believe those rosebud lips capable of such vulgarity. She started to stand up but Buchanan held her down.

'Take it easy,' he muttered, grinning for the benefit of their neighbours. 'They're not coming in here: they're going into the B&B across the road. The Saab's not visible from there.'

'What if they come in?' She had rearranged her alarmed face into a less attention-grabbing expression but her voice was quivery with tension.

'If they do, they do. Making a break for it at this stage won't make things any easier for our defence council. They're not going to give us a doing over in front of witnesses, whatever we're supposed to have done, so we'll have a chance to talk our way out of it.'

McKenzie listened with a vague frown wrinkling his brow, obviously not quite clear about what was going on but convinced that he could catch up with things if he could just sit down and think about it quietly. In silence they watched the two policemen — neither of whom had already crossed their path — ring the doorbell of the house across the road. There were trees in the front garden which made it difficult to see what was going on but, after a moment, someone came to the door and ushered the coppers inside.

Nobody said anything. They all popped out of their seats as if they'd been ejected by the same flick of a switch. Buchanan threw a twenty pound note on the counter as they passed and was rolling the Saab out of the car park in a matter of seconds.

Things were now going from bad to worse. There must be a police report out on the Saab and instead of a couple of wacky cops it appeared that they now had the full force of the law to contend with. That left only two options: back to the main drag and the higher risk of road blocks, or onward towards the barely inhabited seaboard of Wester Ross where everyone who knew a Saab from a Model T Ford would spot them and call the authorities. Either way, the odds didn't look all that great.

6

They had to wait, halfway up a stalkers' track that scarred the beautiful face of Sgurr Maiseach, for the short night to fall.

Fizz couldn't believe the mess they were in. Whichever way they turned, it seemed, the outlook was appalling. Handing McKenzie over to the police would — presumably — solve most of their immediate problems but Buchanan bilked at the suggestion and, if she were honest with herself, so did Fizz. She was pretty certain, from the way that policeman had glared at her, back in Ullapool, that if she walked into a police station with McKenzie it would be a long time before she emerged. Precisely how she had become known to the police and whether Buchanan was similarly implicated was anybody's guess.

There was nothing in the radio news reports they were able to pick up on the car radio that they could tie-in to their current predicament. No murders, no terrorist attacks, and no further mention, even on the local station, of the burned out car. The breaking story of yet another royal scandal had crowded out most of the smaller items from the updates on both the Scottish and the national news, and reception on the smaller stations was smothered by the surrounding mountains.

They left McKenzie sleeping in the back seat and passed the time walking up and down the track as far as they could in each direction while still keeping the car and its occupant, in sight. Neither of them had any suggestions for breaking out of the situation and, from the look of him, the whole business was beginning to get to Buchanan.

'We're being held over a barrel!' he growled, tramping along with his eyes on the ground, oblivious to a sunset like a Bloody Mary. 'That's what's doing my head in. It's like we don't have any free will. Events are just manipulating us like glove puppets.'

'Uh-huh. You're right. We have to regain control.'

He looked at her with one eyebrow hooked up in polite interest. 'And how do you suggest we do that?'

'I just come up with the ideas. It's up to you to make them work.'

'Great. Just give me a couple of minutes.'

'There must be steps we can take,' Fizz insisted.

'Sure. Fax me the list.'

Ten minutes pacing uphill produced no inspiration. Fizz had ceased to grieve over her ruined weekend and wanted only to be back in Edinburgh, but who could tell what might be waiting for her there? It sickened her to think that she could win back to her little eyrie in the High Street to find a welcome party awaiting her arrival — armed police, for all she could bloody tell, ready to shoot her down on sight.

As they turned to walk back down to the car Buchanan said, 'There's not a damn thing we can do till we've discovered what they want us for. It's got to be something pretty heavy. Some sort of violent crime, I guess.'

'Violent?' Fizz repeated, wondering how bad things could get. 'How do you work that out?'

'Those two who chased you up the hill had their batons at the ready. They must have thought we were dangerous.'

'If they thought we were dangerous they'd have called for help, not come plunging in after us.'

'I'm not sure about that,' Buchanan muttered. 'They were being forced to act fast, remember, like you said. They'd have had to figure that if they wasted any time we'd be able to get over the other side of the hill and disappear into the wilderness. They had us in their sights, or thought they had, and they could have caught up in a matter of minutes, no doubt about it. Two big guys like that, armed with batons? They didn't need reinforcements.'

'Unless we'd had guns,' Fizz objected. 'How'd they know we weren't armed?'

Buchanan shrugged. 'They didn't. Maybe they thought that if we had a gun we'd have used it earlier.'

'We can't be sure that they were real policemen, Buchanan. Okay, they were different guys from the original two, but we could be up against any number of fakes. The whole Northern Division can't be after us, can they?'

Buchanan's face said he wished he could be sure of that.

The recollection of McKenzie's experience at the hands of the first two policemen was stuck in Fizz's head like a hatchet. He hadn't been given a split second's opportunity to explain, or to claim his innocence or even to beg for mercy. If they didn't establish which of the policemen were goodies and which were baddies it could be all three of them who copped it next. Which didn't encourage one to sally forth with one's hands up.

They passed the car, where McKenzie was still in the Land of Nod and continued on down to the foot of the hill. The red had all but faded from the horizon now, leaving only a few gleaming streaks on the lower edges of some baby cumulus. On the other side of the valley Fizz spotted a lookout stag on the skyline and presently picked out a group of hinds and yearlings grazing across the shadowed slope below it.

To the south they could recognise several of the Torridon peaks: bald Maol Chean-dearg and the crest of Ben Alligin still pink in the last rays of sunset.

Buchanan looked at them for a long time then turned his back on the sight with brisk determination and started back up the hill.

'Okay,' he said. 'We stop running away. We have to find out what we're up against and the only way we can do that is to discover what Scott McKenzie has been up to. He's the root of the trouble: he has to point the way out.'

'You're wasting your time, compadre,' Fizz had to tell him. 'Nothing short of trepanning is going to get anything worthwhile out of McKenzie. His brain's like tapioca.'

'Granted, so we have to follow the only clue we've got.'

Fizz turned her head to look at him. 'We have a clue?'

'Sure we have a clue. The news item. You heard it yourself.'

She had more or less forgotten the report and, in any case, she felt that it had already yielded all the enlightenment they were likely to gain from it. One didn't have to admit this to Buchanan, however.

She said, 'Oh, yes. Of course,' in a judicious manner.

'It's a long shot, of course, but we have to try everything we can.' Buchanan zipped up his fleece against the chill breeze that was drifting down from the tops. 'We know precisely where the car was stolen from — a doctor's surgery in Huntly Street, Inverness — so there's chance that the sight of the place could jog McKenzie's memory. Even if he doesn't recognise the doctor's surgery he might latch on to something else that does ring a bell.'

'Right,' Fizz agreed, happy to go along with anything that had a hope of breaking the deadlock. 'Well, if that's what you want to go for you'd better keep an eye on Lucky Jim. I wouldn't mind betting he still has some booze about his person and we'll want him sober when we get there.'

'He can't have much left,' Buchanan surmised, looking a bit more cheerful now he'd found a way forward. 'If we make sure he doesn't get any fresh supplies for a few hours we'll be doing as well as we can hope for.' He looked at his watch and then at the sky. 'This is probably as dark as it's going to get. Let's hit the road.'

McKenzie didn't wake as they got back into the car and Buchanan took care not to disturb his slumber as he gently let in the clutch and rolled slowly back to the road.

The only route available was through Glen Torridon and Strath Bran but they passed only a couple of lorries on the road and the roadblocks they dreaded failed to materialise. Buchanan drove cautiously, nosing round every junction with every muscle tensed, ready to whip the Saab into reverse, and when they reached the outskirts of the city he kept to the minor roads as much as he could. This slowed them up so much that it was broad daylight before he was able to find a parking spot in a residential area where the car was unlikely to attract attention.

McKenzie woke bright-eyed and bushy-tailed. He shared Buchanan's razor and hairbrush and made only a token fuss about postponing his first nip of the day till they reached the doctor's surgery. The appalling orange cap caused a difference of opinion but he eventually acceded to Buchanan's request that it should be left in the boot of the car, though not to Fizz's suggestion that it should be donated to the blind.

There weren't enough people around to be used as cover so Fizz walked on one side of the street with her hair covered by a scarf while Buchanan and McKenzie trailed her on the other side, one a good twenty paces behind the other. Buchanan, who was in the rear, was ambling along, pausing to look in shop windows, allowing other pedestrians to come between McKenzie and himself and managing to look like your average tourist, but the way McKenzie was stumbling along gave Fizz the eebie jeebies. Any policemen who came along would spot that he was still tiddly and run him in faster than he could say 'Cheers'.

Huntly Street paralleled the course of the river Ness on the opposite side from the castle. Buchanan took over the lead at the Ness Bridge and piloted them past a row of restaurants, gift shops and the like till they reached a building set back from the pavement and identifiable as the surgery of one Peter McLaren, M.R.C.G.P D.R.C.O.G D.C.H.

Fizz stopped and pretended to be studying the surgery hours advertised beneath the name. Buchanan nervously scanned both sides of the river. McKenzie furrowed his brow helpfully.

'Well?' Fizz prompted him. 'Anything look familiar?'

'Shush,' said Buchanan. 'Give him a minute.'

Fizz gave him a minute and then another one. He finished staring at the facade of the surgery and started turning around on his heel taking in the view.

'Well?' said Buchanan this time.

'I know that bridge,' McKenzie said, indicating not the Ness Bridge but the suspension bridge further along. 'There's a pub on the other side.'

This struck Fizz as definitely promising but Buchanan looked dissatisfied. 'What about the surgery? Wasn't that where someone got shot?'

'Oh no, dear chap. That was somewhere completely different. Bigger. Great high ceilings.'

Buchanan stared at him, almost willing him to continue.

'Echoing,' McKenzie obliged with an effort that clearly scraped the bottom of his memory barrel.

Buchanan stuck his hands in his pockets and looked at the sky, probably praying for deliverance. 'Okay,' he decided after a minute. 'We may as well take a gander at the pub.'

That idea grabbed McKenzie immediately and he set off, with only a trace of unsteadiness and at a speed that took neither of them by surprise. Fizz fell in behind him but was in no hurry to catch up because she was fairly sure that, had he looked at his watch, he'd have realised that no pub would be opening for business for at least another hour. Drinking might be the hobby of the Highlander but Inverness was run by God-fearing folk who weren't going to encourage them. Not at this hour in the morning.

The rush hour was barely underway as they walked across the suspension bridge and converged at the doorway of 'The Persevere.'

'That's right!' McKenzie enthused, flapping a hand at the sign. 'That's right! The Persevere! Great place. Lovely barmaid.' His face fell as he saw the 'Closed' sign on the door. 'Well, bugger me — saving your presence, m'dear.'

Fizz scanned the street and found a café a few doors down on the other side. 'Let's have some breakfast while we wait for opening time. It'll give you leisure to think about the pub and see if anything comes back to you.'

Buchanan was in agreement and, although McKenzie had counter suggestions to offer, they were voted out and he was escorted across the road with firm resolution.

Due to the early hour they were the only people in the café but they eschewed the window table in the interests of stealth and settled themselves where they had a clear view of the doorway and of the pub entrance up the road. Fizz went up to the counter and ordered everything on the breakfast menu for all three of them, there being no certainty where or when they'd see their next meal.

When she got back to the table Buchanan was gently teasing through the tangled skein of McKenzie's memory, separating out what might be recent events from those of long ago.

'So, was it this pub that you remembered having the comfortable chairs and the nice lampshades?'

'Good God no, Tam.' McKenzie blew out his cheeks with a sort of snorty laugh and stood up like a gentleman to hold a chair out for Fizz. 'No, no. That was another place altogether. The Persevere isn't that sort of place at all. More your spit-and-sawdust type of watering hole, y'know what I mean? None of your airs and graces. Probably hasn't had a lick of paint since D-day; brass foot rail; old mirrors. Atmosphere to the rafters.'

'Bit of a change from the jolly old golf club,

95

what?' Fizz couldn't resist remarking. Buchanan scowled and McKenzie pointed a finger at her and said, in several installments and largely by accident,

'Stone walls . . . do not a boozer make . . . nor iron cage a bar,' which amused him so much he nearly choked himself to death.

Fizz tried to exchange a speaking glance with Buchanan but he had an elbow on the table and a hand across his eyes as though the milk of human kindness had turned to yogurt in his breast. McKenzie was beginning to pall on both of them, which was a shame because he was basically such a nice guy. He was at present almost totally sober and you could see that, minus the influence of hard liquor, he still showed traces of intelligence and an occasionally appealing sense of fun.

'Scott,' Fizz said, in a reasonable kind of voice, 'if we're ever to get out of this predicament you've got to remember how you got into it. Please try very hard, if not for your own sake, then for Buchanan's and mine. I don't know how it happened but somehow or other we've become embroiled in the mess and if we get into trouble with the police the consequences to our careers could be horrific.'

'But I don't remember a damn thing . . . '

'Yes, well we're going to sit here till you

do,' she ground out, the reasonable tone already biting the dust. 'Look at that pub over there. You remember what it was like inside. Now try to remember who you were with. Did you know them before you met them in the pub or did you meet them there? What were you talking about? Were you happy or were you uneasy? Who was paying? Just keep focused on the pub and let your mind wander over these questions. Something will float to the surface.'

'Fizz, my darling little cherub, ask of me what you will, even unto half my kingdom and it shall be yours.' He smiled up at the waitress who was delivering their breakfast. 'Thank you, my dear. That looks delicious.'

'Just do it, Scott. Okay?' Fizz insisted.

'Absolutely. It will have my full concentration.'

Fizz made sure of that — or as sure as she could be — by refusing to allow further conversation while they put away as much food as they could accommodate at one sitting. She was in no hurry to vacate the café which was still empty and conveniently dim. The waitress showed no interest in them and it seemed likely that, if the police were still looking for them it would be on the other side of the country.

Buchanan was still on the *qui vive* and couldn't take his eyes off the window but he willingly dawdled over his third cup of coffee while McKenzie made at least a pretense of riffling through his memory banks.

'Marianne wasn't Fergie's girlfriend,' appeared to be the best he could offer. 'I had a feeling she might have been but now I think I'd got that wrong.'

'What makes you think so?' Buchanan asked.

McKenzie hummed a bit, waggling his head uncertainly and dabbing his serviette at a drop of coffee on the plastic tabletop. 'Marianne was top drawer. Lovely girl. Educated. Fergie . . . Fergie was a nice enough chap and generous to a fault but . . . not Marianne's type, if you follow me.'

'I'm right behind you,' Fizz nodded. 'He was scruff, right?'

McKenzie looked pained, but Fizz took it as a 'yes' anyway.

'His intelligence, shall we say, was not on a par with Marianne's.' He drew a line in the air with one forefinger as though to indicate that he had said all he cared to say on that subject. 'I have the impression though — it's just an impression and I may be completely wrong — I have the impression that they were connected somehow . . . colleagues, maybe.'

'You mean, he might have been her employee?' said Buchanan.

McKenzie waved his hands about. 'I get the feeling they were both employees. Of someone else. It's only a feeling, you understand.'

They sat hunched over their coffees for a while like three wise monkeys, staring out at the pub as it opened for business, and picking over these new facts for another lead. Fizz was trying to invent some sort of scenario that would include a foxy lady like Marianne, a thicko like Fergie, a drunk like McKenzie and, apparently, some kind of business concern, organization or criminal alliance. It wasn't easy.

One thing she couldn't get her head round was Fergie's generosity. If her picture of him was accurate — and she was fairly sure it was, for all McKenzie's political correctness — it was unlikely he'd have had all that much money to throw around. Certainly not enough to impress even a totally blootered McKenzie with his munificence. Which would mean that somebody was bankrolling him to keep his drinking buddy happy. Or smashed.

She relayed these thoughts to Buchanan and McKenzie, both of whom looked much struck by the implication.

'By George,' McKenzie muttered, 'but that strikes a chord, you know. It's the worst blinder I've ever experienced, I can tell you that. I don't mind admitting I've had the odd lost weekend now and then but nothing on this scale. To tell you the truth, chaps, it gave me a bit of a scare.'

'Think about it,' Fizz advised, always willing to organise someone else's life. 'That's what you're heading for sooner or later. Brain death. Addictions don't stand still, they get stronger day by day.'

Buchanan pursed his lips and intervened before she got into her stride. 'At least things are coming back to you, Scott. If you can keep working at it I'm sure you can piece some more together.'

McKenzie answered with a pessimistic grunt but he returned to his scrutiny of the bar with what looked to Fizz like renewed resolve.

'We can't hang around here much longer without drawing attention to ourselves,' Buchanan said. 'If nobody has a better idea, I vote we should move to another vantage point.'

Fizz would have voted for going home. She was due back at the university tomorrow and she was almost as determined to get back to her responsibilities as Buchanan was, but it clearly behoved them both to get this mess cleared up first if they possibly could. They had only the one small lead so they'd no choice but to squeeze it till the pips squeaked.

She and McKenzie waited in the doorway while Buchanan went to the counter to pay the bill. As far as Fizz could tell McKenzie still had almost all of his roll of banknotes but, like a lot of financially gifted people, it didn't seem to occur to him to put his hand in his pocket, and Buchanan was too much of a gentleman (sucker, some might say) to remind him.

Fizz was on the point of rectifying matters when McKenzie suddenly stiffened and turned his back on the street.

'Those chaps over there,' he hissed over his shoulder. 'I know one of them and I'm damn sure I've seen one of the others before too.'

'Fergie?' Fizz prompted, stepping back into the shadows.

'No — the other one who was drinking with us. That's him with the leather jacket. And the bald chap — I've run into him somewhere. Maybe not in The Persevere, but somewhere. Sodding hell — saving your presence, Fizz — but it's damn frustrating.'

The bald chap had a face that would lodge in anyone's memory, Fizz reckoned, particularly in the memory of anyone who chanced to get up his nose. His eyes were almost invisible behind a layer of scar tissue that identified him as a boxer and his clamped-shut mouth had all the charm of a gin trap.

The other one, allegedly Fergie's sidekick, looked like Little Lord Fauntleroy by comparison but even he wasn't the kind you'd take home to Mummy. In fact any judge worth his salt would have given all four of the group twenty-one days before asking any questions.

'For pity's sake, McKenzie,' she muttered, 'what have you been getting yourself into? You were drinking with these guys? You're lucky you have a penny left to your name.'

While she watched the men, who were standing talking at the pub door, her mind was dancing ahead. These thugs had obviously seen McKenzie as an easy mark: a helpless drunk with a pocket full of cash and all the signs of more cash within access. They must have been planning to milk him white.

Buchanan emerged from the café and twigged immediately that something was up. He pulled back into the recessed doorway while Fizz brought him up to speed, and hummed under his breath when he saw the group across the road split up: Baldy and The Other One going into the pub and the remaining two heading down the hill towards the river.

'I'm going to tail those two,' he said quickly. 'You stay here and keep an eye on the pub. If the other two come out don't follow them, just try to get a good look at them and note which direction they head in.'

Fizz didn't think that was a good idea but nobody asked for her opinion.

7

It wasn't difficult to keep the two men in sight. They weren't as tall as the two they'd parted with but one of them was wearing a yellow sports shirt which kept flashing in and out like a beacon between the other pedestrians.

They were in no hurry to get where they were going. At points where Buchanan allowed the gap between them to close a little he could detect an air of weariness about them. One of them yawned repeatedly and both of them appeared to be in need of a shave. If Buchanan had been one to leap to conclusions he'd have put them down as night shift workers on their way home.

He expected momentarily to see them hop into a car, which would have put the tin hat on it since the Saab was a five minute sprint away, but they reached the river without incident and turned right along River Walk. There were fewer pedestrians there so Buchanan was forced to loiter outside a restaurant, pretending to read the menu in the window, while the two got further and further ahead.

They were still in sight, however, when they disappeared into the driveway of a big detached house with turrets and a garden full of tall trees. It appeared so unlikely that they would have business at such a flash address that Buchanan half suspected they were lurking out of sight behind the wall, waiting to grab him as he came by. He crossed the road and paced casually along, looking at the river, till he reached the gateway and saw the garden to be empty.

The house itself had a seedy look to it, the curtains untidily drawn, the windows grimy, a pair of dirty trainers drying out on an upstairs window sill. There was a car just inside the gateposts, a beat up, unwashed old Ford, and beyond that, at the end of the driveway, he could see the rear end of a van that looked like a Ford Transit.

The set-up looked familiar to Buchanan. Where the owner of such a property wanted to hang on to it as an investment he or she had either to live in it or rent it out and tenants for such big houses were hard to find. From time to time, usually as executor of estates, he himself had been forced to accept tenants who were less than ideal; itinerant sales forces, workers on a building project, or similar transients. This, he surmised, was the sort of situation he was looking at. He hated to see a beautiful Victorian building go downhill but the eventual purchaser would inevitably want to turn it into offices so the interior was doomed to be vandalised one way or another.

He hung around for a minute or two but there was nothing much to be gleaned from the exterior of the building and nothing showed through the dirty windows so he zapped back to where Fizz and McKenzie were awaiting him in the café. They both looked flatteringly relieved to see him.

'They didn't lead you very far, then?' Fizz said.

'Just down by the river walk. A big house showing signs of multiple occupancy. Maybe divided into flats or bedsitters, it's difficult to tell. Either that or it's some bunch of short-term labourers.' Buchanan, sat down at the table they'd reoccupied and raised an optimistic eyebrow at McKenzie but he elicited nothing but a shrug. 'Doesn't tell me anything, sorry, Tam.'

'Maybe if you saw the place for yourself,' Fizz insisted.

'Anything is possible.' McKenzie bent a look of adoration on her baby face. 'I have to say, a big house doesn't figure in my recollections but one never can tell.'

Fizz's expression was as boot-like as its

106

cherubic contours permitted. She drew a slow breath and turned to Buchanan.

'I've been thinking,' she said. 'If you're right about Scott — and now, presumably, us — being mixed up in some serious crime, the chances are that the crime will have been reported in the papers somewhere. We should get on the Web and start sussing out back numbers till we find something that matches what we know.'

That struck Buchanan as a good idea. 'Uh-huh,' he said, and then thought about it for a minute. 'Uh . . . what *do* we know?'

'Well, we know that it probably took place in an echoey building with high ceilings and we know that somebody was shot. There can't be too many incidents like that per week. Not in Inverness.' She glared at McKenzie. 'And maybe Scott could come up with something useful if he put his mind to it.'

McKenzie was draining the last drops from a cup of coffee and failed to register her irritation.

'Yes, well it's certainly worth a try,' Buchanan agreed. 'I'll get onto it as soon as we get home.'

'Yeah, and also I want to talk to you about getting home.' Fizz pushed her empty cup towards McKenzie. 'How about getting in another round, Scott, dear old chap?'

'Another? You want another coffee? Certainly, certainly.' He wandered off in an aimless fashion towards the counter, while they both kept him under close examination in case he got up to something.

'What do you plan to do with him?' Fizz asked. 'Take him back with us?'

Buchanan profoundly wished he had a choice in the matter. 'That's where he lives,' he said. 'I think we have to offer him transport at the very least. Maybe things will clarify themselves once he gets back to his own home.'

Fizz gave him a wan smile. 'Anything's possible. What worries me is getting him there without finding ourselves completing the trip under police escort.' She tucked a long spiral of hair behind her ear and frowned at McKenzie's back. 'It's a long drive from here to Edinburgh and the police may be on the lookout for the Saab.'

That thought had been irking Buchanan too. 'I'm not abandoning it, if that's what you're about to suggest,' he said. 'I think there's a good chance they haven't got the license number.'

'That's what I think,' Fizz nodded. 'So, if you're stopped on the road you can bluff your way out of it. I can phone Grampa and warn him to give you an alibi if it comes to the nitty gritty.'

'No, you bloody can't, Fizz!' Buchanan exploded, taking his eyes off McKenzie for a moment to roll them in horror. Fizz's readiness to embroil those nearest and dearest to her in the most dire situations never ceased to appal him. 'The last thing we want is for Grampa and Auntie Duff to become involved.'

'Well, someone else, then,' Fizz returned, tossing her curls impatiently. 'I'll get the folk at the Clachan Inn to say you stayed there the last couple of nights — if anyone should ask them, which they probably won't. The point I'm trying to make is that you are possibly in the clear thus far. Those two coppers who chased us out of Ullapool didn't get a close look at you. I don't see how they could have known you were with Scott and I and they didn't seem to be looking in your direction at all.'

Buchanan didn't share her optimism. He had to agree that the coppers hadn't appeared interested in him at first but they'd indubitably spotted him running Scott down the road. He said as much to Fizz but she wasn't perturbed.

'They only saw your back, and from a good fifty yards away, between cars. They might suspect you but I doubt if they could pick you out of a police line-up.'

Buchanan's stomach muscles knotted at the thought. 'I hope to God you're right, Fizz, but for some unfathomable reason they appear to be able to identify you without much trouble and Scott is obviously known to them.'

'That's what I was about to say.' Her eyes followed McKenzie as he left the counter and headed for the gents, but she hesitated only for a moment and then went on. 'With Scott and I in the car with you there's no way you could talk yourself out of it. We have to split up.'

Buchanan knew that his immediately negative response was irrational but she didn't allow him time to voice it.

'Just don't start, okay? You know it's the only sensible choice available to us. Scott and I can take the train and you can meet us at Waverley Station. The worst that can happen is that we'll get nabbed but, if we do, at least you'll be on the outside and able to pull strings for us.'

Even at the best of times, optimism was not one of Buchanan's strong points and in situations involving Fizz it dwindled to a barely detectable minimum. The idea of saving his own skin at the expense of Fizz's, and to a lesser extent McKenzie's, was deeply distasteful yet he couldn't deny the reality that further implicating himself would do nobody any good.

While he psyched himself up to agree to the proposal he divided his time between watching for McKenzie's reappearance from the gents and eyeing the pub up the road. There was a balding chap in shades apparently looking in at the window but, on closer inspection, he proved to be reading the menu.

Finally he said, 'Okay, Fizz. That's how we'll do it. I don't like leaving you with the heavy end but as long as McKenzie stays reasonably sober you should be able to handle anything that comes up.'

'I think he'll stay reasonably sober,' Fizz said, tipping her head towards Scott's reappearance at the counter. 'He's been doing very well all morning. He's only been in there three times so far, hadn't you noticed?'

'You mean, he's topping up?' Buchanan had noticed nothing amiss but put it down to having his attention concentrated on too many different things.

'Just little by little, I think. He's an alcoholic, certainly, but not quite the hopeless case we thought he was, and he's doing his level best right now. I reckon he's a lot more scared than he's letting on.'

So was Buchanan, for that matter, but he felt that now was not the time to admit it.

They killed another hour in the café, eating the substantial lunch that Fizz considered appropriate to their uncertain state and watching the pub for the re-emergence of Fergie and The Other One. When they did emerge Buchanan tailed them to the corner of the riverside walk from where he could be certain that their destination was the same house that their friends had entered. Then, since no one else had any other option to suggest, he escorted Fizz and McKenzie, at a distance, to the railway station and watched them till they boarded the train for Edinburgh.

Fizz had her woolly hat and sunglasses on, a combination which turned no heads in the capital of the north, and she was careful to enter McKenzie's compartment several minutes after he did. Buchanan had to accept that she had all the cunning, and more, to finagle her way safely to Edinburgh, if anybody could, but there was a cold and empty void below his ribs as he walked back to the Saab.

★ ★ ★

Fizz was, in a way, rather glad to be rid of him.

In situations such as this one didn't necessarily want someone like Buchanan looking over one's shoulder, prophesying everlasting doom every time a small stretching of the truth became appropriate, and complaining loudly if one stepped over the line dividing the expedient from the strictly legal.

With only McKenzie to occupy her mind she felt more in control of the situation. She was very much at home on trains, having passed a large part of her misspent youth travelling on them and, since she had only rarely bought a ticket, she was adept at avoiding the interest of the authorities.

McKenzie had chosen a good seat, one at the end of a carriage and facing a bulwark so that, thanks to the high seat backs, he was observed only by the youth who shared his table as far as Aviemore and by Fizz who had rudely spread herself and her belongings across the four seats across the aisle. The train, in any case, was abnormally quiet, probably because it was the slow one that stopped at every hamlet, so there were plenty of other seats.

From Aviemore onwards they were left alone but Fizz refused to communicate, even by sign language and McKenzie, soon after another visit to the toilet, sank into his usual afternoon stupor.

Fizz relaxed as much as she could, read the free magazine and tried to concentrate on the case in hand. People got on and off, passengers passed by on their way to the toilet, every one of them potentially a plain clothes copper or one of McKenzie's dodgy pals. Some of them appeared to stare closely at McKenzie or herself and although she knew that people do that anyway when they're bored rigid, she tensed up each time it happened.

Each time they approached a station she got up and stuck her head out of the window between the carriages so that if she saw anything worrying on the platform as they pulled in, she'd have a few minutes warning. It was hard, even now, to accept that the police might board the train — so hard, in fact, that when two policemen came aboard at Dunblane she was quite prepared to believe that they were merely travelling home after the day's graft.

McKenzie was deeply asleep, propped in the corner of his booth, so she left him there and hurried forward to the front of the train where the police constables had boarded. It didn't do her heart any good when she saw, from the adjacent coach, that they were not sitting down but moving slowly towards her, subjecting each passenger they passed to a close, albeit bored, scrutiny.

Her first impulse was to dive into the ladies and abandon McKenzie to his fate, but at that moment a fat woman rose from her seat just behind her and barged past her into the loo. Balked, Fizz hesitated for a moment. The fat woman had left a feathered hat and a shawl-like scarf lying in her booth, which was otherwise empty. It was the work of a split second to grab them as she rushed past, staggering back to McKenzie as fast as the rolling of the train would permit.

McKenzie was still snoring softly as she crammed the hat well down over his brow and tucked the scarf over the front of his jacket. His legs were hidden by the table and Fizz was convinced that he made a better looking woman than the one who'd beaten her to the toilet. Seconds later she was two coaches further down the train and slipping into the next toilet, which was fortunately free.

It took two or three minutes for the coppers to reach her and, although she was waiting for it, her whole body spasmed at their knock.

'What is it, for goodness sake?' she said, in

a fair imitation of an elderly voice which was enhanced by a wonderfully convincing quaver.

'Sorry, madam. It's the police. Just checking.'

'Well, dearie me! Can a body no' get peace to visit the toilet? Go away!'

'Sorry to bother you, madam.'

Fizz couldn't be sure whether they had moved on or were still waiting outside for her to emerge. Past experience led her to expect the former since she had come across few officials who took their jobs seriously enough to double check, but she waited a minute or two to make sure.

Sure enough, they were now working their way down the next carriage, their backs conveniently turned, giving her the chance to scoot back to McKenzie.

The hat and scarf posed a problem that demanded immediate solution. If she didn't return them soon — hopefully before their owner returned from the toilet — the woman would start complaining about being robbed and the policemen would know that something was up. But, at the same time, it was dangerous to denude McKenzie of his disguise while the cops were on the train since they could easily decide to work their way back up again just to make sure they

116

hadn't missed somebody.

She dithered for a few seconds — a few seconds too long, she realised, as the fat woman reappeared and took her seat at the end of the carriage. Fizz looked back down the line of coaches as far as she could see, which wasn't far. There was no sign of the constables and it seemed a fair bet that they wouldn't come back. The next station was only a few minutes away so it would scarcely be worth the effort of starting a re-check. Hastily, she grabbed the hat and scarf and hauled herself back up the carriage.

The woman was half under the table searching the floor for her lost belongings. There was a split second when Fizz could have dropped them on the table and disappeared without being seen, but her reflexes let her down and she had to tough it out.

'I'm most dreadfully sorry,' she said in her best Morningside accent. 'I do hope you'll forgive me — I've made a terrible mistake!'

A flushed face rose above the edge of the table like a Turner sun and two hard brown eyes fixed themselves on hers.

'Pardon?'

'So stupid of me! I thought these were my mother's. She just got off at Dunblane and when I saw them lying there they looked exactly like what she was wearing. Luckily my husband noticed that Mum still had her hat and scarf on when she got off so I've brought them straight back. I really am most terribly sorry. So embarrassing.'

The woman reclaimed her things and examined them as though to assure herself that Fizz hadn't cut out any bits for a patchwork quilt. Then she said, 'Thank you,' very coldly with her lips and 'Liar!' very hotly with her eyes and turned huffily away, probably not sure what had happened but imagining the worst.

Fizz felt she'd got off as lightly as she could have hoped and was beginning to draw a breath of relief when she looked back towards McKenzie and, to her horror and disbelief, saw the two policemen about to come through the door at the end of the carriage behind him.

It was quite obvious to Fizz in that first instant that there wasn't a damn thing she could do to save McKenzie. He was still lying as she had left him, wedged into his corner with his naked face tilted up and angled towards the aisle, and if he'd had a placard with his name on it slung around his neck he couldn't have presented a more conspicuous vision.

In such a situation Fizz's thoughts turned

invariably to Numero Uno. She had about three seconds to get the hell out of it. Happily, the toilet door was only a couple of paces away and she was already at the door as the policemen moved forward into the other end of the carriage. In the split second she managed to snatch for a last look, they were all but level with their target.

McKenzie lay helpless on their left but the leading constable looked first towards the empty seat on his right. Then, in the time it took him to turn his head, a small, balding man in sunglasses rose from his seat, just forward of McKenzie's, and tried to squeeze past them, evidently in a hurry to reach the far toilet. There was a momentary reshuffling while the man leaned back into McKenzie's booth to allow the coppers passage, then they all went their separate ways without a backward glance, leaving McKenzie to slumber on.

Fizz dived into the toilet, threw the bolt with shaking fingers, and fell back against the door.

'Bloody hell!' she whispered to her wide-eyed reflection in the mirror. 'I can't take much more of this.'

This time the coppers didn't bother knocking on the door, which was something of a disappointment since it would have been fun to pretend to be the same incontinent old lady and claim police harassment.

She sat there till her knees stopped knocking and emerged only when the train drew into the next station, fairly sure that the policemen would get off there and take the next train back to Inverness. This assumption appeared to be correct and she was able to watch at least one of them ambling off towards the waiting room while she staggered back to her seat.

The sight of the second policeman, slouched in the seat forward of McKenzie, the one vacated by the guy in the sunglasses, made her stomach clench. Had it not been for the fact that he was, at that moment, searching for his place in a paperback, he must have seen Fizz approaching, but she made it past him before he looked up and sank, panting and light-headed, into her seat.

McKenzie was still unconscious. Fizz sat there for a couple of minutes, feverishly trying to think what to do. If she woke him and tried to hustle him into another carriage she'd be running the risk of attracting the constable's attention. McKenzie's voice was pitched to carry and God only knew what sort of noise he'd make if woken suddenly from such profound depths of insensibility.

The bald chap returned from the toilet and

seemed about to smile at her in passing but then he saw that the copper had pinched his seat and he passed on with a glower.

Finally Fizz decided that it would be safer, all things considered, to leave McKenzie where he was. Weighed against the virtual certainty of causing a fuss, she preferred to take the chance that the copper would not look behind him when he got off.

She moved quietly across the aisle and sat across the table from McKenzie, separated from the copper only by the thickness of the seat back. From there, should McKenzie wake suddenly and start to sound off, she could reach across and slap a hand over his mouth.

For the rest of the journey she passed the time by biting her knuckles, trying to breathe, and looking for ways to camouflage McKenzie. Since Buchanan had taken all her luggage she had no spare clothing with her and she needed her woolly hat to effect her own paltry disguise. Searching her pockets she discovered nothing but a black felt-tipped pen, which wasn't much help since, regrettably, a Groucho Marx moustache and horn-rimmed specs wouldn't make McKenzie any less conspicuous. He did, however, have a pair of sunglasses of his own, somewhere about his person and those, if she could find them, might at least help.

She had to be fairly rough in her search of his pockets, and just as she located the shades in the inside pocket of his jacket, his eyelids lifted momentarily to half-mast and he stared blearily out at the passing scene.

'Christ,' she heard him mutter as he settled down again. 'Train journeys are bloody boring.'

8

Buchanan only just made it to Waverley station before the other two. His journey had been uneventful, possibly because he had taken a back road whenever one presented itself, but this had cost him time and wreaked havoc with his nervous system.

Edinburgh had never looked so beautiful nor had Fizz, striding down the platform in her Docs and, even more surprisingly, nor had McKenzie. It was such a relief to see them again, alive and unfettered, that he could have hugged them both. Well, almost.

He was about to hurry forward to meet them when the sight of a uniformed police officer, approaching the barrier ahead of them, halted him in his tracks. He had plenty of time to shuffle back into the crowd of waiting travellers behind him but, in any case, the officer passed by without a sideways glance, obviously off duty.

McKenzie was right behind him, moving like a cheetah with an urgent appointment, and would have rushed straight past Buchanan had his arm not been grabbed.

'Scott! You made it without trouble then?'

'Ah . . . Tam! Good to see you, laddie. Trouble? Not a smidgen. Hellish tedious, though.' He swung his head around and appeared to sniff. 'Is there a bar around here?'

Buchanan's knotted stomach muscles relaxed another notch. For the first time in three days a small ray of optimism shone through his gloom. Maybe things weren't as serious as he'd feared. There was a good chance they'd shaken off the police and now that they were all back on home ground they could slip quietly back into their own lives and set about covering their tracks. McKenzie might still be at risk but it would be possible to . . .

His train of thought hit the buffers as Fizz's fast approaching face came into focus.

She didn't often work herself into a rage. Buchanan had seen her lose her temper only twice and both times she'd been scared stiff, not aggravated. Most women he'd known resorted to tears when they'd had a fright, but not Fizz. He doubted if anyone had seen her cry, but there was something in her present tight-lipped scowl that made him hurry forward to meet her.

'Fizz. You okay?'

'No, I'm not bloody okay,' she snapped, not breaking her stride. 'I'm getting too bloody old for this bloody business. I've been shitting bricks since Inverness.'

'But Scott just told me . . . '

'Scott slept all the way.' She used both hands to replace the strands of gold that had wriggled their way out of her knitted hat. Her face wasn't made for expressing hatred but she was doing her best as she glared down the platform at McKenzie. 'Look at him! Another couple of paces and he'd have overtaken the copper! I can't take my eyes off him for a second.'

'What's been happening?' Buchanan demanded, striding out to keep up with her choleric haste.

'There were two coppers on the train, checking people out, and if it hadn't been for a miracle — a bona fide miracle, I'm telling you — they'd have nabbed him.'

'Dear God.' Buchanan suddenly felt himself the focus of a thousand eyes. 'If that's the case we'd better split up till we get to the car. Follow me.'

With the briefest of explanations to McKenzie he headed for the car park, thinking: Checking out train passengers? What is this, a manhunt? If so, why is there nothing on the news?

It was, of course, quite possible that if some serious crime had taken place last Friday, or even before that, the newscasters had already milked it dry. There was certainly enough fresh-breaking news to negate the need to rehash the story, especially if there were no new developments to report. However, if the crime had taken place in the north of Scotland — which surely had to be the case — the story was bound to be in last Saturday's *Scotsman* or, at the very least, in the *Inverness Courier*. Somebody had been shot, maybe even killed, so the newspaper report would be easy to pick out. It wasn't Chicago, for goodness sake.

It might have been safer to allow Fizz to walk home, her flat in the High Street being barely ten minutes away, but Buchanan felt it was worth the risk to have the peace of mind inherent in knowing for certain that she was safe in her own home. He parked the car a little way up the street and waited for ten minutes before he let her out: watching to make sure there were no suspicious characters keeping the entrance under observation and listening as she wound up her harrowing account of the train journey.

When he returned to the car after escorting her up the one hundred stairs to the door of her tiny eyrie, Scott had moved into the front seat. There was an air of contentment about him that made Buchanan wonder if he could possibly have had time to nip into the licensed grocers during his absence but he didn't smell of booze — not any more than usual, anyway — so he didn't feel the need to inquire. As long as Scott was more or less *compos mentos* Buchanan felt fairly justified in abandoning him overnight.

'I'll contact you tomorrow,' he said as he followed Scott's directions across town to the bungalow-ville area that climbed the lower slopes of Corstorphine hill. 'Fizz is going to check out last Saturday's news stories first thing in the morning and I'm pretty sure that will clarify matters quite a bit. In the meantime, I think you'd be well advised to stay indoors.'

'Absolutely, Tam,' McKenzie responded, affably enough but with perceptible lack of conviction. 'First right past the bus stop. I don't know if I ever mentioned how much I appreciate . . . '

'Yes, you already thanked us enough, Scott. If you want to show your gratitude just keep a low profile and, if the worst comes to the worst and you get arrested, try not to mention Fizz and me. Give me a ring as your lawyer, if you like, but don't say anything that could incriminate us.' Buchanan drew up half a block away from McKenzie's bungalow and turned to face him. 'The police may know both of us by sight — they probably have a good description of Fizz — but maybe they don't know *who* we are. It's possible they don't even know who you are. But if they take you in just refuse to say anything till you speak to your lawyer.'

'No problemo.' McKenzie smiled placidly and let his eyes dwell fondly on his home patch. 'All quiet on the western front for the moment, thank God.'

It did look quiet, Buchanan thought. As quiet as only an Edinburgh suburb can look, late on a summer Sunday. The few cars parked along the gutter were empty and no residents showed in their front gardens. He could hear the distant sound of a lawn mower but apart from that the entire population of Corstorphine could have been wiped out by a mystery virus or snatched up to Alpha Centauri by a transporter beam. No matter. McKenzie wasn't getting out of the car till Buchanan was certain nobody was lurking somewhere out of sight.

He waited ten tedious minutes and then pulled forward to the appropriate gate and took a walk down the drive for a quick recce of the garden area before he permitted McKenzie to let himself in. Everything looked as sedate and innocuous as your dear old grannie.

Retracing his route to the end of the road,

it felt like a weight had been lifted from his soul. The roughly forty-eight hours he'd spent in McKenzie's company seemed like a week with an angry mob. What one needed now was a long hot bath, a therapeutic quantity of Glenmorangie, and an early night.

Being a careful driver, he checked his mirror when he came to the junction, and for a good thirty seconds his brain refused to accept what his eyes were telling him. Stunned, he actually got out of the car and stood, watching helplessly as, some five hundred yards away, two men in jeans and leather jackets escorted McKenzie out of his front gate, thrust him into a grey Rover, and took off in the opposite direction.

Every expletive in his lexicon, most of them learned from Fizz, flooded into his mind as he leapt back into the Saab and swung it in a U-turn. What a bloody fool he'd been not to have checked the interior of McKenzie's bungalow! They'd been waiting for him inside — whoever they were — and although some CID officers dressed like that, these two looked more like the type of thug he'd watched going into The Persevere.

Before he'd speeded ten yards past McKenzie's gate the Rover had turned the corner ahead and disappeared into the warren of bungalows that led to the main

Glasgow Road. There were at least four converging routes it could have taken, all of them bristling with side turnings, and Buchanan could see that, short of choosing one at random and chancing his luck, there was nothing he could do.

Vacillating between choices, he had slowed momentarily to a crawl when he realised that a short bald man in sunglasses was running alongside the car and trying to attract his attention. Buchanan slowed still further, allowing him to catch up and shout through the open window,

'Take me with you — please — take me with you.'

Buchanan shut his eyes and gave his head a brisk shake but, when he looked again, he was still there. The sheer audacity of the guy's request coupled with his quite evident expectation of it's being acceded to, struck Buchanan as so bizarre that it clearly had a place in the current maelstrom of events. He sprung the catch on the passenger door and the guy dived in and did some serious panting.

'Who the hell are you?' Buchanan demanded.

'Mate . . . mate of Scott's. Phew! Did you see which way they went?'

'No. I thought you were going to tell me.'

'Don't you know who they are?'

'Dammit, no! Don't you?'

'Oh, Helen Blazes! That's all I needed! I thought you'd — oh well, let's just hope it's the police. Otherwise he's a dead man.'

Buchanan was too aghast at what he'd allowed to happen to know when he was beaten. He chose a junction at random and accelerated down a steep hill as empty as the street they'd just left. He took a right then a left, but the grey Rover didn't show. There wasn't much point in prowling around the side streets but he did it anyway since the main road offered an even punier prospect.

After a few dead ends he started to calm down a bit and his attention returned to his passenger. He took a closer look at him and suddenly something went click in his brain.

'You were in Inverness,' he said. 'Where was it . . . in the café? Yes, I saw you reading the menu in the window.'

The chap removed his sunglasses, wiped the steam from the lenses with his hanky and replaced them. 'Watching you, actually. Sorry, but I didn't know whose side you were on.'

Buchanan spared him a hopeful glance. 'What sides are there?'

He smiled, displaying a collection of large crooked incisors and reminding Buchanan of McKenzie's remark about someone with 'teeth like tombstones'. Not Buchanan's

131

choice of simile, Stonehenge would have been more apt, but clearly this was the same guy: the guy who had escaped, with McKenzie and Marianne, from some place or another after someone had been shot. He was probably in his late forties: a thick set, competent looking chap with something about him of the ex-soldier.

He was saying, 'Well, there's Scott's team, I hope. And those buggers in The Persevere. And the police, of course.'

'What d'you know about The Persevere?'

'Me? Nothing. They hang out there, that's all, the guys who're trying to kill Scott and me. I was staking it out when you turned up with Scott and the young girl.'

'They're trying to kill you too?' Buchanan found himself in a cul-de-sac and finally admitted defeat. He parked in the turning area and twisted round in his seat to face his passenger. 'Remind me: you're not Fergie, right?'

'No. Fergie was one of the guys at The Persevere. I'm Hector McSween.'

Buchanan toyed for a second with the idea of giving a false name. Fizz would have insisted on it but Buchanan could never shake off the conviction that the road to perdition was paved with prevarication.

'Tam Buchanan,' he said. 'But don't tell the

world I'm mixed up in this, Hector. I'd like to keep it quiet if at all possible. I'm not what you could call a mate of Scott's but Fizz — the girl you saw — she and I fished him out of a car crash last Friday and kind of got stuck with him.'

'Yeah. The Mitsubishi. I heard about it on the news.' He used his hanky again to dab his brow. 'I was sorry about Marianne. She saved our lives, y'know.'

Buchanan had more or less guessed at something of the kind but it was enormously encouraging, at this low point in the proceedings, to have contact with someone who could clarify that episode at least, and possibly much more. If there was any chance at all of saving McKenzie's life, this guy was his only hope.

'Look,' he said, 'we have to talk and I'm ready for my dinner. What do you say to getting a Chinese takeaway and taking it round to my place?'

Hector being amenable to this suggestion, they headed for the New Town, taking in the Lee On en route. Selina, having heard the car being put away downstairs, was on the transom of the front door to greet them and startled Hector horribly by dropping, purring, onto his shoulder as he passed into the hallway.

Buchanan had brought her a small portion of stir-fried prawns with plenty of monosodium glutamate as compensation for being left in the care of a neighbour for three days. Pooky, his other cat, was less adventurous in his tastes and preferred a little chicken without sauce.

Both of them were glad to see him back and had to be petted and reassured for a few minutes before they settled down to their meal. By which time Buchanan could see Hector looking at him somewhat askance and had to say,

'Looks bad, doesn't it, Hector? You're thinking I should wear an anorak to complete the picture of a total nerd.'

Hector tried to act very understanding but he was no Gielgud. 'Plenty of guys like cats. Good company.'

'Yeah. Well, I can take them or leave them, to be honest. I just sort of came by these two. It's a long story. Want a lager with this?'

They got settled down with their various tinfoil dishes and talked only intermittently till they had satisfied the inner men. Buchanan was clinging tightly to the hope that McKenzie's abductors were CID. The fact that they had not killed him on sight seemed to strengthen this possibility since his friends from The Persevere had no reason to procrastinate.

Hector, minus his wraparound shades, was lean-faced and long-nosed and saved from real ugliness only by very luminous and permanently amused brown eyes.

'It's a funny business, this with me and Scott,' he said after a while. 'I was hoping he'd be able to straighten things out for me. Tell me what was going down.'

'Maybe we can jigsaw some pieces together between us,' Buchanan proffered, trying to sound positive. 'You tell me what you know and I'll tell you the fragments Fizz and I've been able to glean from Scott — in the few brief intervals during which he's been almost sober.'

Hector grinned his tombstone grin. 'Yes. He can't half put it away, old Scott. Helluva nice guy though.'

'Absolutely. So where did you meet up with him?'

'In The Persevere.' Hector burped genteelly behind his fist and set his empty lager can on the coffee table. 'I didn't know who he was — still don't for that matter — but he was there with the rest of the crowd, Fergie and Skip and Willie and that lot, drunk as a monkey from morning till night. I don't think I ever saw him sober.'

'You knew the others then? Fergie and . . . Willie and that lot?'

'Not what you'd call *know* them, not really.' Hector clasped his hands and leaned over to prop his elbows on his spread knees. 'This is where it gets ... well, kind of awkward, Tam. Sorry, but I don't know who I'm speaking to and there are things I wouldn't like to go any further. Like you not wanting to get into trouble for helping Scott, see?'

'Right.' Buchanan was a step ahead of him, though he hadn't till that moment registered the thought. Ten years in the law business gave a guy a sort of sixth sense about people, particularly those who had seen the inside of Her Majesty's Prisons with any regularity. Hector was reasonably respectable at first glance but the signs were there for those who knew where to look for them.

He said, 'I'll come clean, then, Hector. I'm a solicitor. In fact, I'm training to become an advocate. But that doesn't mean I'm going to drop either you or Scott in the shit. I don't believe he's done anything criminal, not intentionally, and even if he has — if either of you have, come to that — you don't need to tell me about it. Just tell me what you can so that we can figure out a way to find Scott again and get him out of this mess.'

Hector didn't look all that reassured by these words so Buchanan left him to think it over while he got another couple of lagers out of the fridge. When he got back there was another long silence and then Hector said,

'Okay, I may as well tell you, cos it's no secret anyway. I've got a record. Nothing serious. But that was years back.'

Buchanan lifted a shoulder. 'So, we're both in the same position. It would do neither of us any good to be embroiled in something criminal. I won't tell on you if you don't tell on me.'

'Fair enough.' He nodded, lifted his chin and drew a long breath in through his nose. 'I don't want you to think I'm a crim. I'm not a crim. I found Jesus when I was inside and I don't do nothing violent. I've got a job. I work for a kitchen fitter, but it doesn't pay much and it's not regular and I've got four kids so sometimes I do a job for some guys I know. Neighbours of mine. Nothing . . . nothing nasty, like I said, just a bit of driving, a bit of B&E — commercial, not private,' he added, as though that made breaking and entering someone's property little more than a misdemeanor.

As far as Buchanan was concerned that matter was between Hector and Jesus. 'And that's how you'd met up with Fergie and co.?'

'I'd seen them around.' He pulled the tab off his can and took a swallow. 'I don't know for sure what their line was but I gathered — just from a word here and a word there, right? — that they were in the same business as me. I thought it could've been for the same outfit, even. See, in that line of work you don't always know who you're working for. As far as I was concerned I was working for these neighbours of mine, but they were working for somebody else and maybe their contact was working for somebody higher up the ladder. Same with Fergie and the others.'

'But it was an organisation of some sort, right?'

'That's what I reckoned.' Hector nodded. 'Had to be. Some of the jobs they pulled . . . I was just the driver but somebody was making a whole lot of cash. I mean, millions. Had to be somebody with an organisation.'

Pooky jumped up on the couch beside Buchanan but Selina was right behind him and shouldered him aside before he could usurp her place on his lap. Buchanan tried to stroke them both simultaneously to keep the peace while he said,

'You think Fergie and Willie and . . . er . . . Skip, was it? You think they're part of the same organisation?'

'Probably. I hadn't worked with them before but that didn't mean much. They hung around with the guys I knew, did a lot of chatting behind their hands, but they could've been freelances like me, just recruited for the job, like. I don't ask too many questions, you get more jobs that way, but you get to know things anyway. The police have a pretty good idea who some of them work for, see, so the word gets around. I done a sixer for accessory coupla years back so they've got me branded for life, anyway.' Hector bared his gnashers in a grimace. 'Which might not be long. It looks like somebody up the line a bit is trying to put me out of commission. I must have done something to annoy somebody and they want me dead. Scott too. Maybe they think we were planning to cause trouble for somebody. Whatever it is, it's all a mistake. If I did something it was an accident. I don't need that kind of trouble.'

Buchanan freed a hand to drink some lager. 'How d'you know they're trying to kill you?'

'Scott didn't tell you what happened?'

'Scott remembers virtually nothing. He must have been pissed as a newt.'

Hector rubbed a hand across his eyes and chuckled long and hearty. 'That guy's something else. The amount of booze those guys poured into him would have floored a rhinoceros.'

'You didn't try to restrain him from taking it?'

Hector lifted his brows. 'I am not my brother's keeper.'

'No, of course not,' Buchanan said, suspecting his brother's keeper was, more likely, HM prisons. 'I didn't mean that as criticism, I just wondered if he was under duress. But, apparently he was only too delighted to comply.'

'Absolutely. He was either drinking or sleeping. He slept through the whole episode on the train while that young lassie bust a gut to hide him. He doesn't know he's born.'

Buchanan sat up. 'You were on the train?'

'Sure. Followed Scott and that young girl till you whipped them away at the station. I'd have managed to speak to Scott somewhere along the way if it hadn't been for the coppers.'

'It was you who arranged the 'miracle'.' Buchanan nodded. 'Fizz told me about that. I don't believe in miracles but I suppose it was something of a miracle that you were even at hand.'

'God helps those who help themselves,' said Hector with a devoutness rare in one of his vocation. 'That wee lassie deserved a miracle.'

Buchanan started to say that Fizz was not

as young as she appeared to be but couldn't be bothered. Instead he said,

'You were about to tell me how you discovered that you and Scott were on someone's hit list.'

'Oh, aye.' Hector licked his lips, darting quick appraising glances in Buchanan's direction. 'Okay. Well, I don't know how long Scott had been working for the outfit but — '

Buchanan stopped stroking Selina's whiskers and sat up. 'Scott was working for the outfit? Are you sure?'

Hector blinked a couple of times, waggled a hand uncertainly and then said, 'I'd better tell you how it happened, then you can judge for yourself.'

'I think you'd better,' Buchanan muttered, wondering if he really wanted to know.

'A couple of weeks back I got asked to do a job. Driving.'

'A getaway car?'

'Uh-huh. These guys I was telling you about, they said something was being set up for last Friday, in Inverness, and did I want in. It was a building society heist and it was all set up sweet as a row of dominoes with a guard paid off to open the vault and all your orders.' Hector sucked the last drops from his can and leaned forward to put it on the table. 'I needed the cash so I said okay and we went up to Inverness in a van on Friday morning and met up with some other lads I didn't know.'

'Where did you meet?' Buchanan asked. 'At The Persevere?'

'No, at a big house down by the river but we went up to The Persevere later and that's where I met Scott. He was stewed to the gills. Totally blootered.' Hector shook his head, smiling like a picket fence. 'But he's a damn funny drunk, you know, and you could tell he was well in with the rest of the bunch. They all seemed to know him well and there was this lovely girl, Marianne, who just couldn't get enough of him. Treated him like her dad.'

'Marianne, yes. Was she with the outfit?'

Hector started to say 'yes' but then changed his mind. 'I don't know if she actually helped with anything but she was somebody's girlfriend. Somebody with clout, I reckon, from the way she was treated by the others. She had a real soft spot for Scott. Kept trying to stop him drinking too much. When we got back to the house she got Skip and Fergie to put him to bed.'

Buchanan got another couple of lagers and found a few packets of crisps. The takeaway had had only a temporary effect on his appetite and he was starving again.

'Right,' he said, when he got back. 'Tell me

about the building society job. Scott was in on that?'

'Yeah, and that was a surprise because the last I'd seen of him was Skip and Fergie putting him to bed, back at the house.' He stopped talking for a minute or two and sat staring at his lager can and fingering his brow. 'Marianne couldn't have known he was meant to be there either or she'd have made more of an effort to sober him up. Anyway, we get to the building society right after closing time, the guard opens the back door and in go the lads. I'm waiting down at the end of the street in the van when out comes Skip and says I'm needed inside to help carry the stuff out.'

He got up and walked over to look out the open window, jamming one hand into his pocket and using the other to lift the lager to his lips.

'You hadn't signed on for that, had you?' Buchanan prompted. 'Just a driver, you said.'

'Damn right,' said Hector. 'I was right pissed off, because I don't like that kind of job, but Skip said there'd be a bit extra in it so I left the van and went down the lane where the back door was, at the side of the building.'

He turned around and propped his behind on the window sill and his face was grim.

'When I got inside the first thing I saw was the guard. He was on the floor, half under a desk, but I knew right away he was dead and, I don't mind telling you, I was shit scared. I wanted out. I'm not in that league. Never was. And now I've seen the Light . . . '

Buchanan waited for him to go on but when he could wait no longer he said, 'So?'

'So, I backed up. Fast. I just turned and nipped out smartly into the hallway and that's where I saw Marianne and Scott. She was trying to get him away, half carrying him. When she saw me she said, 'Run for it, Hector, they're going to kill you.' I couldn't take it in really, but I knew there was something iffy about the way they'd called me in. I said, 'What?' or something, and she said, 'They're going to kill you and Scott. Run!'. But I couldn't do it.'

He took a couple of long pulls at his lager and threw the empty can out of the window, causing considerable pain to Buchanan's civilized soul. 'It would have been a serious sin to leave her struggling like that. If she'd been caught doing what she was doing — throwing a spanner in the works — she'd have been crucified. I knew I'd be in the shit for doing a runner but she was really going out on a limb for Scott and I couldn't leave her to it. I just grabbed him by the other arm

144

and we beat it down the lane as fast as we could. We couldn't get back to the van without somebody spotting us but we headed in the opposite direction and got round the corner without anyone coming after us.'

Buchanan forgave him the discarded can. Ex-con he might be; criminal he undoubtedly was, but like a lot of chaps who got into trouble, he had his own moral code. He pushed another bag of crisps across the coffee table and waited to hear the rest.

'Marianne had a car across the river at the big house where all the guys were staying but Scott could hardly put one foot in front of the other and we would never have made it. Then we saw the Mitsubishi drawing up outside a doctor's surgery — and that really was a miracle because the driver jumped out, leaving the engine running, and ran inside. We made a dive for it just as two coppers came round the corner behind us.'

'Two big guys,' Buchanan asked. 'One of them with greying hair?'

'That's them,' Hector nodded, not bothering to ask how he knew. 'I thought they were genuine so I — '

'Sorry? You're saying they're bogus?'

'Bogus or bent, I reckon. When I got closer to them I recognised one of them from The Persevere. They must have been dressed up like that to act as lookouts or something. I don't know.'

Buchanan wasn't at all surprised by this revelation. He said, 'But on Friday you thought they'd help you?'

'Yeah. I thought God had answered my prayers. I mean, how often do you see a cop when you need one? Anyway, I started to run up to them but before they noticed me they must have spotted Marianne nicking the Mitsubishi because they just ran right past me and made a bee line for her. She took off like it was the start of the Grand Prix so I did the same: through somebody's garden and over a hedge.' He lifted his shoulders, 'That's the last I saw of any of them till you turned up at The Persevere with Scott.'

It all tied in very neatly with what McKenzie remembered, Buchanan decided, but it didn't actually clarify a whole lot. It didn't explain how McKenzie had managed to infiltrate a criminal gang and it begged the question of how he had managed to become such a danger to them that he had to be eliminated. And what of Hector? Why had he hung around in Inverness instead of going into hiding? He put this question to Hector who waved his hands in a helpless gesture and spoke through a mouthful of crisps.

'Where could I run to? I couldn't go home:

that's the first place they'd look for me. I had twenty quid or so in my pocket but that wasn't going to go far towards a flight to the Bahamas.' He chewed, swallowed and de-crumbed his lips with a delicate knuckle. 'I had to find out who was after me and why. I'd got quite pally with one of the guys and I thought he might lend me a few quid but every time I saw him he was with the others. Then, when I saw Scott I reckoned he was my last chance. Doesn't he know what's happening?'

'Even less than you do,' Buchanan said, wondering if that were really true. And, supposing Scott *had* known more than he'd been willing to admit, what were the chances of hearing it now? Probably not too good.

9

Fizz was impatient to get into the office, not only to start checking newspaper files on the computer, but to assure herself that Buchanan had not been arrested since parting from her the night before. However, because of commitments at the university plus certain private matters she had determined upon during the journey from Inverness, it was almost mid-day when she got there.

Buchanan was quite frequently in the office around that time, particularly if he'd been in court that morning and had an hour free for lunch. He had evidently heard the screams from the typists in the outer office, because he was halfway to his door when she stepped through it.

'Good God!' he said, backing up several paces till his butt hit the edge of his desk. 'Oh, *no*, Fizz!'

Fizz had expected some expression of surprise but never this degree of shock and revulsion. It cut to the quick, especially after the money she'd spent.

'That good, huh?' she said, giving him a twirl. 'Glad you like it.'

Buchanan looked quite ill. His eyes kept sliding away as if he couldn't bear to look at her. He said,

'In God's name, what made you do that, Fizz?'

She dropped into a chair and kicked off the high-ish heels that were doing her ankles in. 'Well, obviously, I'm changing my image. If the cops are looking for a teenager with hair like an explosion in a mattress factory, that's exactly what I don't want to look like. And, anyway, I've wanted to do it for years. That mane was nothing but a bloody nuisance but I couldn't afford to get it cut every few months. Now I can.'

Buchanan came round the desk and sat down, looking across at her and clearly trying to think of something positive to say. 'It's just . . . just such a change. It's just not you any more.'

Fizz gave him an evil smile. 'I fear it is, Buchanan. Don't let a haircut fool you.'

He tried to smile back but not with any degree of success. 'Actually, it's very nice. Suits you.'

Fizz was tiring of the subject. 'Okay. I'll go and check the newspaper files. You haven't done it already, have you?'

'No. Actually . . . ' He waved at her to sit down again. 'There have been developments.'

Fizz eyed him uneasily, getting ready to be horrified.

'Uh-huh?'

'You want the good news or the bad news first?'

'Oh God. Hit me with the bad news.'

'I'm afraid McKenzie's disappeared. Some guys were waiting for him last night and whisked him away in a car.'

Fizz felt as if she had been run over by a tractor. She couldn't even summon up the will to berate Buchanan for not taking better care. But close on the heels of her despair came the thought that it wasn't entirely bad news. At least they were shot of the bugger.

'They must have got inside his house and were waiting for him,' Buchanan was saying. 'I tried to follow the car but they had a good start on me and I never really had a chance. However, someone else was waiting for Scott. A short, balding bloke wearing sunglasses.'

Fizz straightened up. 'Just a minute — I know that bloke. He was on the train. He was the one . . . '

Buchanan lifted a hand to stop her. 'Yes, I know all about that, we had a good long chat. Put your feet up and I'll clue you in.'

Fizz's spirits went up and down like a yo-yo as she listened to him summarise Hector's story. Much of it came as no surprise, the worst shock coming with the realisation that the police had got onto them because the money McKenzie had been throwing around in Ullapool and Inverness had been red hot. Typically, Buchanan was still smelling of violets having played no part in the shopping spree. It was also disconcerting to learn that McKenzie had been on the wrong side of the law all along, or at the very least, consorting pretty closely with those who were. Close enough to earn a pretty hefty fee. All of which was fairly academic now, since he had probably been offed already by whoever it was in the organisation that he'd aggrieved. Tough, of course, but every cloud had a silver lining.

'Well, Kimosabe, that's bad news for poor old Scott,' she said brightly, 'but it more or less lets us off the hook. Right?'

Buchanan, old softie that he was, winced. 'That's one way of putting it, yes. Probably. But, for Scott's sake, I'd like to have another talk with Hector before we throw in the towel. He may have recalled some information regarding this bunch of crooks that could help us nail them.'

Fizz thought that unlikely, given the guy's alleged position on the fringes of the organisation, but she was cynical enough to suspect that maybe Hector had been more

151

embroiled than he was admitting.

'Where is Hector now?'

'He's gone back to Corstorphine to keep an eye on McKenzie's house.' Buchanan fidgeted with some papers on his desk. 'I had to let him crash out on my couch last night. He can't go home and he has no money for accommodation. I expect to see him this evening.'

Fizz didn't know whether to smile at his gullibility or slap him round the head. It evidently hadn't yet dawned on him that he'd just swapped one hot potato for another.

She was impatient to meet Hector largely because, whatever his failings, she had rather liked old Scott and if there was anything to be done to revenge his murder — or even to prevent it, though that was perhaps too much to hope for — she was up for it.

What she'd seen of Scott's toothy chum in action, now that she appreciated it fully, inclined her to hope that he was a man who could think on his feet and therefore somebody who might be an asset rather than an encumbrance to further investigation. The fact that he was a petty criminal made him an ally whose collaboration could reflect pretty badly on one supposed to be on the side of the angels, but there was no doubt that he could bring skills to the job which could prove valuable.

She didn't bother sharing that thought with Buchanan since it would only have given him palpitations, but she made sure that when he went home at five o'clock he could do no less than invite her to dinner. That turned out to be a chinky as usual, but one couldn't look a gift horse in the mouth.

As it turned out, Hector had beaten them both back to Buchanan's place and, Buchanan having trusted him with a key, he had busied himself by making a pot of magnificent tomato and beetroot soup which he served topped with a scoop of crème fraiche.

'Least I could do to repay you,' he told Buchanan as he whipped off his butcher's apron and joined them at the table. 'There's a couple of nice chicken fillets there as well but they'll keep in the fridge till tomorrow.'

Buchanan's eyes flickered a little, probably with the realisation that Hector was intending to be there to share them, but he just smiled weakly and concentrated on his soup. 'This is superb, Hector. Where did you learn to cook so well?'

Hector ducked his head modestly. 'I always enjoyed cooking. When I'm out of work my wife sometimes gets a job at the supermarket while I watch the kids and look after the house. I prefer being the house person, matter of fact. The trouble is so does she.'

'If you ever split up you can marry me,' Fizz declared. 'Is there any more?'

It appeared there was. Hector went back into the kitchen, followed closely and affectionately by both Pooky and Selina, a sure sign that he had been buying their favour with tidbits.

His day's surveillance of McKenzie's bungalow had produced nothing, which seemed to be depressing him unduly, since he could scarcely have been all that optimistic.

'They'd gone off and left the front door unlocked,' he reported as they started on the chinese. 'I went in and had a good look round but there wasn't much to see. No sign of a fight, or that sort of thing, but you could tell there'd been a couple of guys waiting for Scott for maybe a couple of days. Beds been slept in, kitchen in a mess, fag ends and beer cans everywhere.'

'But nothing that would give you a lead on who they were?' Buchanan suggested.

'I don't know. Probably not.' Hector got up and crossed the room to where his jacket was draped across the back of a chair. 'I found this stuck to the seat of a chair.'

Fizz craned over to see the minuscule oblong of paper he handed to Buchanan. It was one of those adhesive price tickets with the trader's name printed across the top. Fizz couldn't make out the heading but Buchanan read it out.

'Braehead Garden Centre. Is that significant?'

Hector poked at a piece of bean skin stuck between his front teeth. 'I know the place. It's fishy.'

'How d'you mean 'fishy'?' Fizz asked.

'I don't know how, exactly, but I've heard it mentioned. Not a lot. Two or three times maybe, over the years, but by guys who were on the job, you know? Just the odd remark like, 'I saw Jimmy down the garden centre'. It's maybe a place you could sell stolen goods, or a money laundering business for some big operator, something like that.'

Buchanan looked interested. 'We'll check it out. Where is it?'

'That's the problem, I don't know. I looked it up in the Yellow Pages but it's not listed.' Hector helped himself to a modest amount of lemon chicken. 'If it's not in Edinburgh it could be anywhere, but I've got the feeling that it can't be all that far away. I reckon half an hour with Directory Enquiries would locate it.'

Buchanan pushed his chair back from the table and struck pay dirt in less than ten minutes.

'It's just outside the Edinburgh directory

area,' he said. 'Near Kinell golf course.'

Fizz's Lowland geography was confined to larger towns. She said, 'Where's Kinnel, then?'

'It's no distance from Bo'ness,' Hector told her. 'Way up river past the oil refineries.' He started to clear the table of the remains of the meal and looked at Buchanan uncertainly. 'I'm not saying it's a sure bet or anything like that, but I'd be willing to keep an eye on the place for a few days in case anyone I know turns up there. You never know.'

Neither Fizz nor, apparently, Buchanan was wildly excited by this possible lead but since it was the only chink of light in a particularly dark tunnel it had to be explored. Hector was raring to go without delay since, he said, if anything nefarious were taking place there it would not be taking place within business hours. Fizz couldn't see that there was any immediate rush. If Scott wasn't already dead — which was by far the most likely scenario — it was unlikely they were going to kill him now, but she fully agreed that it wouldn't hurt to be sure. There was, she realised, the added advantage that the plan would present the opportunity for a pleasant evening drive and possibly, if she played her cards right, a stop at some picturesque country inn on the way. She should, by rights, have spent the evening preparing for her exams, but there would be other evenings.

It took forever to find the place. Buchanan located Bo'ness easily enough but they wandered round and round a labyrinth of thickly wooded country roads and farm tracks before Hector spotted the glint of sunlight on the glass roofs of greenhouses.

It was below them, on a secondary road that curved around the base of the hill they had just climbed by another route, and it covered about four or five acres. Fizz had half expected to see a run down establishment with sickly plants and rubbishy plastic garden furniture, but this place would have made Kew Gardens look like a window box.

The main building was still recognisable as having been a farmhouse at one time: a big, nineteenth century pile that was now hidden behind a welter of so-called improvements that gave it the appearance of an elderly matron in a frilly tutu. The windows had been enlarged and replaced with tall modern panes, some of them underscored with window boxes or ineffective little wrought-iron balconies. Curtains showed behind the casements giving the upper level a lived-in look but the ground floor had been extended to provide a sales and display area. It formed a pentagon of glass and cedar from which radiated long displays of shrubs and trees, tables of bedding plants and perennials, planters, troughs, sundials, fountains, arches and all the usual paraphernalia considered necessary to modern garden design. Around the perimeter, which was edged by a tall chain-link fence, were huts and greenhouses, trellis, paving slabs and stacked bags of compost. Every path was swept clean, every greenhouse glittered, and the whole aspect was one of well deserved prosperity. Scarcely the average den of thieves.

'You're sure about this place, Hector?' Fizz had to ask. 'It doesn't look shady to me.'

Hector pursed his lips and took a long stare down the hill at the layout. 'There's something shady about it, I'm damn sure there is. It'll bear watching, anyway.'

'Where will you stay?' Buchanan asked him. 'It's warm enough just now but when the sun goes down you'll be frozen to death.'

'Don't worry about me, Tam, I'll find a place. I served my time at this game, you know.' He swung his head in a slow arc that encompassed the entire view. 'Look at that culvert down there by the spruce trees. An army could hole up for a week in a place like that. Enough cover for a tank. Let's go down and take a closer look.'

They got back in the car and drove down the hill, losing sight of the complex as the trees closed around them, and then emerging about quarter of a mile from the gates. Buchanan drew the Saab into the opening of the culvert and parked it in the lee of a tall hedge. The sun was already well down behind the hills, and although the summits to the east were still glowing, the garden centre lay in a pool of dark blue shadow.

Hector climbed to the rim of the culvert and took a long look around. There was an air about him that Fizz had not seen him exhibit before but which was recognisable as the confidence of a man doing a job he was familiar with. When he was satisfied that there was no one around he beckoned the other two with his head and set off, not towards the gate but at right angles along the side of the chain-link fence.

Buchanan caught up with him quickly but Fizz, staggering and swearing her way uphill, through tussocky grass and in her unaccustomed heels, was still way behind them when they stopped at the back of the lot. They appeared to be holding a discussion but by the time she came within earshot a decision had been made without her input.

'What — ?' she started to say but Buchanan held up a warning finger.

'Shush. Look over there.'

Fizz looked and, after a minute, located what he was pointing at: a large wooden outbuilding, some fifteen feet away, where she could see a sliver of dim light showing at the lower edge of a window. She turned her head to look at Hector and he sent her a triumphant smile, his teeth ghostly as a graveyard in the half light.

'What'd I tell you?' He buttoned his jacket. 'I'll take a closer look.'

That sounded like an empty boast to Fizz, the fence being at least ten feet high and topped with barbed wire, but with Buchanan's help he was over the top and drifting through a grove of potted cherry trees in a matter of seconds.

It was as silent as the grave as they waited for him to come back. Not even a breath of wind stirred in the long grass but Fizz fancied she could feel the twilight itself moving, cool and soft, against her cheeks. She couldn't follow Hector's passage through the trees but she saw him appear beside the strip of light and his head blotted out a section of it as he stooped down to lay his eye to the crack.

For a long time he stayed there, bent over and motionless, while Buchanan ground his teeth and Fizz fidgeted nervously, then he turned and ran soundlessly back to the fence.

'He's alive. They've got him in there, under guard.'

'McKenzie? My God!' Fizz whispered. 'Is he okay?'

'Pissed as a newt and happy as a sandboy. There's three other guys in there with him. Probably to keep him quiet.'

'Crumbs! What — ?'

'Recognise any of them?' Buchanan interrupted.

'I may have seen one of them before — down the pub, maybe — but they weren't in on the Inverness business. They could be armed but, if they are, I couldn't see anything and they're not expecting any trouble, just playing cards. Looks to me like they're trusting to the alcohol to keep Scott sweet and don't expect any trouble.'

'What d'you think of our chances of getting him away?'

Hector nodded in brisk approval of the idea. 'Pretty good, I reckon. Like I said, they're well laid-back and not keeping much of a watch on Scott. There's plenty of stuff lying around that we can use as weapons so if we get in fast we can take them by surprise. They're in the middle of a card game and I could hear a radio or a tape playing, so they won't hear us coming.'

Fizz was trembling with excitement. The idea of bursting in on three thugs and possibly letting them have it with a flowerpot didn't really grab her but if it had to be done she was up for it. One should never turn down new experiences.

Buchanan, however, had other ideas and when he dug his heels in there was no arguing with him.

'No chance, Fizz. Hector and I can handle this and I don't want you getting under our feet while we do it. Besides, we could need you free to call the police if anything were to go wrong.'

'You could bring the car closer,' Hector suggested, bringing his face up against the fence and speaking in a stage whisper. 'Scott won't be able to put one foot in front of another by the look of him and I don't fancy carrying him any distance.'

'She can't drive,' Buchanan said.

'Yes I can. Not on main roads, maybe, but I've watched you often enough and I've driven a tractor.'

She held her hand out for the keys and Buchanan, groaning under his breath, handed them to her and started to climb the fence. He wasn't as good at it as Hector and something ripped like a pistol shot as he crossed over but he made it to the ground without major injury and followed Hector into the shadows.

Fizz wasn't happy about leaving them to it and hesitated as long as she dared as they moved around the assorted piles of fence posts and fancy bricks searching for suitable blunt instruments, but after a minute it became too nerve-racking and she had to get into action.

It was even tougher going downhill in her court shoes than it had been coming up. It also appeared that her balance was knocked haywire by the unfamiliar lightness of her head so she was virtually out of expletives by the time she reached the road below. It was typical of her luck that this had to happen on the one day in years that she had worn anything but her Doc Martin boots. By the time she got back to the car her ankles were giving her gyp.

There were so many keys on Buchanan's key ring that she had to waste valuable minutes finding which one opened the driver's door and then she had to get her head together and figure out the sequence of moves that would actually get her moving. Buchanan had resisted mentioning the fact that the Saab was practically factory fresh and that he loved it dearly (for which she was willing to allow him the Brownie points such restraint deserved) but the distress it would cause him if she damaged it was making her nervous.

'Okay,' she said, giving her fingers a good wriggle preparatory to turning the key in the ignition. 'Here we go.'

She had wound down both front seat windows to cool her fevered brow, which turned out to be phenomenally lucky because if she hadn't, she wouldn't have heard the approach of another car. It was moving quite slowly and very very quietly, so quietly that had the night not been so still — and, maybe, if her nerves hadn't been so stretched — it would have passed the junction of the farm track with the road just as the Saab was emerging.

Her hand fell from the ignition key as the shark-like shape drifted past the end of the track, and the shock kept her sitting there open mouthed for long shivery seconds. Then she jumped out and ran to the corner to see where it had gone.

It hadn't gone far. Even as she stuck her head round the corner it was drawing to a halt at the gates of the garden centre and disgorging a group of large and exceedingly purposeful-looking men.

10

Hector found himself a short stake, not unlike a baseball bat. There were several dozen of those in the same pile but their lethal potential, when hefted, gave Buchanan the creeps. Nervous as he was at the thought of what he and Hector were about to do, he didn't think he could actually bring himself to apply such violence. He could already hear the crack of cranium and see the spurt of blood, and his stomach rebelled.

Nearby, however, he found bundles of metal rods some three or four feet long, evidently component parts of wrought iron railings, and these offered a viable alternative. He had joined a fencing club at school and, although he had never been very good, he felt confident that he could fend off anyone who cared about their eyesight. Okay, the guards might have guns but it was unlikely and, supposing they did, even a baseball bat wouldn't be much of a deterrent.

The glass of the window through which Hector had made his original recce was painted black but someone had opened it a couple of inches allowing a reasonable view of the gloomy interior. Much of the area inside was used for storage. There were piles of bulging plastic sacks around the walls plus a few pallets of paving slabs and garden ornaments. But in the middle of all the merchandise there was a collection of old chairs plus a trestle table which supported an electric kettle, mugs, the desk lamp which was the room's only illumination, and three men playing cards.

Scott was slouched in an armchair a few feet closer to the window, quaffing from a half pint tumbler that was nearly full of whisky and talking loudly and incessantly to himself. Buchanan didn't need a Breathalyzer to discern that he was on the brink of complete blackout. He appeared to be otherwise unhurt but this was the first time Buchanan had come across alcoholism used as a murder weapon. It seemed that if these guys wanted Scott McKenzie dead they weren't in any hurry.

If Buchanan had half doubted the wisdom of mounting a rescue mission against superior odds, the sight of Scott's vulnerability convinced him that he had no choice. He was a tough old bird, no doubt about that, but right now he was no more able to defend himself than a babe in arms. The men at the table knew that and treated him with corresponding disdain, ignoring him completely as they got on with their game of poker.

Buchanan could see no sign of weapons of any kind, either conspicuous or covert, and began to estimate their chances at slightly above fifty-fifty. It would depend on how determined the guards were to hold on to their prisoner, of course, but with Hector's ferocity and Buchanan's defence tactics plus the advantage of surprise, the chance was there and they had to take it.

Hector spent a long time staring through the gap under the window. Buchanan had expected him to spearhead a frontal attack straight through the double doors at the far end of the building but that was evidently not what he had in mind. He waited a full five minutes before he did anything at all and then, taking advantage of a burst of shouting and laughter from the card players, he slid the window up a couple of inches. It made a bit of a noise which brought Buchanan out in a sweat, but nobody looked in their direction. A couple of minutes later, during another bout of vociferation, up it went again, this time to a little over a foot.

The window sill was at chest height but luckily — or, more likely, due to Hector's forward planning — a plant trough beneath it formed a step from which they could quickly haul themselves over. Hector stepped up, silent as a shadow, and without leaning in moved his head slowly into line with McKenzie's bleary gaze.

McKenzie blinked at him placidly and took another slug of whisky. 'Greatesht ... greatesht bloody ... greatesht banjo player 't ever lived,' he announced, eliciting no response either from the card players or from his fellow prisoner.

'Bloody was!' he insisted with a show of irritability. 'Best ever heard. Y'can keep y'r Lonnie Donnegan! Y'can keep y'r ... keep y'r ... others.'

He scowled, cross-eyed, at Hector while his arm slid off the arm of the chair and swung limply an inch off the floorboards. Hector waved at him, keeping a careful eye on the guards and choosing a moment when the only one facing them was studying his cards. McKenzie kept on staring at him but not as though he believed his eyes.

'Fingers like ... bloody ... bloody ... Fingers like ... Bloody fingers a foot long I'm telling you. Bloody ... '

Hector waved again, grimacing with frustration, and this time McKenzie's face changed. His eyelids lifted and he smiled dreamily, as one who sees visions. 'Bloody tombstones! S'right . . . Dashed decent bloke, though.'

'Give us a break, McKenzie,' said one of the guards but none of them bothered to look at him.

'Hellish glad t'see y',ol' chap,' gargled their prisoner, bringing fear and despondency to Buchanan to whom this was the stuff of nightmares.

Hector didn't turn a hair. The man was steady as a rock. He waved again, beckoning to McKenzie and after a minute or two it had an effect. McKenzie levered himself out of his chair, spilling most of his whisky down his front, executed a heart-stopping sequence of fast sideways skitters and halted, straddle-legged and swaying, in the middle of the room.

One of the guards spared him a sneering glance. 'Sit down you stupid old fart.'

McKenzie stood there wobbling for so long that Buchanan risked popping up beside Hector and adding some frantic beckoning of his own, which appeared to have an encouraging but not what you could call galvanising effect.

'Dear boy! Dashed glad . . . dashed . . . dashed . . . '

Time was running out. It could be only

seconds before someone noticed a draught from the open window or Hector would be spotted, or McKenzie passed out. Buchanan was suddenly a lot less optimistic of their chances, particularly if Hector hoped to get this raving old lunatic out through the window without being observed. There had to be a fracas at some point in the proceedings and it would be comforting to know how Hector planned to handle it. Or even if he had planned anything at all.

Finally, with both of them waving feverishly, McKenzie stumbled a few steps closer to the window. He had fallen silent, as though all his faculties were focused on reaching his friends. One of the guards glanced at him over his shoulder and sniggered. The other two didn't even raise their heads from their cards. The pile of money in the centre of the table was impressive enough to ensure their concentration.

Buchanan felt as if he were watching a slow motion replay as Hector edged the window further open and McKenzie began to shuffle across the room at roughly the speed of continental drift. Whisky slopped from his tumbler as he lurched from leg to leg.

'Dashed deesh . . . deesh . . . decent . . . great ol' chum . . . takesh a good dram . . .'

Buchanan had stopped breathing. Ten paces away . . . five paces . . . in a matter of seconds McKenzie would be in grabbing distance. He could hear Hector breathing a prayer.

Then with a crash that went through Buchanan like a sword thrust McKenzie dropped his glass and instantly one of the men at the table dropped his cards and let out a roar.

In a blur of movement all three were on their feet. The one nearest bounded down the room towards McKenzie. The other two were slower to react and their progress was impeded by the length of the trestle table which was across their path.

Hector went over the top in a rush and seized McKenzie by the arm. Buchanan, right behind him, grabbed the other arm and with a strength born, on Buchanan's part at least, by sheer panic they threw him headfirst through the window and turned to meet their assailants.

But, in the seconds it took for them to clash, the double doors behind the trestle table burst open and a bunch of burly strangers charged into the room, laying about them with implements that made Buchanan long for a baseball bat. Suddenly everything was in total chaos. The table lamp went spinning, reducing the ensuing violence to a phantasmagoria.

Hector hesitated not at all. He took a flying dive through the window and Buchanan followed suit, landing on top of him and also, it turned out, on top of McKenzie, who was rendered pretty well out of the game by the experience.

The noise of mayhem reverberated from the room behind them, crashes and curses and the crunch of club on bone, and each noise was a whiplash urging instant flight. But, in the gathering darkness, it took a moment to get one's bearings and, belatedly, to consider the problem of the chain-link fence.

There was no way they were going to get the flaccid sack of whisky that was Scott McKenzie over the barbed wire topping. Even in the advanced state of intoxication that Buchanan had seen him in on previous occasions he had been pretty active for his age, but his present condition had reduced him to a state of total helplessness that neither of his would-be deliverers had taken into consideration.

Hector was a brawny enough chap and Buchanan considered himself to be pretty fit but McKenzie had to weigh at least as much as either of them and was in no state to help in the undertaking. One could hope, as Buchanan fervently did, that the attacking force might have McKenzie's health and safety in mind but, when one remembered the impulsiveness of the two policemen on the bridge, one was not inclined to hang around to enter into negotiations. They had probably only seconds before one or the other factions got the upper hand and came after them but Buchanan was not hopeful of covering any appreciable distance in that time.

Hector too seemed to be at a momentary loss. As they hauled McKenzie upright he was looking around him with a jerky desperation that fell short of being reassuring. His previous confidence had swept Buchanan along in its wake but it now began to appear that perhaps his strategic thinking was not all that it might be.

In an ungainly knot, they shambled around the corner of the building and found a long black car standing outside the doorway. Away beyond it, near enough half a mile away, Buchanan was astonished to see the gates to the complex standing wide open. Hector's hotline to God had paid off, it seemed, and with a rapidity that merited earnest contemplation, perhaps at a more convenient time.

Hector and McKenzie fell together into the

back seat as Buchanan got behind the wheel and, the keys being conveniently in situ, they got the hell out of there ASAP. Hector was bleeding profusely from a cut on the chin, Buchanan had two skinned knees and one less pair of wearable trousers, McKenzie was — wouldn't you know it? — unmarked.

A weird state of excitement had taken hold of Buchanan. On one level he felt utterly calm, but his mind was working at supersonic speed, reviewing options, planning three steps ahead. He could see the Saab half hidden a hundred yards down the road and Fizz, having spotted what must appear to her to be the precipitous approach of the opposition, was sprinting back to it from what must have been a reconnaissance tour.

He had to toot the horn and flash the headlights several times before she got the message and halted to wait for them, by which time Buchanan knew what had to be done.

'They'll try to follow us, Hector,' he said, as he slowed for the gates. 'So we'll have to take this car with us and leave it a few miles away. You take Fizz in the Saab and follow me till I find a place to lose it.'

'Roger.' Hector leaned across the back of the passenger seat, still panting with agitation and holding a hanky to his bleeding chin.

'What the hell happened back there?'

'Search me. Like you said, Hector, God helps those who help themselves. Right?'

'Amen.'

Buchanan slowed barely enough to let Hector jump out and then accelerated away again before Fizz could complain about the arrangements. Let somebody else answer her questions for once, he thought, he needed some peace and quiet to concentrate on driving and to clarify his thoughts.

The advent of the second bunch of heavies could have several explanations. They might have been pissed off about something that had nothing to do with McKenzie. They might even, he supposed, have been more friends of McKenzie's with the same intentions as Hector and himself. They might have been CID. They might have been the local Neighbourhood Watch, for all anyone could tell. One could only hope that they were not in a position to discover who had stolen their car.

Obviously, the sooner he got rid of the vehicle the safer he'd feel but at the same time McKenzie's condition was also causing him consternation. The noises coming from the back of the car were barely recognisable as snores and they hinted to Buchanan that if McKenzie didn't empty his stomach pretty soon and replace the whisky with strong black coffee, he might slip into a coma.

The stomach-emptying took care of itself a little later as Buchanan spotted a convenient forestry track and swung the car into it so abruptly that McKenzie slid to the floor. The smell was appalling but luckily most of the puke went on the carpet and not on McKenzie. Buchanan dragged him out and slapped his face a bit while waiting for Hector and Fizz to arrive.

'Scott! Wake up, Scott! On your feet, mate.'

It was hopeless: he had no more rigidity about him than wet spaghetti and he now appeared to be wracked with shudders that shook him from head to heel. When Hector arrived Buchanan had him help to support McKenzie while they walked him up and down and Fizz ransacked the boot of the car in the hope of finding a travelling rug.

'Crumbs! It's full of clothes,' she called over. 'Coats and shoes and trousers. Bundles of them.'

She chose a long overcoat into which McKenzie was soon bundled and in another minute they were tooling through Bo'ness on their way home, Hector nursing McKenzie in the back and Fizz — a strange, shorn, elf-like little Fizz — in the passenger seat.

Nothing, for a very long time, had upset

Buchanan quite so much as the loss of her outrageous, rumbustious, obstreperous, glorious hair. Okay, it had never been anything but a mess because she was in the habit of cutting off any bits that got in her eyes and shearing an inch or two off the length with any sharp blade that came to hand. It frequently irritated Buchanan by tickling his face when he came within its rapacious reach and it was far from what the ambitious young lawyer should be wearing. All this had occurred to him in the first few horrendous seconds it had taken him to register its despoilment but none of it erased the hurt and the sense of loss that had weighed on him all day.

That hair *was* Fizz. In some strange way it personified the free spirit that was the core of her being, and it was inexpressibly sad to see it quelled. What depressed him even more was the thought that the hairstyle might not be the only part of Fizz that was ripe for change. All the time he'd known her she'd been a one-off. Uniquely Fizz. Doing her own thing at all times and unswerved by fashion, current ethics, or the expectations of other people. But now her lifestyle was about to be reshaped. In a few months time she would have her exams behind her. He had promised her a place with the firm — not as a favour but because someone would be needed to take his place there and he knew she'd earn her salary. And that very salary would make such a fundamental change in her circumstances that she could scarcely remain the same person. All her attitudes and responses were those of a penniless person with no marketable skills. Buchanan might cavil at her manipulation of other people — mostly himself — and her unswerving prioritising of Number One, but he had come to recognise those sides of her character as, not innate, but as survival strategies forced on her by her conditions.

Now she was on the brink of becoming financially secure, and it was not lost on Buchanan that, at the same time, he himself was facing a year — or several — of comparative poverty. Change was on the agenda for both of them and he didn't much relish the idea.

He saw her safely into her flat, after reassuring himself that no one was awaiting her return, and laid in a course for home accompanied by his two unwelcome but inescapable lodgers.

McKenzie had recovered partial use of his legs by the time they unloaded him from the car but it took both Hector and Buchanan to transfer him from the garage to the flat above and almost two pints of strong black coffee to restore him to something approaching lucidity.

Hector laid him out on the couch and covered him with a blanket but any hopes of having him keel over and go to sleep perished in infancy. He wanted to talk and Hector was impatient to listen to what he might have to say.

'Dashed decent of you chaps to go to such trouble for me. Can't imagine how I came to be wandering around in the dark but it was damned uncomfortable.'

Buchanan exchanged looks with Hector and felt enfeebled by the prospect of going through all this again. 'Is that all you remember, Scott?'

'Don't you remember the storage hut? The guys playing cards?' Hector prompted.

Scott pushed the curls back from his brow with the flat of his hand and gazed helplessly at both of his confederates. 'You speak in riddles, dear chaps. One assumes I've been a naughty boy again, huh?'

Buchanan wanted only to lie down in a darkened room with a cold compress and a bottle of Glenmorangie but Hector had the patience of a saint.

'Not your fault this time, Scottie. Those guys were filling you up with whisky like they had a pipeline to the distillery.' He tucked the blanket tenderly round McKenzie's shoulders. 'Listen. Forget that part of the story and think back to yesterday when Tam here dropped you off at your house. They were waiting for you, weren't they? A couple of guys in leather jackets.'

'Right.' He was visibly relieved to find that he still retained the odd grey cell. 'Bastards. Drank all my Glenfiddich.'

'That's right, Scottie. Now think. Did you recognise either of them? Had you seen either of them on that Inverness job?'

'Ah . . . no, Hector, I don't believe I knew them. Tell you the truth, I don't remember them too clearly but I think I'd have noticed at the time if they'd been from The Persevere crowd. Different kettle of fish entirely. Hellish rude, those two. Food all over m'carpet.'

Buchanan sat down and tore open a little more of his two hundred and fifty pound slacks to examine his knees. 'Yes, well you know, Scott, The Persevere crowd weren't angels either. Or were you aware of that?'

'Seemed decent enough chaps to me.' Scott looked to Hector for confirmation. 'Never a cross word out of them. Generous to a fault. Do I lie, Hector?'

Hector smiled at him fondly. 'No, you don't lie, Scott, but maybe they had a motive for being nice to you. Maybe they were keeping you drunk for a reason we can't make out at the moment.'

'Ah . . . ' murmured McKenzie as though he understood perfectly or expected to in just a moment.

He still looked very ill and his face had an embalmed look about it. Buchanan thought it was probably a waste of time to expect any sense out of him but Hector still had a little fight left in him.

'What did you know about the job?' he asked.

'Job? What job's that?'

'The building society job. The robbery. You were in on it, weren't you?'

Blank stare.

Buchanan said, 'High ceiling. Echo-ey. Guard got shot.'

'Ah . . . Right.' McKenzie blinked rapidly, his eyes flicking from Buchanan's face to Hector's and back again several times. 'Building society. Robbery, you say? Well, bugger me.'

'They were going to kill us both,' Hector said emphatically, as though he hoped the shock might unlock McKenzie's memory banks. 'Marianne got us away.'

McKenzie closed his eyes and drew a long breath. 'Oh God. The wife's going to be furious about this.'

Hector started to tell him he had more to worry about than his wife's ire but got exasperated halfway through and took the first aid kit back to the bathroom.

'What are we going to do?' he asked Buchanan when he got back. 'They'll be looking for Scott at his place and they'll be looking for me at mine. We can't go on crashing out here with you.'

'We'll move into a nice cheap hotel till it all blows over,' McKenzie assured him regally. 'Don't worry about the expense, old chap. I'm pretty solvent at the moment.'

'No you're not,' said Buchanan. 'That roll of banknotes you've been subsisting on must have come from the robbery. I've been wondering how the police got onto us so fast in Ullapool and again in Inverness, but now it looks as if they knew the numbers of the notes. You'd better give them to Hector to get rid of before you're tempted to spend any more.'

Hector nodded and went through McKenzie's jacket pockets till he found what was left of the roll of twenties. 'I should have stayed over at Bo'ness tonight,' he said, sliding the money securely inside his sock. 'If something's going down at the garden centre that's the quickest way to find out about it. I reckon

I'll take a trip over there tomorrow and keep an eye on the place for a few days, see what turns up.'

Buchanan was forced to agree. The garden centre was the only lead they had and if Hector was willing to put in long boring hours staking out the place he was willing to let him do it. It would be nice if he could think of a similar plan to keep McKenzie at a distance and out of mischief.

11

Fizz was surprised to find Hector in the office when she turned up for work the following morning. It was not yet nine o'clock but there he was, pacing up and down in front of Buchanan's desk, waiting for him to finish speaking on the phone.

'What are you doing here?' she said.

He waved an arm at Buchanan. 'Just making final arrangements with Tam. I'm going back to Bo'ness to stake out the garden centre for a few days.'

'Right. Good idea.' She fell into the spare chair which groaned at the assault. 'What will you do if you see anything?'

'Phone Tam.' He reached into a pocket and produced the mobile phone Buchanan had been given by a client recently but had never used. 'I'll also be borrowing Scott's car so if I need to move out fast or maybe follow somebody I'll have wheels. Handy for kipping down in too.'

Buchanan finished his call and came round the desk to clap Hector on the shoulder.

'Right then. We know what we're doing, do we, Hector? You'll check in every three hours till midnight and then from nine a.m. onward. If anything happens to you and you can't phone me I want to be alerted as soon as possible. How about food?'

'I'll stock up on the way there. Don't worry, I'll be fine. Like I told you, I've done this sort of thing plenty of times.'

'Of course. I just like to be sure we've got everything covered.'

Hector looked at his watch. 'I'll give you a ring when I get there to let you know the state of play. Around one o'clock, probably.'

'Okay. Good luck, then, Hector.'

Buchanan looked reluctant to let him go and stood, staring at the door for two or three seconds after it closed, as though he were trying to think if he'd left any precaution unconsidered. Then he went back to his seat and shook his head heavily.

'I just hope he's as competent as he looks,' he said. 'Sometimes I wonder.'

Fizz had wondered too, more than once, but not seriously enough to start spreading uncertainty. 'So, who's looking after McKenzie?'

'Dolores.'

'Dolores? I thought you were going to let her go? You said you couldn't afford a cleaning lady anymore.'

He shuffled some of the morning's mail

around with sudden briskness. 'Uh ... yes but Dolores has a daughter getting married next month and her husband didn't get the pay rise he was hoping for. I thought I'd keep her on for a month or two, just till I find her a new client.'

Fizz confined her comments to a pitying smile. Buchanan already knew he was a sucker and couldn't do a damn thing about it so there was no point in nagging. She said, 'You think Dolores will be able to prevent him from going out and getting corn-swoggled again the minute the pubs open?'

'I hope so. He has no money — Hector's getting rid of that roll of twenties he had — and he has nothing to wear but a bathrobe because I took his clothes away and locked my wardrobe. In fact, he was looking so ill when I left him that I doubt if he could make it as far as the front door.'

Fizz nodded approval. 'You can only do so much,' she said. 'I could probably pop round and check on him some time after lunch.'

'That would be a help, Fizz.' He swept the mail into his briefcase, checked his watch and stood up. 'I'd better get a move on. I'm meeting Larry at the High Court but I'll be back here at lunchtime for Hector's call — unless the court is late in rising for lunch and I get held up. If there's anything urgent you can leave a message for me.'

'Wilco. See you at lunchtime.'

Fizz trailed him out of his office, shut herself up in her own, and got on with her day. There was nothing awaiting her attention but some run-of-the-mill conveyancing work so she kept her head down and had it finished before noon, leaving herself time for a little research on the web.

She had already scanned the major reports of the building society robbery, none of which offered anything at all that could be construed as a lead, but there was always the possibility that more could be gleaned from local press coverage. Also, it had struck her as very likely that if a criminal gang were operating in the Highlands there would be reports of other crimes that might show a similar modus operandi. Neither prospect flooded her with optimism but leads didn't always offer themselves on a plate; sometimes you had to scrape around for them. Besides, she liked surfing the web.

There wasn't really a lot of crime north of the industrial belt, not compared to Glasgow, Edinburgh, and Dundee. Inverness and Aberdeen were the only other cities north of the Border and, outwith those two conurbations, nothing had been reported for months other than driving, drinking, or drug offences.

A shipment of cocaine had been intercepted by the coastguard cutter off Aberdeen, an oil worker had been struck and killed by a loaded crane on one of the North Sea rigs, and an Inverness waiter had been charged with handling stolen goods. There could be a connection between The Persevere crowd and any of those items but the accounts gave no details that could be followed up. Even more interesting was the story about the body of a foreign sailor that had washed up Rhubha Coigeach. Rhubha Coigeach wasn't far from Achiltiebuie, and that was the direction in which Marianne and McKenzie had been heading when first encountered. That could be meaningful but precisely *what* it might mean was another matter. No way of knowing without talking to the person who'd found the body.

She stored away the information for further consideration and reverted to scrutinising the local papers. News of the robbery had not reached some of them till yesterday's edition and still others only came out once a week. Only the *Cromarty Mercury and Advertiser* had identified the dead guard as one Donald Mulvey, whose widowed mother, Mrs Rita Mulvey, was being comforted in her Morningside home by friends and family. Mrs Mulvey had much to say about her son's uprightness of character but, reading between the lines, Fizz doubted if she had convinced the reporter responsible for the piece.

She was having a quick game of Free Cell before lunch when Buchanan returned.

'How is it,' he said, 'that every time I come in here I find you playing computer games?'

'Dunno. Maybe it's got something to do with the thick carpet in the corridor.' Fizz tapped a few keys and waved at the screen. 'The guard who was shot during the robbery — he had a mother in Edinburgh. Morningside, it says here. Think I should have a chat with her?'

He leaned across her shoulder and read the report. 'I don't know, Fizz. Could be a bit soon to intrude.'

'We don't have time to waste, Buchanan. If either Hector or McKenzie get offed while we pussyfoot around — '

'Yes, right. I hear what you're saying.' Buchanan swung a chair closer and sank into it, swinging his feet up onto the corner of Fizz's desk. 'Let's wait and see what Hector has to report. He may come up with something we can get our teeth into, in which case we can at least postpone any contact with Mrs Mulvey for a few days.'

'And if he doesn't?' Fizz asked, being reasonably sure they wouldn't be that lucky.

'Well, I suppose we won't have much choice in the matter. We have to push ahead.' He rubbed a hand over his eyes which were showing the effects of anxiety and lack of sleep. 'It's something we can't do together because one of us will have to stay with Scott. If it must be done, I'll do it.'

'I don't think so, petal,' Fizz disabused him with a kind smile. 'Nice try, but I don't think so. I've had dear old Scott up to here and, in any case, you need a quiet night in. Look at you. You look like you've got one foot in the grave and the other on a bar of soap. Give yourself a break.'

'We'll see,' was the best response she could get out of him but when Hector phoned to report all quiet on the western front she dug in her heels till Buchanan admitted defeat.

She was well aware that, however coincidentally, she was doing him a favour, because even before the advent of McKenzie and Hector, he'd been doing two jobs at once. When he wasn't dancing attendance on Larry he was working till late evening in the Advocate's Library; however being Buchanan, he felt constrained to supervise Fizz while she developed into a more useful adjunct to his two partners. He wasn't even getting paid for that, since he was not permitted to moonlight while devilling, but try talking him out of it. An evening at home with nothing to do but chat to Scott would do him more good than it would do Fizz. Much more. Plus, Mrs Mulvey sounded an extremely interesting prospect.

When Fizz spoke to her on the phone she sounded quite youthful but in the flesh, what there was of it, she was clearly well into her sixties. Her face was a small bony triangle, so closely surrounded by a mop of white hair that Fizz was momentarily arrested by the impression of a mouse peeking out of a cat's bottom. It occurred to Fizz that she herself might have looked very similar before her haircut.

'Wipe your feet,' snapped the vision in a voice that grated on the ear. 'That's what the mat's for. I've just had these carpets shampooed and it doesn't come cheap these days.'

She led the way into a small, neat sitting room with photographs of dogs and children and weddings on the mantelpiece surrounded by holiday postcards, condolence cards, a pair of fake brass candlesticks, a half finished mug of coffee and a collection of china thimbles. All three pieces of the old fashioned suite were draped with cotton throws and the air was full of the scent of lavender furniture polish with an underlying tang of bleach.

'Sit yourself down there. You'll have had your tea?'

'Thank you, yes,' Fizz said perceiving that, whatever her answer, she wouldn't be getting any.

'That's good, because I'm about finished mine.'

She took two large gulps from the mug on the mantelpiece and pushed it out of sight behind a picture frame. The room felt unnaturally still and airless. Even the sound of traffic from the busy street outside seemed muffled. There were no motes dancing in the shaft of low sun that lay across the carpet.

Fizz said, 'I'm really sorry to have to intrude on you at this time, Mrs Mulvey.'

Without answering, Mrs Mulvey settled herself in the opposite armchair and arranged the folds of her skirt. She was dressed in black; black dress, black cardigan, black stockings, but her shoes were an unlikely ruby red. She eyed Fizz with deep dislike.

'You said you're a solicitor,' she remarked with profound scepticism and, without giving Fizz time to answer, went straight on, 'If that's the case, why is it you're interested in Donnie's death? That's for the police to deal with, nobody else.'

'Actually, it's the robbery itself that concerns my firm, not your son's death.' Fizz got a card out of her shoulder bag and handed it to her but it didn't sweeten her sour expression any. 'We have a client, whose details I'm not at liberty to reveal, of course, but who is possibly in danger from the people who committed the offence. Anything we can discover that might lead to the arrest of these people would be of enormous value to us.'

'Well, you've come to the wrong place.' She straightened up as though she were getting ready to show her visitor to the door and her small, mean mouth curved a little in the pleasurable anticipation of getting rid of her. 'My Donnie wouldn't have known the first thing about those thugs, so I certainly don't. Oh, I know what's being implied in some of the papers: that Donnie was bribed to let them in and then shot in case he talked. Rubbish. Total rubbish. Nobody's going to tell me that my son would let himself be drawn into anything like that.'

Fizz hadn't expected this to be an easy interview but it was already clear to her that if she got anything out of Mrs Mulvey it wouldn't be Mrs Mulvey's fault. She took a deep breath of furniture polish and said,

'I wouldn't want you to think that I, or my firm, hold any such suspicion. Your son's liability, one way or the other, really has nothing to do with our inquiry. Even if we

193

turned up any incidental evidence that might be damaging to your son's character we'd be under no obligation to reveal it to the police or anyone else. On the other hand, it would be possible to pass on to you any facts which would help you to establish his innocence.'

'I don't need to establish Donnie's innocence,' she snapped. 'Anybody whose opinion matters to me, or to him, knows he'd never get mixed up in anything wicked like that. It's just pure evil to be hinting otherwise. I don't hear the police saying it so the papers have no reason to be putting it in people's minds. He was never in trouble in his life, that boy. I never lost an hour's sleep over him.'

Fizz glanced at the family pictures on the mantelpiece and wondered if all Donnie's siblings had been so angelic. There was a faint edge to his mother's voice that made her suspect otherwise.

'You're lucky to be able to say that, Mrs Mulvey,' she murmured. 'There are so many temptations for young people these days. I know that from my own family.'

'You don't have to tell me that, Miss Fitzpatrick,' said Mrs Mulvey with a sharp jerk of her head. 'Dear me, no, but Donnie was never a worry to me. Far too smart. So you're not going to get me to believe that he opened the door for that bunch of hoodlums. Not you nor the papers nor anybody else.'

'I don't think that for a minute,' Fizz lied, fixing her with wide, honest eyes. 'What worries me — and what is probably worrying you too, Mrs Mulvey — is whether he was somehow forced to do what they told him to do. Blackmailed. Threatened. Intimidated in some way.'

An insignificant speck of dust on the table beside her chair had distracted her for a moment but at these words she stopped flicking at it and her bony face tightened in anger.

'What are you saying? Do you know something I don't?'

'No. Absolutely not,' Fizz assured her hurriedly, shaking her head to underline her denial. 'There's not a scrap of evidence that Donnie was involved in the crime. Not a scrap. But, all the same, I'm sure it must have crossed your mind that some sort of compulsion could have been brought to bear on him. Everyone's vulnerable in some way or another. I mean, supposing someone I loved was under threat, I don't know that I'd have the bottle to say, 'do your worst'. Would you? But security guards must be open to that sort of pressure. Surely it's at least a *possibility* that Donnie was coerced?'

'No,' she declared flatly, looking down her nose with all the confidence of one who'd heard it from a burning bush. 'I don't think so. I don't think anyone would go that far and, in any case, Donnie doesn't have anyone they could threaten. He doesn't have a wife or children or even a girlfriend.'

'What about a sister or brother?'

'He doesn't have a sister, Miss Fitzpatrick,' she sneered as though that discredited the entire theory. 'And I can assure you that his brother is quite able to take care of himself, thank you. Anybody threatening Keith — or any of his family come to that — would very quickly regret it.' She leaned forward and the tip of her tongue appeared between her teeth at every digraph as she added, 'And that's the truth.'

Fizz was instantly gripped with a desire to know more about brother Keith. She said, 'So, if anyone were threatening Donnie, Keith would be the person he'd turn to?'

'Like a flash, and damned right too,' said their dear white-haired old mother. 'If Donnie had been intimidated Keith would've been the first to know about it and I'd have been the second. They don't keep anything from me, my boys. That's how I know it didn't happen.'

'Well, I'm sure that at least is a comfort to

both you and Keith,' Fizz said, nodding as if she totally accepted the possibility of two grown men sharing all their secrets with Mum. 'Keith sounds like a handy man to have in the family. Was it you or your husband who taught him to look after himself?'

'Life taught him that,' she said soulfully, folding her hands in her lap like a Mother Superior. 'Keith has a market stall selling jeans and jackets. Travels all over the place with it: Manchester, Birmingham, Glasgow, Ingleston, the Borders. That's a hard life and you have to be able to take the knocks. That's his wedding picture up there.'

Fizz stood up to take a closer look, her interest thawing only the extreme edges of Mrs Mulvey's frostiness. Neither the groom nor the blushing bride looked like the sort you'd care to get into a pub brawl with. Keith was big and brutish and hard of eye while his beloved looked as tough as old boots, with brassy hair and a cleavage like a builder's bum. If his face had a lived-in look, hers had been let to students.

'What a lovely couple. And are these their children?'

'Yes. That's Andy, he's two and this one's called Ian after his granda; he'll be starting school in September. A couple of wee monkeys.'

Fizz kept on looking till she was sure that she could pick out Keith when she saw him. She knew that most of the bigger country markets were on a Wednesday which meant that he'd be at the one in Peebles tomorrow. Definitely worth a visit.

She let Mrs Mulvey rattle on about her grandchildren for a while. It was fairly obvious that a threat to his nephews, had any threat at all been necessary, would have had Donnie over a barrel, but nobody was going to get his doting mum to countenance such a possibility for a second. Or, at least, to admit to it.

'I don't suppose that Donnie saw a lot of the boys,' Fizz said, 'what with them being in Edinburgh and him being in Inverness.'

'Oh but he was up and down every other week.' She was one of those women who couldn't put somebody right without managing to imply that their assumption showed a total absence of insight or forethought. 'The wee ones were awful fond of him, always round here right away to see what he'd brought them.'

Fizz nodded and smiled and made appropriate noises while she pursued her own line of thought. Obviously, Donnie had been ideally suitable for coercion. A threat to his mother or his nephews would carry a lot of weight and any self-respecting hoodlum would have had no trouble making sure he didn't bleat to the police or to his brother. It was even possible that someone had set him up in the job with the idea of using him when the time was ripe.

'Had Donnie always been in that line of work?' she asked.

'No. Donnie was in the army right up till the year before last. Catering Corps.'

'So he'd been working at the building society for how long? Over a year?'

'A year past last Christmas.' Mrs Mulvey clearly wondered why this was of interest to Fizz but wouldn't give her the satisfaction of admitting to curiosity.

'I just wondered how you'd go about getting a job like that,' Fizz told her anyway. 'Do they advertise in special recruitment bureaux or magazines like the *Police Gazette?*'

She sniffed and one shiny red shoe tapped a brief tattoo on the fireside rug. 'I'm sure I've no idea. Donnie heard about the job on the grapevine. From some trader friend of Keith's who bought some old computers from the firm.' She gave the impression of trying to get the facts right for her own satisfaction rather than for Fizz's, a trait Fizz had observed in a lot of old people who were starting to suffer memory loss — not least Grampa and Auntie Duff who could argue all the way through a film about when they'd last seen the star.

'I don't suppose you'd remember his name?' Fizz harried her in a small voice.

'Now why would anyone want to know that?' She pursed her lips with exasperation but she wasn't knuckling under to amnesia without a fight. 'I'm quite sure I know it. I never forget a name. Em . . . he sells second hand computers. Reconditioned. That thing there came from him. Keith brought it in. I never touch it but you should see the wee ones with their video games. What is it they call him, now? Something daft. Something out of a comic.'

She spent a couple of minutes worrying at it and getting increasingly irritated by Fizz's helpful suggestions till it became evident that they were flogging a dead horse.

'I suppose he'd have a workshop somewhere,' said Fizz.

'You're expecting a lot, young lady, if you expect me to know that. You'll be asking me what he had for his breakfast next thing! And what possible interest it could possibly be to either you or your employer I cannot imagine. You're sure you're not from the newspapers?'

Perceiving that a breakdown in relations was imminent, Fizz announced that she had to be going. Once witnesses got into this sort of mood there was no chance of getting anything worthwhile out of them so it was better to give them time to cool off and try again later.

'If I should come across anything I think you'd like to be informed of,' she said ingratiatingly, as she re-slung her shoulder bag, 'I'll be in touch.'

'Don't bother. I already know that Donnie did nothing to be ashamed of. I don't need anybody to inform me of that.'

Mrs Mulvey couldn't wait to see the back of her. She strode ahead to the front door, skirt flouncing and shoes twinkling, like the Wicked Witch of the West. 'Good day to you.'

Fizz had been thrown out of better places than this but never with such implacable determination.

'Thank you for — ' she started to say but the door was shut firmly in her face.

She dawdled up the road to the bus stop, swithering about maybe popping round to Buchanan's to report on her conversation with Donnie's mother. The thought of having to put up with McKenzie's wittering wasn't much of an incentive, however, so she decided to phone instead.

'Buchanan.'

'Hi. S'me.'

'Hi. What d'you want?'

'What d'you mean 'what do I want?'? Aren't you interested in knowing what I got out of Mrs Mulvey?'

'What did you get out of Mrs Mulvey?'

'Nothing.'

'Right. See you tomorrow.'

'I'm taking the morning off.'

'Okay. See you in the afternoon.'

'I'm going to Peebles market to talk to Mrs Mulvey's other son. He has a stall there.'

'Uh-huh? Any particular reason?'

'It looks like he's the one Donnie would confide in. I reckon he probably knows much more than his mother does.'

'Couldn't it wait till I can come with you?'

'If that means the weekend — no. But I reckon I should take McKenzie with me in case he might recognise Keith from a previous occasion.'

Long silence.

'Okay.'

'I'll pick him up at nine o'clock, then.'

'Suits me.'

'Roger and out.'

Buchanan was never what you'd call the chatty type but Fizz had seldom known him quite so laconic. But then, if it had been she who'd drawn the short straw and been cooped up with McKenzie for the evening, maybe she'd be laconic too.

12

Buchanan replaced the receiver and smiled into the long-lashed hazel eyes that regarded him from across the room.

'That was Fizz,' he said. 'Just checking in.'

'She's not coming over?' McKenzie said, drawing those eyes and, reluctantly, Buchanan's to his own face. 'I wanted Kerry to meet her. Sweetest little poppet you ever saw, Kerry, and as sharp as a tack. I told you how she shook off those two coppers.'

'You did, Daddy.' The long-lashed eyes widened a fraction in polite interest as Kerry swung back to Buchanan. 'A colleague of yours, you said, Tam. Was it some sort of company outing that took you both to the west coast?'

Buchanan had anticipated this question and had already crafted his reply with considerable care. Not that he had anything to hide, but for some reason things frequently went wrong at this stage.

'No, we were just doing a bit of hillwalking in the area. It's a new sport for me but Fizz is an experienced climber. She was brought up among the mountains and was at one time a member of her local Mountain Rescue team, so she's showing me the ropes, so to speak. It suits her to have the transport and it suits me to have a competent guide.'

'And who better to have been on hand just at the right moment! Daddy is so lucky to have fallen into such capable hands! It's amazing!'

She shook her head and her wonderful strawberry blonde hair swished and sparkled like sequinned satin.

Buchanan had never been a fan of Titian hair: the entire range of shades from carrot to auburn were too often matched to a pallor that he found dreary. But nobody could have called Kerry dreary. She was vibrant and animated, with an intelligent expression and the cutest little pointed chin. Her skin shimmered with a golden tan that seemed to reflect the radiance of her hair and her greenish-brownish eyes were dark enough to give her face real character. In the gathering shadows she appeared, to Buchanan's besotted gaze, to have ingested what light remained to the day only to radiate it again like an exquisite lantern.

She said, 'I'm not at all sure that I totally grasped what you told me on the phone about Daddy's adventures. I know he managed to get himself mixed up with a group of hoodlums who robbed a building society, but why did they attempt to kill him? Are they afraid he might report them to the police?'

Buchanan got up and walked across to top up her glass of tonic water. 'The bald truth, Kerry, is that we really don't know anything about these people other than that they are using a big house in Inverness as a headquarters and that they drink at The Persevere. I suspect that they latched on to your father here in Edinburgh, and took him to Inverness because he was of use to them in some way.'

Kerry laid a hand to the delightfully low neckline of her blouse. 'But, what possible use could he be in a robbery?'

'Maybe all they wanted was someone who looked . . . I don't know . . . unthreatening . . . innocent. Maybe he had some other special qualities that wouldn't be apparent to us.'

Both Kerry and Buchanan turned their heads to look at McKenzie who was slouched in his chair in an attitude of half-witted apathy. The only special qualities Buchanan had noticed him display was a talent for getting drunk and staying drunk for prolonged periods. He did look disarmingly guiltless, which might make him valuable as a front man, but he was hardly unique in that dimension and one would have thought his equal could have been found in Inverness.

'You'll think me incredibly dense,' Kerry said, 'but I can't get my head round who's who. There are the policemen who tried to kill Daddy on sight.' Her hands bracketed two imaginary policemen and set them tidily to one side. 'And there are the people at the garden centre, who *didn't* try to kill him but merely kept him prisoner.' The guards were deposited on the other side. 'Then there are the people who burst into the shed. Would they have killed Daddy if you hadn't rescued him?'

Buchanan was disinclined to dwell on that particular incident. In retrospect, his rescue attempt struck him as an act of sheer lunacy and in spite of, even now, being unable to devise an alternative solution to the direct action that had seemed necessary at the time, the memory embarrassed him.

'To be honest, Kerry,' he said, 'I don't know who they were or whose side they were on. They might have been trying to rescue your father, for all I know. In that situation we had to get Scott away first and ask questions later. They were certainly two different factions. If they hadn't been busy knocking lumps off each other we'd never have got away.'

Kerry's eyes took on a lambent glow. 'It takes a very special person to go to such lengths for someone they'd only known for three or four days.'

'We didn't have a lot of choice,' Buchanan disclaimed. 'You can't stand by and let someone be killed and there was no time to go for the police.'

'Thank God for that,' McKenzie put in from the depths of his armchair. 'Don't know what they've got on me but it looks like something that would put me away for a hellish long time. Don't even think of handing me over, Tam.'

Buchanan, who had spent much of the day considering that very option — never mind what he had promised Marianne — now found that the idea had lost its appeal. He smiled at Kerry and she said,

'I suppose what we should be doing is engaging a professional investigator to track down these thugs.'

'God, no, Kerry! I'm not having some cowboy trailing me from place to place. Tam's doing fine.'

'But Daddy, Tam has other things to do.' She turned a look of exasperation on Buchanan. 'Daddy can well afford to pay someone, you know. He sold his business only last year and he can't have drunk all the money yet. The least he should do is pay you for your time.'

'That's really not necessary,' Buchanan said firmly. 'Expenses, maybe, if they become too onerous but the rest is on the house. It's possible we may need extra help but there are one or two avenues still open to us before it comes to that. For a start: Fizz is going to Peebles market tomorrow morning to suss out one of the stall holders. I don't know why, Scott, but she thinks there's a chance you may remember this chap from somewhere so she wants you to go with her.'

McKenzie had been looking down in the mouth, probably because he'd had only one medium-sized Glenmorangie in almost twenty-four hours, but he perked up at this news. 'Really? Who is he?'

'The brother of the security guard who was shot. Can you be ready to leave about nine?'

'Nine *a.m.*?' said McKenzie with dismay but his daughter ignored the protest.

'Of course you can, Daddy,' she said. 'You'll come home with me tonight and I'll make sure you're ready in time.'

'I'd much rather stay here with Tam, pet. We're getting along just fine and I'm no trouble to him. Am I, Tam?'

'Daddy . . . don't you think Tam's doing enough for you already? He and Fizz have been absolutely wonderful, looking after you — putting themselves in real danger for you. We can hardly ask them to be responsible for you twenty-four hours a day — and you know you need some support if you're not to go off the rails again.' She leaned closer to him and touched his cheek with such affection that Buchanan twinged with jealousy. 'I won't be merciless to you, Daddy. You can have your tipple if you must, but we can't have you wandering off again — not with someone trying to kill you.'

'I feel bad about passing the buck to you,' Buchanan said. He was aware of her eyes following him as he walked over to switch on the overhead light. 'If I could handle the situation alone — '

'Don't be silly, Tam. With Mum away on holiday Daddy's my responsibility and I'm well used to it, I promise you. The nice thing about being an accountant is that you can work from home for a few days at a time without causing too much disruption.' She reached down a hand to stroke Selina who was stropping herself against her legs. 'You've been so amazingly selfless. I only wish I could repay you for what you've done already.'

Buchanan had been wishing much the

same thing but this was hardly the time to say so. 'No need,' he said, briefly reviewing the possibilities behind a bland face. 'Fizz is calling here at nine o'clock so I'll drive her over to pick up your Dad and then take both of them to the bus station. That suit you, Scott?'

Scott muttered that he supposed so and looked soulfully at his empty glass.

'I'll give you my address,' Kerry said, and opened her bag with delicate fingers, as dainty as a Geisha performing a tea ceremony. Buchanan had always found something inexplicably sexy about a woman riffling through her handbag. There was a hint of the esoteric about it. Something to do with the perfumes that drifted forth, and the stolen glimpses of jewelled or lacy objects inside. It was a profoundly feminine action and Kerry was a mistress of the art. She held out a card with fluted edges. 'Gilmore Place. Do you know it?'

Buchanan knew it well: a street of Georgian villas and spacious flats in an upcoming area just south of Princes Street. A mere ten minutes away by car. He wondered if she lived alone but couldn't quite formulate an innocent-sounding query. She wasn't in a relationship — not as far as her father was aware — but there could be a flatmate which was, in Buchanan's experience, often a bind.

'Fine,' he said. 'I should be there not much after nine.'

'The parking can be awkward at that time in the morning but I'll watch for you from the window so that you can double park for a few seconds.' She started making ready to leave. 'You're so very kind, Tam. I'm sure I wouldn't know how to handle this situation on my own, but it's such a comfort to know you're taking an interest. I don't know why you should feel obliged to do so but — '

'He promised Marianne he'd look after me,' interposed her father, laying a privileged hand on her bare knee. 'I told you. It was the last thing she said to him: 'Look after Scott.' That right Tam?'

'Well, something like that,' Buchanan agreed, fighting embarrassment. 'But I could hardly have left you to your own devices. Can I run you and Scott home, Kerry, or do you have transport?'

'I have my car downstairs, thank you, Tam. Come on, Daddy. Upsadaisy.'

McKenzie collected the plastic bag containing his few belongings and they all went downstairs together, escorted by Pooky and Selina who were completely bemused by the sudden influx of visitors.

Kerry got her father into the car and

started up the engine before leaning out, all shiny-eyed and smiling.

'We'll be all ready and waiting for you in the morning, Tam,' she said, unaware of the effect of her words on an imaginative, sex-starved guy of Buchanan's disposition. 'I'll look forward to seeing you then.'

Buchanan waved them off, grinning like a pillar box, and stood there gazing after them for some time after the cats had deserted him and the sound of the car's engine had died away. He could smell the peppery scent of nasturtiums from a neighbour's window box and a blackbird was singing loud and clear from the eaves. The world was a beautiful place and full of pleasant surprises, he thought, as he climbed the stairs.

There had been damn few such surprises in the last couple of years and those that had come his way had somehow failed to come to fruition. At times he was totally convinced that this had something to do with Fizz but, of course, it would be indulgent to assume she was entirely to blame for his lacklustre love life.

She didn't fancy him herself, she left no room for doubt on that score and, although she kept that side of her life strictly private, Buchanan suspected there had been at least one man lurking in the shadows over the last few years. He'd encountered her outside her flat early one Sunday morning with an obnoxious Bruce Willis type with whom she claimed to be bent on climbing Ben Alder. Knowing Fizz, she could have been in it solely for the lift but the sight of the two of them emerging from Fizz's entryway at crack of dawn, laughing and intimate, hinted at a more personal relationship. Buchanan felt she deserved better than Bruce Willis but it was none of his business any more than his relationships were of interest to Fizz.

He looked in the hall mirror as he closed and locked the front door. He was fit enough. He still had all his hair. His teeth were good and girls had said nice things about his eyes, so how come he'd lost his appeal? Time was — and not so long ago — when he didn't even have to try, but these days . . .

There didn't seem to be a logical explanation other than the 'Fizz-effect' but in the heart's deep core he knew that idea appealed to him only because it was the least depressing alternative. No matter, he'd take damn good care to keep her away from Kerry.

★　★　★

It was barely eight-thirty in the morning when the bell at the foot of the stairs shrilled, sending Selina dashing excitedly for the lintel.

Buchanan flicked the switch on the entryphone.

'Fizz?'

'Lothian and Borders Police, Mr Buchanan. We'd like a word with you regarding an armed robbery in Inverness.'

Buchanan recognised the voice so he wasn't fooled for a second but the words gave him a sick feeling all the same.

'Come on up.'

He was back in the bedroom getting his tie by the time Fizz reached the door but as she entered he heard her say,

'Don't even think about it, you mangy little rat. Where are you, Kimosabe?'

'Here. I'll be through in a minute. You're early.'

'So I am. Any coffee left in the jug? Where's Scott? Don't tell me he got away?'

Buchanan didn't like shouting so he pretended he didn't hear her till he'd finished knotting his tie. He'd had a wet shave this morning and selected the lilac shirt that made his eyes look bluer. A haircut would have been an improvement but the overall effect was, he thought, pretty damn good. If Kerry went for the lean and hungry look he was in with a shout.

He found Fizz in the kitchen making a

fresh brew of coffee under the close observation of both cats.

'You haven't eaten yet, have you?' she asked hopefully, then glanced over her shoulder and did a double take. 'Crumbs! Something special on this morning?'

'Uh . . . ' Buchanan was almost never tempted to lie to anyone but Fizz. 'Why d'you ask?'

She raised an eyebrow. 'The silk tie. The good shoes. The aftershave. Muchacho, you've never looked so lovely.'

Buchanan shrugged. 'Got to spruce up once in a while. There's a few oatcakes left in the packet.'

The mention of food distracted her enough for him to swing the conversation onto less personal subject matter by saying,

'The good news is: I got shot of McKenzie last night, thank God. Made him phone round his family till he found one of them willing to give him house room. His wife's on holiday in Venice and his son is married and living in Dundee, but he got his daughter to come and take him away. The bad news is: we now have to go over to Gilmore Place to pick him up. You can drop him off at the office when you get back to Edinburgh and I'll run him home. As far as I'm concerned it's a small price to pay to get him out of my hair.'

She gave him a nod of approval. 'Well done. I had a horrible feeling that I was next on his list of prospective keepers. What's the daughter like?'

'Very nice,' Buchanan said, hoping that an assumption of pseudo-generosity would look less suspicious than indifference, and hurried on, 'No luck with Mrs Mulvey, then? I must say I didn't expect a major breakthrough there. How did she strike you?'

'Not what you'd call a prime example of Scottish hospitality.' She sandwiched two oatcakes together with cream cheese and licked the knife. 'Okay, I didn't see her at her best but even at her best, I reckon, she's not the hostess with the mostest. A poor second to Lady Macbeth, I'd say. Virtually kicked me out.'

Buchanan was scarcely surprised at all. He hid his smile behind his coffee mug. 'But you think her son might offer better prospects?'

'Sounds possible to me. Keith — that's his name — is the muscle of the family. That's the implication anyway. You don't spit into the wind, you don't tread on Superman's cloak, you don't whip the mask off the Lone Ranger, and you don't mess around with Keith.' She removed a flake of oatmeal from her chin, examined its antecedents, and nibbled it off her finger. 'Donnie was the wimp of the family. Anybody bullied him, he got his big brother to sort them out.'

'His mother said that?'

'More or less. Sounds like a bit of a thug, don't you think? Somebody who's possibly no stranger to the seamier side of life. He's certainly more likely to have been involved in the robbery than Donnie.'

'It could be risky. I'm not at all sure — ' Buchanan started to say but she was ahead of him as usual.

'Yeah, I didn't think you would be, compadre, but I'm sussing him out whether you're sure or not. I'm not gormless enough to do anything stupid. If I have any doubts about Keith I won't even speak to him, but I do want to see if McKenzie can place him. It could be the lead we're desperate for.'

Buchanan forced himself to disregard the hollow feeling in the pit of his stomach which he always experienced when Fizz did something problematic. Making a fuss about her participation in chancy assignments was, as she had frequently pointed out, insulting to her intelligence and a symptom of chauvinism of the most porcine sort.

However, in this case he felt that being the muscle of a defenseless old lady and sissy brother did not necessarily brand Keith as a danger to the populace. The chances of

McKenzie recognising him were not wonderful but if Fizz thought they were worth the bus trip that was up to her. Buchanan wished they could be granted a lead that was something less of a long shot. Sometimes Fizz's optimism was a trifle hard to share but at least her new game plan would have the advantage of keeping McKenzie out of mischief for an hour or two, not to mention certain other payoffs of which she knew nothing.

'You will bear in mind,' he had to say, 'that Scott's photograph may have been circulated to the Lothian and Borders police. You'll have to be very circumspect.'

She gave him a one-fingered answer and spread herself another oatcake.

They had to hang around till Hector phoned in, with nothing to report, but managed to reach Gilmore Place before quarter past. The problem of preventing Fizz from spotting Kerry at the window had been exercising Buchanan's mind since he woke up but, probably through lack of practice in the art of dissembling, no solution had presented itself to him. It must have been the sudden rush of adrenaline on seeing that luminescent hair behind the glass (What light at yonder window breaks?) that inspired him to say,

'Give me my sunglasses out of that glove

compartment, would you, Fizz?'

Fizz rummaged unsuccessfully for the few seconds it took him to smile and wave and then said,

'They don't seem to be in here.'

'Oh, sorry. They must be in mine. Yes, here they are.'

He waved again at the now empty window knowing that Fizz would assume she'd been just too late to see McKenzie.

'You'd better take this for your bus fares,' he said, partly to distract her, and got a couple of notes out of his wallet. 'I think Hector got most of the hot money away from Scott but, keep an eye on what he tries to spend.'

'Scott's first stop is the bank,' Fizz said, buttoning the notes into the pocket of her shirt. 'It's time he started forking out for his subsistence. We should be bloody charging him for the service he's getting. I've had enough of his toffs-is-careless attitude and if he doesn't start — '

She broke off and allowed her expression to complete the sentence as McKenzie loomed up at the nearside window beaming like a Cheshire cat who'd just become sole beneficiary of its owner's millions. Buchanan had been unable to come up with a contingency plan for use if Kerry had come downstairs with him so he was much relieved to see Scott unaccompanied.

'God, but it's busy out here. Is it always like this in Edinburgh at nine o'clock in the morning?'

'I fear so, Scott,' Fizz told him and swivelled round to look at him as he slid into the back seat. 'You're a little rosier-cheeked than when I last saw you.'

'And you, my little sweet thing, are a joy to behold. Almost worth being pitchforked from my bed at this ungodly hour. Tam, dear chap, never have a daughter. They wrap one round their little finger at an early age and grow up to have no filial respect whatsoever. Better to expose them at birth and raise only boys. Sons are a different kettle of fish entirely. They go off and get married and leave one to get on with things as one sees fit.'

Buchanan, anxious as he was to get the conversation onto something other than daughters, was attending to the task of getting back into the flow of traffic and couldn't concentrate on both things at once.

McKenzie sat himself sideways with an arm along the back of the seat, giving himself a better view of Fizz and disappearing from the rear view mirror entirely.

'Before I forget,' he said. 'I'm to ask both of

you if you'd like to come for dinner tomorrow night.'

Buchanan felt safe enough in snapping on an oh-god-no expression in time to forestall Fizz's knee-jerk acceptance of free nourishment. She turned with a 'y-y-y-y . . . ' trembling on her lips but caught sight of his face and paused, giving him the chance to say,

'I'll have to pass on that one, Scott. Another time would be lovely, but I'm afraid I've got something on tomorrow evening.'

'Too bad. How about you, Fizz? Would you care to come or would you prefer to wait and come with Tam at another time?'

'I . . . um . . . '

Buchanan had never known her to take so long to make up her mind where food was concerned. He was convinced she was doing it to torture him. Finally he slid his eyes towards her and gave her the tiniest twitch of a frown, which appeared to convince her.

'I think I'll take a rain check this time, thanks Scott. I'll come when Tam can make it.'

Buchanan maintained a deadpan contemplation of the flow of traffic but already he was wishing he had let things take their course. There was a very narrow line between his infantile miming and blatant deceit and it would only take one glimpse of Kerry, one minute in her company, for Fizz to know that he had been misleading her.

She'd wonder why, and since his social life was no concern of hers, how the blue blazes could he explain himself without looking neurotic? Good question that.

13

Fizz didn't just like markets, she was addicted to them.

Part of the reason was that she'd never been able to afford to shop at high street stores and, since moving in to her first student flat, she'd discovered that markets provided the bare necessities of existence at a fraction of the price she'd have had to fork out elsewhere.

The entertainment value of a good market — the characters, the banter, the chance to pry into other people's treasures — was a bonus, but an important one for someone who couldn't afford to pay for entertainment. Ingleston Sunday market in Edinburgh had introduced her to a habit that had persisted for upwards of ten years and led her by the nose through the Athens flea market, the Saint Sophia market in Istanbul and the Souk in Morocco plus every little village market she could access en route.

Peebles market came nowhere near her Top One Hundred list. The stalls were almost all selling traders junk: cotton carpets, everything-under-a-pound haberdashery, shoddy costume jewellery, dermatitis in tubes and spray cans. The last two rows, however, held the genuine junk so close to Fizz's heart. Most of those were manned by traders too, of course, but there were one or two non-professionals clearing out their own attics or getting rid of granny's earthly possessions.

'I thought you said this chap we're looking for sold clothing of some sort,' McKenzie mentioned placidly as she locked on to her first target.

'We'll get to him in a while. He's not likely to pack up and go before closing time.'

He found an old fashioned kaleidoscope and started twiddling with it and holding it to his eye while the stall holder eyed him like a pointer dog.

'Bugger me — saving your presence, Fizz — what magical things these were. Nothing like the dingy plastic things you see nowadays. I used to have one like this when I was . . . oh, ten or so. I think I'll have it.' He beamed at the stall holder. 'How much for this wonderful object?'

'Seven fifty,' said the woman, who knew a mug when she saw one. 'It's an antique.'

McKenzie coughed up without a blink and strolled on cradling his bargain and radiating satisfaction. It was very possible that the toy was worth a couple of pounds, Fizz thought, but antiques were only worth spending money on if one knew where to sell them. She could have bought it for a fraction of what McKenzie had paid but, never mind, if it was keeping his mind off booze for a couple of minutes it was a snip as far as she was concerned.

He clearly imagined she hadn't noticed him sipping from the flask in his hip pocket but she was simply indifferent. She knew he could function well enough at a medium level of intoxication and as long as he stayed more or less rational till she got him home he could do what the hell he pleased. She wasn't Alcoholics Anonymous.

By the time they had exhausted the possibilities of the junk stalls McKenzie was carrying two plastic bags full of assorted rubbish. He had called at his bank before they arrived at the market but was in danger of having to go again before he got home. Fizz tried to dissuade him from the acquisition of a straw hat and a dowdy, middle-aged pair of shoes for his no doubt dowdy, middle-aged daughter, but he was enjoying himself too much to heed her and only transportation difficulties restrained him from purchasing a mountain bike and a twenty foot extending ladder.

Fizz saw nothing at all to seduce her other

than a couple of office binders which she really needed for her course work. Three art students who were about to finish their degree course were selling off their redundant supplies and Fizz spent a few minutes fingering half empty tubes of oil paint and psyching herself up to spending a pound or two. She hadn't done any painting since her ignominious departure from art school nine years ago but the time was fast approaching when she'd have time for a hobby again. Not yet, though. She saved her money.

The rain that had been threatening all morning held off till almost noon and then came on with such a rush that it caused a minor panic around the stalls that were uncanopied. Fizz and McKenzie had to dart from one shelter to the next till they spotted Keith. Luckily both he and his lady wife were tall and striking so it would have been hard to miss them.

Their canopied stall occupied a double site and their merchandise consisted of cheap denims and leather jackets with a few anoraks thrown in for the more discerning customer. They were doing very little business, probably because most of the punters who had not gone home for lunch were being chased away by the rain. Fizz paused at the adjacent stall and asked McKenzie if Keith looked familiar to him.

McKenzie took a long time to say 'no', so long that Fizz's hopes had started to rise, but finally he shook his head.

'No. There was a chap with a shaved head like that. I'd forgotten about him, but he was shorter and not quite so ugly. That's not him.'

'What about before you went to Inverness?' Fizz persisted. 'Remember the people you went to Inverness with? Was he one of them? What about the three guys who were playing cards in the storage shed at the garden centre — or the other prisoner? Don't you remember what they looked like?'

'Ah . . . can't say I do, no, but I bet I'd recognise them if I saw them.' He mimed abject despair. 'Sorry, darling, I don't know the chap. Pretty sure I never clapped eyes on him in my life.'

'What about the woman?' She indicated the heavy figure that was huddled in a corner, sipping a mug of tea. The bulging bosom had sagged out of sight and the brassy hair was now like coconut matting but Keith's bride was still hanging on in there.

'No.' McKenzie was sure about that. 'The only woman I saw with any of them was Marianne.'

'Okay.' Fizz took a minute to suss out the

situation. She hadn't held out all that much hope that McKenzie would recognise Keith but it was a bit of a downer all the same. Donnie's big brother looked even meaner in the flesh than he'd done in the photograph and the idea of picking his brains was not one that turned her on to any great extent but having come all this way some sort of overture was definitely called for.

'I'll go and have a few words with him,' she told McKenzie. 'You stay here where I can see you and keep out of sight behind that rack of carpets. I'll only be a couple of minutes.'

McKenzie puffed a whisky scented sigh.

She edged casually closer to Keith's stall, pausing to browse through the videos and CDs on his neighbour's display and then moved over and started sorting through a rail of jeans. She was pretty confident that Keith was, as she had assured Buchanan, on the side of the goodies but all the same, she jumped when he appeared beside her, watching her like a hawk.

'All big sizes there, doll. Eights and tens on this rail here. Them's yer baggies, them's yer bootlegs.'

'Thanks,' said Fizz and gave him a chummy nod as if they'd met before. 'I was sorry to hear about your brother Donnie.'

'Aye, well.' He took a good look at her.

'How'd you know I was Donnie's brother?'

Fizz fiddled with a pair of jeans. 'I met him at Ingleston one Sunday and he pointed you out to me.' She smiled. 'Said you'd give me a bargain.'

'Were you a friend of his, like?'

'I saw him around. I worked in a bar that he used to drink in, up in Inverness. He was a nice guy. Always good for a laugh.'

His chin, which he had tucked in, the better to look down at her, started slowly to rise till his head was tipped back and he was regarding her almost down his nose. 'What bar was that?'

Fizz was about to invent a name but decided to see if she could surprise a reaction out of him by saying, 'The Persevere. It's just round the corner from the river walk.'

Keith was either unfamiliar with the name or he would have made a good poker player. He merely looked politely interested and asked casually, 'And Donnie was a regular in there, was he? What was he drinking? Sticking to his whisky and green ginger?'

Fizz was too good a liar to fall for a loaded question like that. If Keith had told her in so many words that Donnie was a tee-totaller she could not have been more certain but even so she wasn't going to take chances.

'Actually, I never served him myself, but I

don't think he was much of a drinker. The boss used to say he only came in to chat up Louise, one of the other girls. I think he really fancied her. He always waited for her to serve him, anyway. She'll be really gutted, Louise will.'

A couple of teenagers started working their way down the rails but Keith wasn't for moving.

'Lorraine,' he called to his wife and jerked his head at her till she swore under her breath and moved forward. The instant she did so the teenagers abandoned their shoplifting attempt and sidled out into the rain.

'Did you know any of Donnie's other pals in Inverness?' Keith asked, attempting a smile that would have been better left unborn.

'No. He always came in on his own,' Fizz confided, holding a pair of denims against her waist. She rather liked the interest Keith was showing in Donnie's lifestyle. As she had expected, he was turning out to be the type who wouldn't rely on the due processes of the law to avenge his brother's death.

She was thinking about how to lay the foundation for a free and frank exchange of ideas when she realised that Keith's attention had abandoned her in favour of something a few stalls away. Even as she turned to look she had the feeling that it must be McKenzie he was looking at, and it was. He had crossed over the aisle between the two rows of stalls and, engrossed in the variety of exotica, was now visible from Keith's emporium.

Fizz's brain went haywire. McKenzie might have no recollection of seeing Keith before, but Keith sure as hell knew McKenzie and not, judging by his expression, as a dear friend. Another second and she'd have blurted out something totally horrendous to this guy with consequences which would probably have been highly injurious if not lethal.

She flapped the jeans she was holding to draw Keith's attention, if only fleetingly, back to herself. 'I think they're all much too long for me,' she said and then drew in a quick breath and pointed at a youth hurrying past the opposite side of the site. 'My God — look — he took an armful of jeans!'

Keith did a quick about turn and without wasting energy on more than a single — but quite powerful — expletive charged off in pursuit of the now vanished suspect. With equal speed, Fizz exploded into the near aisle, darted through a thicket of punters and grabbed McKenzie with both hands.

'Move!' she snarled in his ear, shoving him forward with infuriated strength.

'My dear girl . . . '

'Just move it, Scott. This is serious.'

It took a few seconds for the message to get through but within a few paces he started to totter forward at a reasonable speed and Fizz could let up the pressure. Running any faster would only draw attention to them. She chivvied him through and out of the more open-plan stalls, darting across the aisles and quickly putting pursuit behind them. There was still enough of a crowd to melt into but a sign advertising public conveniences seemed to offer the best temporary concealment.

McKenzie had never been in a ladies toilet before but, as he was roughly informed, there was a first time for everything and it was one place they could be fairly sure Keith wouldn't look. Fizz bolted them both inside a cubicle and ceded the seat to McKenzie who needed it more than she.

'I can't take my eyes off you for a minute,' she snapped, her patience tested to destruction. 'What on earth were you playing at, crossing over the aisle to where Keith could see you?'

'Did I?' He looked the picture of perplexed innocence as he thought it over. 'Was that the stall with the floor polisher?'

'Scott,' she said, leaning her back against the door and keeping an ear open for the arrival of other patrons. 'In God's name, what would you do with a floor polisher?'

'Fizz, it was only one-fifty! Must have been worth — heavens, even second-hand it must have been worth a hundred pounds!'

Fizz was too disheartened even to roll up her eyes. She had only herself to blame for putting any reliance on McKenzie. From now on she'd have to abandon all hope of rationality from him and start thinking of him as having a mental age of, at a generous estimate, three. That meant she couldn't leave him in the cubicle while she made sure the coast was clear, she'd have to hover in the doorway, or close by, and look two ways at once.

'I do wish you wouldn't, my darling. Really. I don't mind at all having to sit here for a while but I'd be much happier if you were to stay with me. What if someone comes in?'

'If someone comes in she'll go into the other cubicle.'

'What if someone's in the other cubicle? She might look under the door. She might see my feet. She might call the police. What if Keith comes in and looks under the door?'

Fizz gave up trying to interrupt him and considered the matter seriously. He had a point. A small point, perhaps, but if he wasn't content he wouldn't stay there for five minutes. She took his plastic carrier bag from him and pulled out the clumpety shoes he'd bought for his daughter.

'Here, dammit, put these on.'

'Oh dear, I don't think — '

'Too damn true you don't think. If you were capable of thinking we wouldn't be in this mess. So, just get them on. Roll up your trousers and get your feet into them. Come on.'

They wouldn't go on, of course, but they went half on and that was good enough to withstand a moderately fast scrutiny. It was hard not to wish for a camera. He'd have made a wonderful shot, sitting there with his face so ludicrously woebegone and his hairy white shanks tapering into impossibly tiny patent leather pumps. Fizz was sorely tempted to plonk the straw hat on his head, purely for her own amusement, but she was surprised to discover that McKenzie's intransigence had not deprived her of all humanity.

'I'll be just outside, Scott,' she said, trying to scowl at him. 'And, so help me, if you move from that seat you're on your own. I mean that. And listen — take it easy with the hip flask. If we have to hurry again you can't rely on me to carry you, right?'

McKenzie said he supposed she was right so she left him there looking pathetic and not funny at all. Outside, the rain had blown away on the breeze and plastic sheets were being optimistically whipped off the exposed stalls. Keeping in the shadow of the doorway Fizz took a long careful look in both directions without seeing any sign of Keith.

She was not banking heavily on his having lost the supposed shoplifter in the crowd. It was possible of course, but almost certainly too much to hope for. The youth had not been moving all that fast and, of course, he had not been trying to hide, so she had to assume that Keith now knew she had foxed him. That meant he'd be aware that she and McKenzie were in alliance, so he'd be looking for them both.

Obviously, they couldn't afford to hang about till he got fed up and went back to his stall. She'd have to look for him, as well as she was able, and make sure that he was headed away from her before she made a break for the exit.

Because the toilet block was situated in a corner of what was, for six days a week, a car park, she could see a fair distance along two sides and from one of those sides she could look sideways down the aisles of stalls. This gave her a reasonable chance of sighting Keith, the only drawback being that he might see her first.

It wasn't difficult to skulk along from stall

to stall because she was low in the crowd but, for the same reason, it was awkward to get much of a view. Further hampered by the necessity of keeping an eye on the door of the ladies loo, she was on a fast slide to despair when she finally spotted Keith.

He wasn't charging down an aisle, as she had expected to see him, but lurking much as she herself was doing, behind a tall rail of merchandise. He wasn't waiting in ambush for her, Fizz realised right away, but focusing on a stall in the next aisle, which was back to back with the one that concealed him: a stall selling reconditioned computers and sundry accessories. Painted on the backdrop of the stall was a large spider's web which would have been sufficient to give Mrs Mulvey's memory the boost it needed. 'Something out of a comic', she'd said. Well, here he was: Spider-man.

There didn't appear to be much to interest Keith at the stall. It was manned by a man and a boy of about sixteen, neither of them doing anything more suspicious than taking money and putting stuff in carrier bags. Their customers were mostly innocuous young men, clearly more interested in the compara-tive merits of video games than in slipping across wads of notes or packages of illegal substances. Yet Keith was clearly waiting for something.

Fizz was torn by making a fast exit while Keith was intent on his surveillance or staying put to find out what he was waiting to see. She was expecting at any second to be faced with the spectacle of McKenzie tottering out of the ladies' loo in his high heels but she waited as long as she dared, which was about ten minutes. It then struck her, with something of a shock, that Keith was most probably waiting for herself and McKenzie. He evidently didn't trust Spider-man and must be wondering if he was in cahoots with herself and Scott.

Cursing herself for not moving sooner she hared back to McKenzie and found him fumbling his way into his shoes with the clear intention of coming to look for her.

'Fizz! I thought something had happened to you. Christ, I hope I never have to live through anything like that again! Destroyed my faith in womankind, I swear to God. It's sodding purgatory in here — saving your presence, darling.'

This 'saving-your-presence' thing was getting up Fizz's nose. She wasn't one to be shocked by a naughty word. As far as she was concerned words were just words, not magic spells that could wound or dishonour anyone but the user. But the insincerity of the pseudo-apology was becoming profoundly irritating. If he wanted to 'save her presence', whatever that meant, he could bloody save it by not swearing in the first place.

She threw the pumps away, rammed his bare feet into his shoes, and hauled him to his feet.

'Okay, matey, let's hit the road.'

They had two options. One was to forge a way through the shrubbery that surrounded the car park and climb the wall beyond and the other was to skip past the end of the aisle where she'd seen Keith and give McKenzie a look at Spider-man as they passed. Option one was barely viable as McKenzie would have to be heaved over the wall and, even at that, she wasn't sure he could do it. Option two was dangerous but if McKenzie recognised Spider-man it could be the breakthrough they needed.

McKenzie's unsteady gait drew a few affronted looks as he lurched along, propelled and supported by Fizz's grip on his arm. His felicity at being restored to the outside world was so compelling that he had to smile at everyone they passed and it held him inured to the glowers he was receiving from the douce locals.

Fizz halted on the corner of Spider-man's

aisle and checked that Keith was still on surveillance. He was, and by the look of him he hadn't even blinked since she'd left him. Carefully, she insinuated McKenzie's head around the corner.

'See him? Four stalls along.'

McKenzie obediently followed her pointing finger, his mouth open and his eyes slowly focusing.

'Well, bugger me!' he said loudly, and lurched suddenly forward. 'It's good old Fergie!'

14

Buchanan was dismayed to find that Fizz and McKenzie were not there awaiting him when he arrived back at the office at two-thirty. He had intended to have a quick wash and shave before driving McKenzie home to Gilmore Place but he was so worried that he couldn't move from the window till he saw them, at last, weaving their way towards him through the Queen Street shoppers.

He was back at his desk and deep in paperwork by the time they reached his door.

'That's it!' Fizz burst in without knocking and plummeted into the spare chair. 'I've HAD it with this guy!'

McKenzie, beaten into second place, had to make do with propping a hip on a corner of the bookcase. He looked so old and disconsolate that Buchanan gave him his own seat and appealed to one of the typists to rustle up a pot of coffee.

If ever there were a case for saying I-told-you-so, Buchanan thought, one was looking at it now. Fizz was clearly in a vile temper and if she wasn't regretting her insistence on going to Peebles it was only because she made a consistent point of regretting nothing.

'Christ, Tam, we've had a hellish day,' McKenzie groaned. 'Harried from pillar to post. Skulking round corners. Lurking in ladies toilets. Running for our lives. This little girlie here has no concept of what it is to be seventy-four years old.'

Fizz had her teeth clamped over a reply but her eyes boiled with animosity.

'The main thing is, you're back here safe and sound,' Buchanan soothed them both, 'and I take it you managed to shake off any pursuit before reaching the office?'

'We shook off today's quota of McKenzie-exterminators,' Fizz ground out with great bitterness. 'No doubt there'll be more tomorrow. I'm just surprised they're not queueing up at the door with torches and rope and sacks of quicklime. There were times today when I was on their side.'

Perceiving that a total breakdown of diplomatic relations was imminent, Buchanan waited till the coffee and biscuits arrived before pressing for details. Fizz was accusatory, McKenzie was defensive, but the story that emerged only confirmed for Buchanan that he had been seriously remiss in allowing Fizz her head. She was certainly a lot less scatty than she used to be but you could be fairly sure, even now, that left to her own devices, she could manage to transform even the most staid scenario into a scene from a Carry On film in a matter of minutes.

'Okay,' he said, dodging the question of liability altogether. 'At least we can say that the expedition was successful in that you identified the Spider-man as Fergie. You did get a good look at him, Scott?'

'He did!' Fizz put in, doing her Shirley Temple scowl. 'And if I hadn't been there to kick his legs from under him, Fergie would have had a good look at *him*! He shouldn't be allowed out without his mother!'

'I got a little confused, that's all,' McKenzie alleged, waving his arms about like Andre Previn. 'Fergie was always very nice to me whatever those other bloody bastards — saving your presence, Fizz — tried to do to me. There was no need to use such extreme methods.'

'There wouldn't be,' Fizz told Buchanan, 'if he'd stop buggering about like a sodding cretin while I'm trying to keep his balls out of the mangle — er — saving your presence, Scott.'

'Whuh . . . whuh?' McKenzie looked as though he were about to call an exorcist.

'Listen, we haven't time for all this,' Buchanan interrupted. 'Okay, you had a tough day but at least it wasn't a waste of time. You've established two things. One: Keith recognised Scott. That could indicate that he has some connection with The Persevere bunch. Maybe he moves in those criminal circles himself, maybe he's doing his own bit of detection into his brother's death. He certainly associated Scott with Spider-man, right?'

Fizz nodded energetically. 'As soon as he lost track of us he headed straight for Spider-man's stall as though he expected to catch up with us there. I'm ninety per cent certain it was us he was waiting for.'

'And you still have no recollection of seeing him before, Scott?'

'Absolutely not. Could be wrong, of course, but he's not the sort of chap you'd forget in a hurry even if you were slightly . . . anaesthetised when you met him.'

Buchanan wasn't too worried about that. The chances were that McKenzie had met only the bit players in the building society drama, whereas the planners might well have been familiar with him.

'Well not to worry,' he said, 'you've also identified the Spider-man as one of The Persevere bunch which could mean that they are operating here in Edinburgh as well as in Inverness. You reckon it was here that they picked you up — right, Scott? — and, presumably, Spider-man is operating around the Edinburgh area. We have to decide how to follow this up.'

McKenzie was still stunned by Fizz's rhetoric and kept reviewing her with quick glances that blended revulsion with disbelief. Fizz, however, having got some of her vexation off her chest, had cheered up considerably.

'We could put a tail on him,' she contributed. 'I dare say he'd lead us somewhere eventually.'

This was, of course, a classic bell-the-cat suggestion as neither she nor anyone else would volunteer to do it. Hector was the only one of them with that sort of patience and that amount of time to spare, but he couldn't be in two places at once and the garden centre seemed a likelier source of intelligence. It seemed probable, to Buchanan, that Spider-man's retail business had little to do with his moonlighting, however it was something that ought to be checked out sooner or later.

'I'll see what Hector has to say about it when he phones at six o'clock,' he said, and looked at his watch. It was already twenty to four, not too late for Larry to phone him with some last minute research he might need in court tomorrow, yet still early enough for a decent chat with Kerry when he dropped off her father. The Wonderful Beatrice, whose secretarial skills he now shared with Fizz, could, in the first eventuality, phone him at Kerry's number and if he left now he might be able to stretch the second eventuality into an hour or more.

'You two can put on your thinking caps and see what you can come up with. I'll do the same and we'll discuss it tomorrow, okay? Meanwhile, Fizz: the Abernethys have fixed up their mortgage and want a quick completion, so could you go ahead with the search, etc, ASAP. I have things to do also, but I'll drop you off home first, Scott.'

Fizz was still new enough at the job to enjoy even the boring tasks around the office so she dashed off in a hurry, giving McKenzie a pat on the head in passing, either to wake him from his daze or to let him know he was forgiven.

McKenzie's eyes followed her from the room and then swung to Buchanan in a look of piteous denial.

'I can't believe she said that. Fizz! I just can't believe it. Where did she learn that sort of language?'

'Not from me, Scott, I can assure you.' Buchanan whisked his paperwork into his briefcase and walked over to the door. Something — loyalty? — prompted him to say, 'I told you she was no Barbie doll, Scott. She's had it tough from the age of three and there's not much of the dreamer left in there. Behind that baby face there's a very intelligent pragmatist. You should take her seriously.'

That was too much for Scott to take in all at once. As they walked out to the car he kept on mumbling, 'But language like that . . . like a sailor's parrot . . . from a lassie scarce out of her teens . . . what's the world coming to? It's the television to blame.'

'You're a fair linguistic teacher yourself, you know, Scott.'

'Who, me? Well, but . . . from a young lassie — '

'She's twenty-nine.'

'Twenty — ? Really? All the same, it's a completely different kettle of fish when a woman speaks like that.'

Fizz would have wanted to know why, precisely — which was a fair question — but Buchanan had never been able to answer that one himself, either to her satisfaction or to his, so he left McKenzie to figure it out for himself.

Kerry opened the door to them in a floaty tomato-red dress topped by an open shirt the pale apricot colour of Cornish ice cream. She held the door wide and motioned them into a narrow, rather gloomy hallway.

'Come in, Tam. Safe home, then, Daddy? Have you had a lovely day?'

McKenzie tramped resolutely past her without a glance and headed for the stairs at the back of the hall. 'I've had an absolutely ghastly day and I need a drink. A very large drink. And immediately.'

Kerry widened her eyes at Buchanan in half-serious alarm. 'Oh-oh. That doesn't sound too auspicious.'

Buchanan ventured a reassuring pat on the shoulder. Well, not exactly a pat, maybe, but certainly not a grope. 'Not as bad as it sounds, fortunately. And they did make a little progress.'

'Well, that's good news, at least. Come upstairs and tell me all about it.'

Her tanned legs, as she climbed the steep staircase in front of him, were silky smooth and slender with fragile ankles and neat feet in strappy red sandals. As she moved, the hem of her dress fluttered and flirted around her knees, so that Buchanan missed the top step and only narrowly avoided head-butting her in the rear.

The apartment was what was known in the trade as a double-upper flat: the top two storeys of a Georgian terrace house that had long ago been divided into two homes. The rooms were spacious and elegantly proportioned and Buchanan's professional eye estimated that at the current Edinburgh prices, Kerry was sitting on a small fortune.

McKenzie was in the kitchen, getting whisky into a tumbler with lightning speed and a deftness he had rarely evidenced before, but Kerry led the way past the open doorway and into a tall-windowed lounge filled with late afternoon sunshine.

'I won't offer you alcohol, Tam, since you're driving, but there's apple juice and orange juice and some fizzy things. Or would you prefer a coffee?'

'Apple juice would be nice, thank you, Kerry.'

She swirled out of the room and through to the kitchen from where her voice and McKenzie's drifted back in gentle remonstrance and robust justification. Buchanan passed the time by adjusting his tie in the mirror above the fireplace and breathing into his cupped hand to check his breath.

Kerry was laughing when she came back into the room.

'I suspect your colleague found Daddy quite a handful this morning,' she said, setting down a tray of glasses and carafes and sinking into an armchair. 'According to Daddy, Love's last word is spoken.'

Buchanan matched her smile. 'Scott's perception of Fizz was very much at odds with reality right from the beginning, I fear, so he was going to be disappointed somewhere along the line. A lot of people make the same mistake. I'm sorry if she went over the score.'

Kerry wafted that away with an airy hand. 'Daddy is not the easiest person in the world to get along with these days. Even Mummy has more or less given up on him and my brother and his wife simply don't want to know. If I didn't adore him so much I'd probably be the same myself, so I'd be the last person to blame Fizz if she lost her patience with him. Especially as, if Daddy's to be believed, she has located someone he met in Inverness.'

'Fergie, yes. That's a step forward, thank God, but where it might lead us is still a mystery. Your father insists Fergie's a great guy but, I have to say, all the evidence points to the opposite, so Fizz was absolutely right in keeping them apart.'

'Oh dear. So he's one of the people who are trying to kill him?' Kerry's eyes latched on to Buchanan's. It felt like a child's scared hand sliding into his.

'Nothing to worry about, Kerry,' he said, restraining himself from laying a paternal hand on her arm. 'I'm quite confident that Scott's safe for the moment. The fact that you've had no trouble before now proves that none of his murderous chums know of your existence. From what I saw of them, they're not the type to waste any time.'

She nodded, but her eyes still clung to his. 'It's not the first time he's been in trouble like this, you know. Oh, I don't mean he's been in fear of his life, but there have been a few occasions when he has disappeared for days at a time and then reappeared without a clue as to where he's been. Or so he claims.'

Buchanan stretched out a hand and laid it on . . . the arm of the chair quite close to her wrist. 'It must be very worrying for all the family.'

'Horribly. In the end Mummy just couldn't take it, and to tell you the honest truth, I'm sometimes tempted to abandon him myself. I think he gets up to a lot that never reaches my ears.'

'Can't you persuade him to accept treatment? I'm sure a spell in one of the better clinics would work wonders.'

Her bosom rose and fell in a sigh. 'The trouble is, he doesn't want to change. No clinic can help him if he doesn't really *want* to stop drinking.' She leaned forward and refilled their glasses from the carafe. 'The only progress we've ever made was in getting him to phone me every day. That way, if I don't hear from him I know he's on a bender. Usually he's at home or in one of the other lairs he holes up in. It's only once in a while that I can't locate him, and that's a worry.'

'So, you knew last week that he was missing?'

'The last *two* weeks,' she said, looking surprised at his misconception. 'The last time he phoned me was a fortnight ago last Thursday — three weeks ago tomorrow. I'm sorry, I thought you knew how long he'd been missing. Is it important?'

Buchanan didn't know whether it was important or not, but it was vastly intriguing.

He said, 'I'll have to think about it, but right now I can't imagine what value your father could have been to those guys. They found him in Edinburgh, kept him in varying stages of intoxication for two weeks — using him for purposes we can't even guess at — and then, after incriminating him in an armed robbery, tried — with considerable persistence — to kill him. Does that make any sense to you? Because it doesn't make any sense to me, I can tell you.'

Kerry's eyes hung on to his with flattering

confidence. 'I'm sure you'll sort it all out, Tam. One can only hope that nothing too horrific will emerge.'

It was not hidden from Buchanan that his ploy in shunting McKenzie onto his daughter and, hopefully, out of his own immediate aegis, had misfired. Instead of diminishing his involvement in the current mess he now felt, not only ashamed of his chicanery, but wholly committed to protecting and supporting Kerry as well as her father.

'I'll certainly do what I can, Kerry,' he said, leaving his hand conveniently on the arm of her chair in case she needed recourse to it. 'But, in the meantime, it's unlikely that your father is in any immediate danger. If we can prevent him doing anything silly, as he did today — and I admit, I should have envisaged that possibility when I okayed the scheme — it's only a matter of time before we find out who his enemies are. Once we know what they're up to we can go to the police with proof that Scott was set up.'

Kerry nibbled doubtfully at her lower lip and her gaze wavered. 'If he was set up,' she whispered.

'I'm sure he was.' Buchanan didn't have to force his confident grin. He simply couldn't see McKenzie as a criminal. 'But if I'm wrong, I'll keep my mouth shut about it, never fear.'

Light as a wisp of swan's-down, her fingers rested for a moment on his. The effect was slightly less galvanizing than sharing a bath with an electric radiator but it was a start.

'That telephone conversation you had with your father around the time he disappeared,' he said. 'Did he say where he was? Or who he was drinking with? Anything we might be able to follow up?'

'I'm pretty sure he didn't.' She moved her shoulders in a half shrug. 'I know he was in a bar because I could hear the usual background noises but he wasn't too distressingly drunk. Nothing out of the usual, but of course, it was fairly early in the evening — around nine or half past, I think — so who knows how much he drank after phoning me. He was with people, he said, but I don't remember his saying anything that could identify them.'

She squinted her eyes in thought, holding a finger away from her glass in a just-give-me-a-minute gesture. Then she said,

'He'd met them before. The previous evening, I think, but I could be wrong there. Recently, anyway. He said, 'They're on the pipes.' '

'On the *pipes*?' Buchanan repeated but the

words didn't mean any more to him when he said them than when she did.

'I asked him what he meant but he just mumbled something unintelligible.'

'He didn't say where he was calling from?'

'No. I did ask but I didn't get a straight answer. Actually, I got the feeling he wasn't too sure himself, but that was nothing out of the usual. I wish now that I'd insisted on knowing.'

A clock in another room struck five and Buchanan relaxed a little. Now he was on his own time and free of commitments till Hector phoned in at six o'clock. He'd have to be at home to receive the call but that gave him another hour, God (and Kerry) willing, and the way things were progressing, that could be enough.

He said, 'If Scott could be kept under close supervision for a few days — '

And then the phone rang.

Kerry had to go out into the upper hallway to answer it but when she came back she was carrying a cordless extension.

'It's for you, Tam. Your secretary.'

Buchanan had guessed as much, since The Wonderful Beatrice would never have given anyone else the number, and he knew it had to be urgent or she'd never have phoned him at all.

'Hello, Beatrice.'

'Sorry to bother you, Mr Buchanan, but I have Mr McSween here in the office and he claims it's imperative that he speak with you right away.'

It took Buchanan a moment to connect the name McSween with Hector. 'That's okay, Beatrice. Put him on.'

'I'll just switch him through.'

There were various clicks and then Hector's voice came down the line breathless with impatience. 'Helen Blazes, Tam! You're a hard man to reach. That hard-faced bulldog out there would do well in the prison service.'

'You're early, Hector. Has something happened?'

'I've got a lead, yeah, but I can't follow it up. There's something going on back at the garden centre and I could miss something if I don't get back there real quick. When're you going to be home? We need to talk.'

Buchanan swore silently but with a fluency that would have shocked even Fizz. He looked at his watch but it was still showing five o'clock.

'Okay. Give me twenty minutes. I'll be at the flat as soon as you are.'

'Right. Don't be late. I have to get back.'

Kerry's expression emulated his own

frustration but not any more than politeness dictated.

'You will let me know if he has discovered anything significant, won't you, Tam?' she said as she conducted him back downstairs.

'Yes, of course I will.' He thought fast. 'Why don't you and Scott meet me for a quick lunch tomorrow. I have to be in court so I'll only have about an hour but I could bring you up to speed on this new lead of Hector's.'

'That would be nice,' she said, warming him with her eyes. 'Daddy would appreciate some male company too. Where shall we meet you?'

'The Apex International in the Grassmarket has good parking and it's only five minutes from the High Court. One o'clock — though I could be a few minutes late, depending how things go in court.'

Her smile left Buchanan in no doubt regarding her enthusiasm so he was not dissatisfied with his progress. He could award the encounter with no better than a B-minus, but there was always tomorrow.

McKenzie's car was already sitting outside the flat when Buchanan pulled into the mews. Hector wasn't inside it but pacing up and down with his sunglasses on top of his head.

Buchanan pulled into the garage but barely

had time to switch off the ignition before Hector was in the passenger seat, radiating urgency from every pore.

'No point in going upstairs, we can talk here. There's something — '

'What's the big rush?'

Hector's teeth flashed in an irritated grimace at the interruption. He was wound up tight with agitation and impatience.

'There are more staff around the garden centre than usual — maybe six or eight more — and none of the extras are attending to customers. They appeared this afternoon — probably one at a time cos I'd have spotted a van-load — and they're in and out of a big shed near the one they had Scott in. There's stuff in bin bags going in — not too heavy, but bulky. Something's up. I can't guess what it is but I'd lay a pony on it that it's set for tonight.'

'So why aren't you there? I thought that was the whole point of — '

'Because something more urgent came up, that's why,' Hector snarled, visibly restraining himself from telling his audience to shut up and listen. 'A woman went in last night — late — about half eleven. Stunner. Pale blonde. Classy. Big car with a driver. Looked like a boss of some kind so I watched for her coming out, all night and all this morning.

Didn't see her till the middle of the afternoon so I had to follow her, didn't I?'

'Absolutely,' Buchanan affirmed, but it appeared that a reply was neither expected nor appreciated.

'Followed her back to Edinburgh, over by the Gyle — next to the casino, right? Big white house with a high hedge all round it, fancy flower pots shaped like women with turbans on at each side of the door. You can't miss it, there's nothing like it nearby.'

He paused, so Buchanan said, 'That sounds like sterling information, Hector. Probably worth your night's sleep, I'd say. I'll get onto it right away.'

'Right, I'm off. I'll phone you as soon as something breaks at the garden centre.' He paused with the door open and one foot in mid-air. 'This phone doesn't work too good in the car but I should be there by seven so you'd better be beside your phone from then on.'

'No problem. Good luck — ' But Hector was off and running.

Buchanan sat there for a moment, pondering the new information and planning his next move. Foremost in his mind was the thought that Fizz should play no part in it. This was just the sort of situation where she would love to get down and dirty and given half a chance she would be straight into that house like a ferret down a rabbit hole, thinking on her feet and making up outrageous lies to account for her presence there. If there was to be a more judicious way of penetrating to the core of the organisation he would have to move fast, before she could interfere.

15

Buchanan had barely an hour and a half to get to the Gyle and back, which was fine as long as he didn't spend longer at the house than, say, forty-five minutes max. That was probably all the time he'd need to get over the threshold and glean what he could but it clearly behoved him to get moving right away and think of a cover story as he went.

Getting inside a house had never posed much of a problem to him before, largely because his business had always been legitimate but also because a solicitor's business card went a long way towards allaying suspicion. However, he wouldn't be presenting anything with his name on it on this occasion so the situation was a trifle more problematic.

Stopped at a traffic light, he went through his pockets and found the card of an antique dealer he'd once been negotiating with on the purchase of a Charles Rennie Mackintosh mirror. His mind went instantly to the flower urns Hector had mentioned. The owner might not wish to part with them but a sufficiently dazzling offer would surely buy him a parley.

This game plan commended itself to him all the more when he saw the urns in the round. They were beautifully executed bronze nudes, more than four feet high and quite plausibly the sort of thing to catch the eye of an antique dealer.

Emboldened by this sign of divine intervention, Buchanan inserted the bogus credentials into his card holder and drove into the spacious parking area behind the encircling hedge. There was no one about but he spent a few seconds posing in interested attitudes around the urns before climbing the steps to the entrance.

It was slightly surprising to find the door lying open — it was a hot and clammy day but security had to negate that — however he rang the bell and had time for a quick peek at the interior before a stunningly attractive middle-aged woman appeared.

'Darling, you don't have to ring!' she crooned, reaching out an arm in a scooping gesture that wafted him through the doorway and into a large room, the major part of which had hitherto been invisible. 'There's always someone here to welcome you.'

Buchanan's first impression was one of understated affluence. His feet sank into a plush, toffee-coloured carpet, his ears were massaged by soft music, his nostrils assailed by the scent of gardenias. Sunlight filtered through peach gauze drapes illuminating a collection of good watercolours, a piano, and several long sofas with end tables that carried glossy magazines and expensive displays of fresh flowers. A small fluffy dog was sleeping in a patch of sunlight close to where three young women were playing Scrabble in the window bay.

It looked perfectly obvious to Buchanan that he'd been mistaken for someone else but that assumption was short lived.

'I don't believe we've met before,' murmured the older woman, as they waded through the carpet towards the other occupants of the room. 'I'm Sharon and this is Cara . . . Marlena . . . and the baby of the family, Bunny. Girls, this is . . . '

'William Court.' Buchanan provided, quoting the name on the apparently unnecessary card.

This nonchalent reception threw him a little. There being no sign of the blonde that Hector had described, there was nothing to do but hang around as long as they'd let him in the hope that she'd turn up. In the meantime he had a God-given opportunity to find out what he could from Sharon and her family.

Somewhat at a loss, he shook hands with the girls each in turn and was rewarded with unanimous, and rather flattering, interest and approval. Cara made room for him on the couch beside her, a fast move that evidently didn't endear her to the other two.

Bunny was the only blonde, and she was unmistakably much too young to be the one he wanted, however all three were quite outstandingly good looking. They might be wearing a tad too much makeup for so early in the evening, especially Bunny who could be no more than sixteen, but their partiality for flimsy summer dresses with spaghetti straps was exactly to his taste.

He said, 'You have a really charming house, Sharon.'

'I'm glad you like it, William,' said Sharon, sinking into a spindly little lacquered chair and crossing legs that were still as slim and shapely as her daughters'. She struck Buchanan as a rather exotic personality. The affected use of 'darling' implied an actress or an entertainer of some sort: a woman confident enough to be a bit of a flirt without losing her dignity. 'We've only been here since January but I think it's beginning to get that lived-in feeling at last. It takes time — don't you think? — to make a house a home. But it's very important to us to get the atmosphere right.'

'I'd say you've succeeded,' said Buchanan. 'The colours are charming. Where were you before January?'

Sharon made a depreciating little moué allowing Marlena to put in,

'Leith Links. Not nearly so nice. It's much more interesting here, not just for us but for our friends. And quieter.'

'The rooms are bigger and sunnier too,' Cara added.

She was the prettiest of the three but her voice was high pitched and grated painfully on Buchanan's ear so it was disturbing to discover that his thigh was pressing against hers. He slid an inch away and crossed his legs.

'Yes, it's nice to have plenty of room to move around in,' he murmured, drawing glances of warm agreement from all present. 'There's nothing worse than being cramped for space.'

'You're so right, William,' said Marlena, with rather more enthusiasm than the observation really deserved. 'I'm a person who needs plenty of room to breathe. I think most active, energetic people feel that way.'

'We have eight bedrooms here,' Cara informed him, turning sideways to look at him, a movement which brought her thigh once more into contact with his. 'That's three more than we had at Leith, and they're all huge.'

'Really?' Buchanan pretended interest in their real estate while peeling his leg gently away from Cara's, and said brightly, 'No need for you to double up, then.'

'Oh, we do that quite often,' she said, with a giggle. 'It's fun.'

Buchanan wasn't quite sure how to take that. They all had a flip way of conversing: laughing at nothing, watching his face as though they expected some sort of response he was unable to contribute. He'd never had much to do with the arty crowd so he assumed their demeanor to be a chic trend that had so far escaped his notice.

There was a brief silence and they all appeared to be waiting for him to state his purpose so he started to say, 'I hope I'm not calling at an inconvenient time . . .'

'Darling, there's no such thing as an inconvenient time,' Sharon exclaimed, waving a plum-tipped hand in horror at the idea. 'We never have too much company — particularly when it's the company of such handsome young men!'

Her large dark eyes twinkled at him with a roguishness he found quite extraordinary, but far from offensive, in a mature woman. She was perfectly serene: an elegant middle-class woman at ease with her guest. Far from being impatient for him to state his business and go, she showed not the slightest curiosity as to what brought him to her door. Buchanan never ceased to be amazed by the variety of lifestyle and social conduct one met with in a cosmopolitan city like Edinburgh.

'That's a beautiful suit you're wearing,' commented the baby of the family, a pretty little thing with her hair caught up into a bunch above each ear. She leaned forward to see past her sisters and, unfortunately, the front of her dress gaped open, revealing, before Buchanan could snatch his eyes away, considerably more than she realised. 'And your shirt's reflected in your eyes. They look almost purple.'

Buchanan would have felt awkward if one of the others had said it but he could himself remember being every bit as gauche and ingenuous at sixteen and felt as embarrassed for her as for himself. He gave her a grin and said, 'You should be an artist, Bunny. You have an eye for colour.'

'She has an eye for a hunk,' Cara said, with pseudo contempt, and they all laughed merrily.

He said, 'I don't want to take up too much

of your time but I — '

Bunny stood up. 'I'll get you something to drink, William.' She tipped her head to one side and smiled with what could have been juvenile coquetry. 'Or can I call you Willy?'

'I'll pass, thank you,' Buchanan said. 'I'm driving.'

All the girls found that amusing.

Sharon re-crossed her legs, being a little careless of her modesty in the process, and said, 'A small glass of something, surely darling? I'm sure the effects will have worn off before you leave. You're not in a rush are you?'

'No, really, I'd rather not take the risk — '

'A drop of Glenlivet.'

'Thanks all the same but — '

'A tiny gin and a lot of tonic, then.'

'No — '

'How about a glass of wine? We have a lovely Cabernet Sauvignon.'

Buchanan settled for that, since she wasn't going to take no for an answer, but when Bunny came back with it he took one sip and left it, thereafter, on top of some magazines on the table beside him. As he did so he caught a glimpse of a photograph on one of the covers but had barely time to register it as what appeared to be a large area of bare flesh before Marlena said,

'You must be uncomfortably hot in that suit, William. Don't you want to slip off your jacket, and maybe your tie?'

'Actually, I'm fine,' Buchanan smiled, marvelling at the warmth of their welcome. 'As I was saying, I won't take up too much of your time. I'll just be in and out again so there's no point in taking my jacket off. What I wanted — '

'Of course, darling,' Sharon nodded gently, her expression transmitting motherly understanding. 'And that's perfectly all right. Whatever you want and any way you want it, but next time you visit us I hope you'll be able to stay longer. We'd all like that, wouldn't we, girls?'

The girls made it almost exaggeratedly clear that they would be living for that moment. Cara's thigh was now back against Buchanan's and moving in a manner that refuted any possibility of the juxtaposition being accidental. He couldn't remember when he'd made such a categorical hit, but time was marching on.

'The urns outside the front door,' he obtruded into the cosy atmosphere, and smiled apologetically. 'They are extremely attractive.'

Sharon smiled back. 'You like that sort of thing, darling? It's the colour you prefer, perhaps? That lovely dark brown?'

'Er . . . yes, a wonderful colour . . . ' Buchanan sought for more esoteric, more professional phrases to describe his appreciation but Sharon merely nodded at Bunny who got up and left the room.

'I was wondering if there were any possibility of — '

'Darling, please don't be afraid to ask. I'm not going to bite your head off.' Sharon leaned forward and took his hand, giving it a firm squeeze. 'Just come right out with it and say what you'd like.'

Buchanan had to smile. She had obviously interpreted his circuitous conversation as shyness, which was probably the reason he had been treated with such patience.

'Well, as I was saying, I very much like the Victorian urns at your front door,' he said. He slid a hand into the inner pocket of his jacket and was about to produce his card holder when the door behind Sharon's chair opened to admit Bunny, accompanied by a tiny, china-frail Asian girl in a white sari.

Sharon turned round in her chair and reached out an arm to take the girl's hand and draw her forward.

'This is Sita, William. Isn't she lovely?'

Something like a scud missile hit Buchanan

in the chest, flooding his face with hot colour and reducing him to a profound vegetative state for long seconds. His hand shot out, found his glass of wine and emptied it down his throat in a single gulp.

Before the power of speech had returned to him, Sita had shimmied across to him, preceded by the faint aroma of something sensual and spicy, and was proffering a hand like a magnolia blossom.

'Hello William,' she said in a clipped Oxford accent. 'I am so very pleased to make your acquaintance.'

Buchanan got his knees under him and stood up, desperate to cut and run but hampered by the thought of Fizz's scorn if he defected.

'Sita,' he said, shocked and smarting from third degree embarrassment. 'I'm delighted to meet you, but I fear I've caused a misunderstanding. It's very stupid of me but I — '

'Darling, don't be so apologetic,' Sharon said easily, and laughed a gentle, husky laugh. 'You're so sweet! Isn't he sweet, girls?'

The girls agreed, loudly and at length, that he was the sweetest thing since jelly babies.

Buchanan hid his burning face by giving Sita his place on the couch, praying, the while, that the details of this encounter would never reach Fizz's ears. It was beginning to dawn on him that the situation had its possibilities. It was a frightening thought, but if he had the bottle to go through with it, he could possibly buy the time to speak, privately and at length, with the obscure blonde woman. Unless, of course, she turned out to be the madam of this high class brothel, which would be just his luck.

Marlena turned her head lazily to look at Sharon. 'Do you know what I think, Sharon? I think William has someone special in mind. Do you, William? Someone you've met before?'

'Actually, yes,' Buchanan said, and to his own ears at least, his voice shook at the enormity of what he was saying. 'The trouble is, I don't know her name. She's blonde, very pale blonde.'

'Oh, *Celia*.' Sharon nodded her comprehension. 'Darling, you have expensive tastes! Where did you meet her before?'

Buchanan's brain was closely engaged in calculating how much cash he had with him and comparing it to what might be necessary. He had a fair idea — through professional association only — of what charges applied in the city's more upmarket massage parlours but in this sort of establishment, the like of which he had never even imagined, who could tell what remuneration might be expected?

'Sorry?' he said, realising he'd missed something.

'Where did you meet Celia, darling?'

'Uh . . . um, to tell you the truth, I haven't met her,' he stumbled. 'I've just seen her going in and out sometimes when . . . when I pass on my way to the casino. She . . . she's very lovely.'

'Oh, isn't he the adorable one! Love at first sight! Darling you are such a romantic!'

The girls cooed their phoney agreement and gazed at him with lambent eyes, lashes fluttering in unison like pennants at the Clyde regatta.

'It's too bad,' Sharon continued, affecting a girlish pout which did her no service, 'Celia has tonight off. I believe she's asleep, as a matter of fact. But, never fear, you sweet man, I'm sure I can introduce you to someone every bit as charming.'

'Thank you, Sharon, but I'll take a rain check if you don't mind.' Buchanan was still on his feet and happy to have an excuse to vacate the premises. 'It was really Celia I came to see.'

Evidently unwilling to lose a sale, Sharon rose quickly to face him, unobtrusively blocking his way. 'Let me just see if she's awake, darling.' She made a signal to Bunny who headed for the door. 'If you dash away without even saying hello she would be so annoyed to have missed you.'

'She sure would,' said Bunny, exiting on the line with a lascivious wink.

Buchanan, identified as a big spender, was now flavour of the month. The three remaining women were determined he should have the complete customer package and ladled on the flattery and innuendo till it became totally farcical. Buchanan refused more wine, cigarettes, cigars, and a line of coke and steeled himself for the coming ordeal. Sex, he was positively resolved, would not be a part of it. For a start, the idea of battening on an unfortunate woman who, through whatever circumstances, had to sell the use of her body, was profoundly distasteful to him. Likewise, the danger of catching some ghastly disease, although logically no more substantive than in his occasional associations with amateur loose women, acted on his libido like an ice pack.

Even the sight of Celia, proudly presented to him like a chef's speciality, failed to turn him on. She was a stunner, yes, but at close quarters the huge brown eyes were shrewd and the plump lips had a bitter twist. She wore her ash blonde hair in a straight fall that curtained all of one side of her face and as Sharon introduced her she kept lifting her hand in a strange gesture as though to flick it back, but changing her mind at the last minute.

Buchanan went through the niceties that Sharon seemingly thought necessary, smiling and shaking hands and indicating his satisfaction with the merchandise. There was mention of a V.I.P suite with jacuzzi, whirlpool, and Thai bath, plus mixed saunas, videos and unspecified 'executive treatment', all of which he was able to refuse without a great deal of angst. Finally, Celia linked an arm in his and led him out of the speculative gaze of her colleagues, along a short corridor, and into a spacious room with a draped ceiling and a half-canopied king-sized bed.

Flimsy curtains fluttered in a faint movement of air from the open window, and beyond Buchanan could see a long lawn backed by rose beds and the same tall hedge that veiled the front of the house. There was nothing in the room, he was careful to note, that might turn out to be a tape recorder or a one-way mirror.

'Celia,' he said, before she had time to start throwing off her clothes, 'Is it all right if we just talk?'

'But of course, William.' She sat down on

the bed and leaned back on stiff arms, jutting out her considerable bosom. 'There's no hurry. We can talk as long as you like. Is there anything particular you'd like me to talk about?'

'No. I don't mean 'first' I mean 'instead of'.' Buchanan, after the recent debacle was set on having no obscurity of meaning lurking in the background of their dealings. 'I particularly don't want to have sex with you. Nothing personal, of course — you are an extremely attractive woman — but for reasons I don't wish to discuss.'

She sat up and looked at him carefully, raising a hand to touch her hair and then dropping it as though it had been slapped. 'If you're experiencing a little temporary difficulty, darling, I'm quite sure I can overcome it.'

'No, thank you Celia, but that's not on.'

'You mean, it's not temporary? Because, even if — '

'No, really. I wish you wouldn't bother. Just — '

'You mean — ?' Celia's eyes went to his crotch. 'It's . . . gone?'

'Let's just talk, Celia. I'll pay the usual rate but all we do is chat, okay? How long do we have?'

Celia looked a little nervous, probably

wondering if he was some kind of weirdo, but she finally propped the pillows up against the headboard and sat up cross-legged. She was, in fact, younger than she had appeared at first, probably in her early twenties but the skin of her face was thickened and open pored.

'Between five and six it's basically a hundred and fifty pounds. It's Happy Hour. You want me to talk dirty?'

'No. Just chat. And there'll be something extra for you if you keep quiet about it.' Buchanan took off his shoes and sat at the end of the bed, trying to look relaxed. 'Tell me about yourself. Were you born in Edinburgh? What brought you here?'

She leaned over, took a joint out of the drawer of the bedside cabinet, and lit it, drawing the smoke deep down into her lungs and hanging onto it for a good ten seconds. Then, having given herself time to think, she tipped her head back against the pillows and poured forth a cautionary tale of youth despoiled, early genius unnourished, opportunities wasted, and innocence betrayed.

It was a load of codswallop, of course; not that that made any difference to Buchanan, whose only purpose had been to establish a rapport. He let her run on for a couple of minutes, making sympathetic faces, and then edged her closer to the heart of the matter.

'I don't suppose this is a job you'd want to be doing twenty years from now, but it must be quite pleasant living here.'

She pinned on a bright smile. 'It's lovely. And the girls are such fun. And Sharon. Well, she's like our mother. We all love her.'

'Is she your only boss?'

There was a faint stutter of hesitation before she said, 'Yes. Sharon's in charge. But she's gorgeous. Treats us like her daughters.' She squinted at his face. 'Is this doing it for you?'

'Oh, yes, absolutely,' Buchanan faked it, nodding at her encouragingly. 'You're fantastic. Would you like to tell me about your clients? Not specifically, of course, but speaking generally. Do you have to sleep with people you don't like?'

'Not often,' she said, looking more complacent now she supposed herself to be turning him on. 'You can't fancy them all, of course. And, to put it bluntly, William, not many of them are half as dishy as you.'

Deeming this to be what was required, she launched forth on a nauseating selection of anecdotes that would have made Casanova impotent. Buchanan halted her as soon as he could without appearing too squeamish, and guided her onto more profitable ground.

'I suppose you have your regular clients.'

'Uh-huh.' She lowered her lashes modestly. 'I'm the most popular of all the girls here. That's why my time is more expensive.'

'Do you always work from here or do you visit clients at home?'

She straightened up, looking at him narrowly and making that curiously truncated gesture with her hair. 'What do you want to know that for?'

Buchanan backed off, holding up both hands palm out to placate her. 'Sorry. Sorry. I was just making conversation, not prying into your . . . ' He tried to find an alternative term to 'affairs' but failed. 'It didn't seem to me to be a particularly personal question.'

'Well, no,' she said, smoothing her ruffled feathers with a long drag at her joint. 'It's okay. I just . . . well, anyway if it lights your fire . . . Do I visit clients at home? Not as a general rule, no. Sharon doesn't allow that.'

'Not as a general rule.' Buchanan made it an offhand statement, not a question, hoping that she might take it from there herself without having to be prompted further.

She let the hiatus lengthen a couple of seconds and then said, 'No. She likes to know we're safe. Some punters . . . er, clients . . . like it rough, you know.'

'Don't tell me about that,' Buchanan said,

before she could start on her reminiscences. 'Animals like that should be put down. Tell me about what you do in your spare time.'

She gave him a long, smiling look and then shrugged. 'Nothing much. This time of year we sit in the garden . . . read . . . watch TV. Once in a while some of us might go to see a film matinee.'

'But you work every evening?'

'Every evening, uh-huh. Sometimes in the afternoons as well.'

'That sounds pretty tough.' Buchanan picked at an imaginary mark on his trouser leg. 'I thought Sharon said this was your night off.'

'Yes. But that was only because I had a heavy night last night.' She seemed quite moved by his concern. 'You really care, don't you, William? You don't get off on sadism — on hearing about my tough life, that sort of thing, do you? You're really a nice guy.'

Buchanan thought that, if that was all that was necessary to mark him as a nice guy, then yes, he was probably a very nice guy indeed.

Celia got rid of the stub of her joint and leaned forward to lay a hand on his leg. 'You're sure you wouldn't like me to try something different? I'd really love to do something nice for you — on the house.'

For the first time, she looked perfectly

genuine as she said it and it pierced Buchanan to the heart. He didn't want anything she had to offer but, to blunt the edge of his refusal, he lifted a hand to touch her cheek and was shocked when she involuntarily flinched away.

Suddenly, he knew the reason for that hair-sweeping gesture she kept on making. He caught her by the wrist and, with his other hand, hooked back that concealing fall of hair. A livid bruise, partly covered by a thick layer of make-up but extending well beyond the hairline, covered the whole area from eyebrow to ear.

It wasn't just the sight of the brutish abuse that made Buchanan nauseous, though that alone would have been quite sufficient. What really hit him was a replay of Fizz's face in an even worse condition accompanied by the bloodlust that invariably possessed him every time he thought about it. It was now over a year since she'd suffered the attack but the memory was never far from Buchanan's consciousness and his fists — and his stomach — still clenched each time it rose before his mind's eye.

Evidently some of this angst showed in his face because Celia's painted mouth formed a silent 'Oh!' and she put a hand on his shoulder.

'Oh William, don't look like that! It's no big deal. Please don't make any trouble.'

'It's criminal, Celia,' he said, trying to sound composed because she was so clearly afraid of repercussions. 'Nobody should be allowed to do that sort of thing no matter what they're willing to pay for the privilege.'

'William darling, will you just leave it please?'

Buchanan really wanted to leave it. He wanted only to get up and walk away from this evil place where young girls who should be still at school and women who had no other options were sold as toys to any animal with the cash to indulge his perversion. Individually, there was probably little he could do to help these women but, if what he was beginning to suspect was true, there was a chance that he could open the cage door.

'You don't have to do this, Celia. There are other jobs — '

'I do have to do it, darling. Now let's just talk about something nicer, yes?'

'You said that Sharon treated you like her daughter. So why does she allow some sick pervert to beat you up?'

She pulled abruptly away from him and lit up another joint, inhaling deeply and frowning at him.

'Some things are not as simple as they look.'

Buchanan frowned back at her. 'Why does Sharon allow you to be hurt, Celia? Tell me.'

For a moment she pressed her lips together, looking at the glowing tip of her joint and shaking her head slightly as though asking it, 'What's with this guy?' She took another look at his face and decided he wasn't going to go away.

'Because, Nosey,' she hissed, 'Sharon is just the administrator. It's the boss who calls the shots.'

'I see. So it was the boss you were with last night?'

'I'm sorry, I don't want to talk about it. Is that clear?' she said, quite strongly and then, to Buchanan's dismay, dissolved into the most harrowing sobs, tears flowing from her eyes and both hands clamped across her mouth to smother the noise.

Buchanan removed the joint from her fingers, laid it in the ashtray and took her into his arms, whereupon she pushed her face hard into his good suit and let rip for a good five minutes. Buchanan had never confronted such an outpouring of utter despair. He tried to tell himself that it was good for her to let it all out, that it was like lancing a boil, but it was still distressing to witness.

After a while she pulled away and accepted his hanky to wipe the tears plus an amazing quantity of makeup, from her face. Buchanan, perceiving that this was what was required of him, kept patting her arm till she moved it to reclaim her still smouldering joint.

'That was silly,' she said with her lungs full of smoke, and essayed a brave smile. 'You won't tell on me will you?'

Buchanan looked hurt. 'I wouldn't ever do anything that would embarrass you or get you into trouble, Celia. Don't you trust me?'

She nodded, her eyes starting to redden again. 'You're the nicest guy I've ever met.'

'That's very sad,' Buchanan said, meaning it. 'But I'm glad you trust me because I'm going to get you out of here.'

'Forget it.' She was crying again but not with the abandon of the last spasm. 'I owe them a lot of money. I . . . I have a little boy and I needed . . . Oh, God, I'm not going into all that. Just take my word for it, there's no way they're going to let me off the hook till they're paid in full, and God knows when that will be. I can't even pay off the interest.'

'That's not the way we approach the problem.' Buchanan took her hand and held it tightly. 'Listen, Celia, I know the sort of guy who owns these places. They are rarely honest

284

businessmen, believe me. They have other irons in the fire, enterprises they don't want anyone to know about, particularly the police. Are you with me?'

Celia nodded as if she was way ahead of him. 'Yes, but — '

'With your boss in jail, you and your colleagues will be free to do whatever you want, either change careers or find a better employer.'

'Yes, William darling,' she said sadly, 'but that's just a dream.'

'No, it isn't. It's a distinct possibility, I promise you. In my business — no, don't ask! — I have contacts, strings I can pull. Trust me, Celia, if you'll help me there's a significant possibility of nailing this guy without having to implicate you at all.'

She stopped weeping and thought about that for a while, looking deep into his eyes with a despair that changed only slowly to wavering resolution.

'You really believe you can finish him off? Put him in jail? Without getting me crucified?'

'I reckon we have about an eighty per cent chance — depending on what you can tell me about him. But I can guarantee that, win or lose, I can keep your involvement secret.'

She fell back against her pillows, her face

sagging. 'What can I tell you about him? Nothing. He owns a garden centre somewhere out of town — at least that's where I meet him. He tells me to call him Taff. He has a wife called Belle. He has a bunch of minders who escort him to the bedroom door. And that's it. Where's that going to get us?'

Not all that far, Buchanan thought. However, he still had twenty minutes left of his Happy Hour, and Hector could wait for once.

16

It seemed to Fizz to get hotter and hotter all afternoon. It was a moist, unpleasant heat, unusual in Edinburgh where the east wind rarely dropped below a breeze. Even when the sun was low in the west the evening was hot and airless, reminding her of similar evenings spent waitressing in Madrid.

She studied from five-thirty till about nine o'clock by which time her eyes were crossing and it was taking six readings to interpret every sentence. A short break was definitely called for so she donned her Doc Marten's and took a lazy walk down the Mound to drop in on Buchanan.

She knew he'd be glad to see her, since he was more or less confined to base while providing Hector's back-up, however he hid it well and let her in with a grunt.

The minute she saw him she knew he was on edge. Instead of sitting down, as he would normally have done, he started jittering around the room doing an impression of a cleaning lady.

It was Wednesday, which meant it was two days since Dolores had mucked the place out, so it wasn't surprising that it looked like a tip. Buchanan was a spoiled brat whose mother, or some paid menial, or a girlfriend or The Wonderful Beatrice, had picked up after him all his life and he hadn't a clue how to get himself organised. The flat was stuffed with all manner of unnecessary gadgets which needed to be filed and dusted and maintained and, until he threw most of them away, he'd have to pay a Dolores to administer them for him. The thing was: it was a bit late in the day to be to be coy about the tidiness of his sitting room as far as her own opinion was concerned.

'What's the sudden interest in housework?' she said, dislodging Pooky from the armchair and dropping into it. 'You're not expecting *Hello!* magazine, are you?'

He looked at the pile of newspapers he had collected as though uncertain what ought to be done with them, then he threw them behind the couch and stuck his hands on his hips.

'I suppose you'll want a coffee?' he said ungraciously.

Fizz, having glimpsed a glass of something golden on the floor beside the telly, gave him a sunny smile.

'I'll have what you're having.'

'Since when have you been into Irn-Bru?'

'Irn-Bru? I thought it was Glenmorangie. I'll have one of those.'

'No you won't. I remember what happened the last time you were on malt whisky. You can have a small gin and a lot of tonic. I'm not walking you home.'

'Swine! Go on then.'

Pooky accompanied him to the kitchen and back while Selina stared her usual basilisk stare from under the couch. Fizz had never been a cat person, her appreciation of the species being reserved for its marginal superiority over mousetraps. Selina, for her part, was just a feline bitch who hated any female who came near her Buchanan.

'So,' she said, when Buchanan came back. 'Anything happen since I last saw you? You got McKenzie home in one piece, I imagine? Did you speak to his daughter? Still nothing helpful from her?'

He went on wandering about while he recounted an extraordinarily dull conversation between himself and the daughter, going into so much detail that it was obvious he was putting off talking about something else. Fizz smiled at him very sweetly. She loved this game.

'Fascinating. She sounds like she could be a real wow at a party. Anything else world shaking to report? No advances at Hector's end, I suppose?'

Buchanan retrieved his drink and sat on the floor with his back against the couch.

'Actually yes,' he said, with a pinched expression she'd seen before when he felt compelled to tell her something he didn't want to divulge. 'He was here waiting for me when I got home tonight. He'd followed someone from the garden centre to the edge of town.'

'Someone interesting?' Fizz said, sensing a lead.

'I think so. But more immediate than that, he's sure something is about to happen at the garden centre — probably tonight. There are more helpers about and a lot of activity centred on one of their storage sheds. They appear to be transferring some unidentified commodities in plastic bags. I've just been sitting here waiting for him to ring and let me know whether I should join him or not.'

Fizz took a large mouthful of her drink. There was enough gin in it to fit in a nut shell and still leave room for the nut.

'I'll come with you.'

'I thought you'd say that. You can either stay sober and come with us or you can have another drink. Take your choice.'

That was Buchanan for you. Tight as a duck's arse.

'And what about the other lead? The guy

he followed this evening?'

He got up and walked over to shut the window, taking his time about it and straightening the curtains in a fussy way that was just so funny. Watching him trying to hide something from her was the best free entertainment in Edinburgh. She turned her head away to hide her glee and in a minute he returned to his seat and said diffidently,

'According to Hector, a woman arrived at the garden centre late last night in a big car with a driver.'

'A prostitute?' Fizz surmised, and Buchanan blinked at her for a second before nodding. There may have been a faint reddening of his brow but she couldn't have sworn to it.

'Exactly. Hector trailed her to a big house over at the Gyle. A high class brothel close to the casino and the big hotels.'

'Thank God,' Fizz said. 'This is the first decent break we've had. Someone will have to talk to her, ask her who she was seeing, find out if she knows anything.'

Buchanan drained his apple juice. 'I've done that.'

'What — already?' Fizz was so annoyed that he'd grabbed the best lead for himself that it was a moment before the joke hit her. Buchanan in a brothel! You could make a long running situation comedy out of a premise like that. God, what she'd have given to be a fly on that wall!

She started to giggle but Buchanan went straight on in a listen-or-you'll-miss-it tone.

'I managed to speak with her — her name's Celia — and, provided we make completely sure that they don't suspect her, she's willing to help us all she can. She'll do a bit of careful snooping and maybe talk to one of the other girls — someone she trusts. At the moment she knows very little, but she has at least met the head honcho and knows what he looks like. She calls him 'Taff'.'

It was not hidden from Fizz that Buchanan had an eye for a pretty face, an eye that was currently all the sharper for having been blinkered, as far as she herself had been able to contrive, for some considerable time. However, it would be a real foxy lady who could tempt him to pay for sex and even the offer of a freebie from a known prostitute would scare the hell out of him. Which was just as well, because an illogical antipathy towards other women in his life was the one thing she shared with Selina.

'Taff? Is that the best you could get out of her?' she complained. 'It's not the most illuminating pillow talk I've ever heard.'

Buchanan had been expecting a jibe of

some description and didn't rise to it, though he couldn't stop his mouth tightening a bit. 'Pillows didn't figure in the conversation, Fizz, so you can forget the wisecracks. And, no, I hadn't finished telling you what she had to say. She believes that Taff has a wife called Belle and, more significantly, she says he goes nowhere without his bodyguards, so we're probably talking about a big operator. Somebody with enemies.'

'Did you ask her if she'd heard any mention of McKenzie, or Inverness, or market stalls or . . . ' Fizz's creative thinking ground to a halt as Buchanan nodded.

'I asked her all that. None of it rang a bell. She has heard Leith mentioned more than once. The brothel used to be near Leith Links, before they moved up in the world, but she reckons that there's still something going on there.'

'Mmm . . . interesting.'

Fizz could see how that bit of puzzle might appear to come from the same jigsaw, even though its position in the picture was, for the moment, unclear. Leith was home to Edinburgh's only port and minutes away from the heart of the city, but it was a whole separate universe. Until the eighteenth century it had been a town in its own right and it still had a village atmosphere: vibrant, self sufficient, colourful and diverse. The harbour area had been largely yuppified over the past ten years or more, but ships from all over the world still used the docks and there were still, a stone's throw from the chic restaurants and the Royal Yacht, plenty of massage parlours, gambling dens and similar establishments geared to parting sailors from their cash. If one had naughtiness in mind, Leith was the place to indulge it.

'Just 'Leith'?' she said. 'Nothing specific?'

'She's trying to remember anything else she might have heard,' Buchanan said. 'She promised to phone me if she comes up with anything and I think we can be confident that she's going to make a real effort to find out more.'

He went into the kitchen and came back with a bottle of Irn-Bru from which he topped up both their empty tumblers.

'I just hope we can wrap this thing up soon because Taff's giving her a rough time. He beats her up.'

Fizz looked at the muscles standing out on each side of his mouth and knew he was smouldering with anger inside. She knew why too, or at least she knew part of the reason, because she'd seen him like that, only much worse, when someone had done origami on her own face not that long ago.

Buchanan was an old softy but if this case dragged on much longer he'd have more hot potatoes around him than a haggis on Burns' night.

She said, 'Most of these girls are on hard drugs, Buchanan. They're not going to get another job that pays enough to feed their habit.'

'Celia isn't on hard drugs. She told me — '

The sudden ringing of the phone startled both of them. Buchanan lunged for it, alarming both Pooky and Selina, who had been having their tummies scratched, and sending them bolting — Selina up the curtains, Pooky into the kitchen.

'Buchanan here . . . Oh hell, we should have thought of that . . . right . . . right . . . Absolutely. Go for it. Have I time to get there before . . . no, you're probably right. Okay, bell me as soon as you can.'

Fizz eyed his bleak face as he rang off. 'Gimme the bad news first.'

'It's all bad news.' He rubbed his hand down his jaw. 'The whole damn business has been a catalogue of incompetence from day one. I must be losing my touch.'

'Too many cooks, that's all,' Fizz said, because it was probably true, not because she was a bit peeved that, in Celia, he had now enlisted yet another helper without asking her. 'What's happened?'

'All the signs seemed, to Hector, to say that the action, whatever it was, was going to take place in the garden centre; instead of which there are now vans coming out, they've started leaving at intervals of about ten to twenty minutes.'

That sounded just great to Fizz: she couldn't see what the problem was. 'How is that bad news? Hector could follow them and see where they're going.'

'Sure he could — if they're all headed for the same destination,' Buchanan said. 'But if they split up he can only follow one of them. If I'd been with him at the garden centre — as I could have been — we could at least have followed two.'

Fizz wasn't too worried about that. If the vans had been intending to take different routes they wouldn't be bothering to leave a delay between each departure. Obviously Buchanan was just peeved at the thought of Hector having all the fun but, for that matter, so was she.

'So, what's happening, then?' she asked. 'Is Hector tagging on at the back?'

'He's following the next one to leave and, as soon as he knows which direction they're heading he'll phone and let us know. With a bit of luck we'll be able to catch up with them before they get out of range.' He got up and sat on the couch to put his shoes on. 'We'd better be ready to pull out as soon as we hear from him. See if you can find my binoculars, will you? Try the bookcase.'

Fizz found the binoculars and then, for want of something more productive to do while Buchanan got the car out of the garage, she raided his varied and arcane collection of tinned goods and concocted a pack of exotic sandwiches in case malnutrition should strike either of them before they got home.

It was fifteen minutes before the phone rang again. Buchanan listened intently, muttering 'uh-huh, uh-huh, uh-huh' but divulging nothing to satisfy Fizz's curiosity. She could tell by his body language, however, that they were on their way so she laced up her Doc's, collected the sandwiches and was waiting at the car when he galloped downstairs.

'It's a convoy,' he said tersely, doing a Le Mans start that would make him popular with the neighbours. 'The vans are keeping well apart but they're all headed in the same direction, thank God.'

'Where's that?'

'Towards Edinburgh at the moment, which is another piece of good luck. In theory we should be able to wait for a while and let them come to us, but I'm not chancing anything this time. I want to latch on to them while Hector has them eyeballed.'

He was overcompensating for his earlier mistake, of course, but Fizz was all for it. There was nothing like a car chase for spicing up a dull evening.

She said, 'How many vans?'

'Five.' He braked for the A90 junction and then accelerated away at a speed which pressed Fizz back in her seat. 'Hector's doing the smart thing: letting one van pass him and waiting for the next to catch up. He's at the back of the queue now, just coming up to Dalmeny. There are no major turnoffs between there and Cramond and, at the speed they're doing at the moment, we should have plenty of time to catch up with them before then.'

Fizz let down the window. The heat of the evening had not lessened as the sun went down and it was well worth suffering the draught to get a breath of air. It had also clouded over considerably since she'd left home and the moon shone only fitfully through thick cumulus.

They had passed the turnoff to Cramond before they spotted the first van coming towards them. Neither of them could be sure that it was one of the plain black vans that

Hector had warned Buchanan to look out for but, when they passed its twin within a mile and a third some five minutes later, there could be no doubt that they had met the convoy.

Well back behind the fifth van, Hector was tooling along at a modest forty. He raised a finger from the driving wheel in greeting but didn't slow down as Buchanan did a U-turn and tucked the Saab in behind him.

'Okay,' Buchanan said, allowing himself a satisfied grin. 'We made it.'

'One of us should be up front,' Fizz pointed out. 'Right up there behind the front van. No point in us both trailing the same van.'

'Just what I was thinking,' Buchanan nodded. 'But if we move up to the front now one of the van drivers might recognise us as the car that just passed him going in the opposite direction. It'll have to be Hector.'

They closed the few car lengths that separated them from the Rover that Hector had borrowed from McKenzie and signalled him to stop. The road was empty enough for Buchanan to pull up beside his window and allow Fizz to pass on the message, at which Hector nodded and pulled away without wasting a second.

For the first time since witnessing McKenzie's car crash Fizz felt they were actually getting somewhere. They had the enemy in pincers — or would have when Hector reached the head of the well spread out queue — and they seemed almost bound to be heading for a big break. That's the way it worked sometimes: one minute you were floundering about in pitch darkness, and the next, the dawn broke and you wondered why you hadn't managed to figure it all out right at the beginning. But, of course, that was just sometimes: most times you found yourself even deeper in the shit.

It was frustrating to have to creep along at forty miles an hour but that was what the van in front was doing and the road was so straight that Buchanan had to keep well away from it, leaving its brake lights barely visible. Luckily the thick cloud cover made it very dark, much too dark to make the Saab identifiable at that distance.

It soon became apparent that Hector had guessed right: the convoy was headed for Edinburgh city centre. It passed within a stone's throw of Buchanan's mews — which amused neither of them — but then proceeded eastward and carried on down the south bank of the Forth.

'What the hell?' Fizz wondered, having

been confidently predicting, for the past ten minutes, that Leith docks would turn out to be the convoy's destination.

Buchanan started to answer, then muttered something under his breath and swerved to a halt behind the parked Rover. Hector's face appeared at Fizz's window and she could tell by the look on it that something had gone horribly wrong.

'Shit! What are you doing here?' he demanded.

'Where else would we be?' said Buchanan.

'I thought you were following the last van.'

'I am. That's it in the distance.'

'What? That's it?' Hector hauled his head back and made a survey of the road in both directions as though he suspected Buchanan of lying. 'For chrissake don't lose it then. I've lost the others.'

He turned and dashed back to the Rover, leaving Fizz incandescent with curiosity.

Buchanan slammed the Saab into gear and roared away, passing the Rover, halving, in a couple of minutes, the distance between himself and the van, and paying Fizz's volley of expletives no visible attention.

In God's name, she wanted to know, how had Hector managed to lose four vans? One van — not exactly a hanging offence. Two vans — careless, but it was dark and they were well spaced out. But, *four*? He'd have to be blind! Whose side was he on, for pity's sake?

'Fizz, just concentrate on keeping your eyes on that van in front, okay?' Buchanan growled, grinding his teeth with a ferocity that made his jaw muscles ripple. 'If we lose this one I'll shoot myself in the head.'

'But how could that happen?' Fizz insisted. 'Hector doesn't strike me as a total moron and only a total moron could lose four vans without even trying. He could be deliberately stymieing us for some reason.'

'Don't be so quick to blame Hector,' said Buchanan, fast sinking into a depression. 'Keeping tabs on five moving objects isn't as easy as you'd think, especially when there's a mile or so between them. I should have been ahead of that; I've seen it happen before.'

Fizz turned her head aside so that she could relieve her feelings by rolling her eyes without being observed. God, was there any evil in this world that Buchanan couldn't blame himself for? The man should be in therapy. If anyone were to blame this time, Fizz's money was on Hector.

She thought about it for a while, watching the street lights of Fife, which now looked almost as far away as Dover from Calais, glittering like strings of stars across the widening firth. The suburbs had already thinned to a narrow ribbon of houses lining the inland side of the road and soon they would be meeting virtually open country.

Finally she had to say, 'I can't see how Hector could have avoided seeing what had happened. All he had to do was count.'

Buchanan completed a short stint of tooth grinding before he answered. 'If you miss seeing the leading van turning off the road, you don't realise that there are only three cars in front of you instead of four. Hector would have kept on going past the third van till he realised he wasn't going to meet up with the fourth. By the time he grasped that he was ahead of the convoy and decided to turn back, both three and two could have diverted down a side road. If he hadn't spotted us — behind what he must have assumed to be the third in line, he'd probably be back in Edinburgh by now.'

Fizz more or less grasped what he was saying but she was unwilling to relinquish the seeds of suspicion she now harboured against Hector. This was not the time to share them with Buchanan, who would only castigate himself for enlisting someone he didn't know but, hell, they could be walking into a trap. She glanced back at the Rover which was a few car lengths behind them and considered her options.

What did they really know about Hector, after all? He was an ex-con. He'd turned up in Inverness, trailing McKenzie. He followed him to Edinburgh and then reappeared just after the kidnappers had spirited Scott away from his home. Okay, he'd played an active part in liberating him from the garden centre but — think about it — had that all been a bit too easy? Could the fortuitous arrival of the second bunch of heavies have been stage managed specifically to give the scene a cachet of authenticity?

Hector seemed, on the surface, to be on the side of the angels but there was no doubt about it, he could just as easily be a four pound note, so Buchanan had to be alerted to the possibility right now, before they were lured any further into the trap.

She voiced her misgivings in a few terse sentences but Buchanan gave then no more than lip service.

'I hear what you're saying, Fizz, and you're right, we should trust nobody. My gut feeling is that Hector's on the level — his story ties in with what I'm beginning to piece together.'

'Which is?' Fizz said, a touch crisply since she would have expected him to share his thoughts with her as they occurred to him.

Buchanan leaned closer to the windscreen,

squinting at the dark blob hovering at the extreme range of his headlights. 'Are they slowing down?'

Fizz wasn't sure but, a moment later she saw the dim brake lights converge and then disappear as the van turned down a single track road that could lead only to the water's edge. The sight acted on her like a shot of pure gin administered straight into a major vein.

'They're turning! They're turning! Look!'

'I see them, Fizz.'

Buchanan used his brakes to signal Hector and dropped his speed a notch. When they drifted past the road end Fizz could see the lights of the van, still on the move but not as far away as she had anticipated.

'They must have slowed to make sure we passed on by,' she pointed out, earning only a grim nod as Buchanan rounded the next bend in the road and slowed to a halt in the first cover they came to: a piece of waste ground with the remains of some farm steadings leaning together, dark and spooky and full of bats. A minute later the Rover swung in behind them, parking behind the single remaining wall that was high enough to hide the cars from the road.

With both sets of headlights killed it was as

black and sticky as a barrel of molasses. The far side of the firth was low on the horizon and the lights were almost entirely swallowed by the gloom. A long peal of thunder rolled in the distance as the engines died and Fizz slid out of her seat into a night pulsating with an obscure menace. A line from Tam o' Shanter floated into her head: *That night, a child might understand, The De'il had business on his hand.*

She jumped as Hector loomed up behind her and said,

'Did you see? They dropped someone off at the end of the road. Probably a lookout.'

'Uh . . . no. Is that what they were doing? Does that mean we're stymied, then? Or can we get past?'

She heard Buchanan's footsteps as he walked round the car and stopped beside them. 'We can get down to the beach from this angle and work our way round,' he said. 'It may be a bit of a scramble in the dark but I reckon we should be able to get close enough to see what they're up to.'

'I'm up for it,' Hector said. 'Will we need a rope? There's one in the boot.'

'If it's a small one, bring it,' Buchanan decided. 'It probably won't be necessary but it's as well to be prepared.'

He dived back into the Saab to get the

binoculars while Fizz, making best use of her time, grabbed the sandwiches and armed herself with one of Buchanan's walking poles which she had long scorned but recently come to love. They might look naff, but when one was descending a steepish cliff in the dark, naffness was relative.

She was much more on edge tonight than she had been the night before last at the garden centre, but then, she was always jumpy when there was thunder about. The static electricity made her hair stand on end and that phenomenon alone, even acting on the short crop she now sported, tuned her nerves to a high C.

Even at the best of times, the slope she found herself descending was not one she'd have chosen to attempt in the dark but the stick proved invaluable, both in balancing her, in forging a way through brambles, and in feeling her way ahead where the terrain was doubtful.

They were barely twenty feet from the slabs of rock that edged the beach when Hector, who was bringing up the rear, gave a prolonged hiss to halt them.

'Quick! Look over there.'

Straight ahead of them, close to the point where the firth met the sea, a white light like a meteor escaped from the constellations of

Fife, winked once . . . twice . . . three times, then disappeared.

'That was a signal,' Hector informed them, quite unnecessarily. 'They'll likely be sending a boat ashore for the stuff.'

'What stuff?' Fizz asked, looking at him sharply.

'The stuff they were loading into the vans. Stuff in black bin bags.'

Fizz supposed she should have made that creative leap for herself. So that was what they were up to. Smuggling. Drugs, no doubt, although one would have expected the trade to be going in the opposite direction. Ian Fleming, Buchanan's tame policeman, had told him recently that the drug squad had — thanks in no small measure to Buchanan and herself — closed down a major operation, but there would seldom be staff vacancies in that line of business and, evidently, someone had already filled the gap.

Excitement and impatience goaded her into taking chances on the descent and she paid for it by covering the last stretch in an unintentional scurry with her arms flailing and gravel erupting from under her feet.

The next stretch lay along the high water mark which hugged the foot of the cliff. It was comparatively easy although the tide was almost fully in and they were forced to paddle across a couple of shallow bays.

It was impossible to hear anything above their own footsteps because of the sound of the waves, so it was only a dazzling flash of forked lightning, exploding out of the blackness with a heart-stopping crack, that warned them of what they were about to stumble into.

17

Buchanan spent the next few seconds flattened against the cliff face, momentarily expecting a torch beam in the eyes and a fist in the solar plexus. He could feel Fizz, rigid as the rock behind her, on his left and he could hear Hector panting energetically on his right but his night vision didn't even stretch to his own feet.

It seemed impossible that they had not been spotted, because there was no scrap of cover between them and the two men waiting on the beach ahead. The snapshot which the lightning had printed on Buchanan's consciousness placed them at no more than fifty yards away — if that — and although both men were staring out to sea, the three intruders should have been well within the scope of their side vision.

Making an immediate dash for safety was not an option. The men were close enough to hear the clatter of boots on rock so it was clear to Buchanan that his retreat would have to be slow and careful, not an easy matter when you couldn't see a yard ahead. At the same time, a second bolt of lightning could, at any second, illuminate the whole beach like a film set, so procrastination wouldn't help any.

As thunder boomed deafeningly across the water Buchanan gave Fizz a nudge and she led the way back along the cliff till they came to a niche that was deep enough to accommodate all three of them. It probably took less than one minute but Buchanan felt he had lost a third of his body weight in sweat before he reached safety.

Hector's breath was now laced with an underlying wheeze.

'We'd be dead by now if they'd spotted us,' he gasped, sliding down to a squatting position with his back against the rock. 'The good Lord is looking after us this night and that's for sure.'

Buchanan was glad to hear that Someone was sharing the responsibility for their safety and wondered if that division of blame would pertain if things started to go pear-shaped.

Two more blinding zigzags followed by two peals of thunder passed over them before he felt safe enough to risk edging one eye around the corner of their haven. As he waited for the next momentary illumination his ears caught a rattle of pebbles. He whipped his head back hastily but, hearing nothing further he was just leaning forward again when another bolt flashed into the sea, showing him one man still at the water's edge and the other, only a dozen paces away and tramping steadily towards him, his eyes concentrated on his unsteady feet.

Buchanan lurched backwards and threw out an arm to warn the other two to keep still. In another minute the guy would be on top of them, barely time enough for Buchanan to reach down to his feet and get a grip on a handy rock.

His mind was zapping ahead, already living the next episode in the drama.

Buchanan: Oof! (Fells Thug 1)

[FX: sound of bone crunching.]

Thug 1: Aaaagh! (collapses and dies.)

Thug 2: You okay, Reggie?

[Getting no reply, Thug 2 approaches and is struck down by Buchanan. He dies slowly, screaming in great pain, a deluge of his blood gushing over Buchanan's shoes, and his brains oozing onto the pebbles.]

Buchanan: Oh God! (Vomits.)

Thunder rolled but the darkness remained impermeable as they waited, holding on to each other to maintain some sort of communication and trying to keep their breathing under control.

Silence.

Then a rustling sound close — close! — at hand.

Silence again.

Then the smell of hot piss assailed Buchanan's nostrils, sweeter to his senses than all the perfumes of the orient. He risked moving to give Fizz's hand a reassuring pat but stayed otherwise immobile till long after there could be any immediate danger of discovery. Even then it was clear that none of them had any comment to make that was worth breaking the silence to give voice to.

The next brilliant thunderbolt was a super deluxe model. It unzipped the sky in the west, seeming to give a glimpse of divine glory beyond. The two men were shown once more intent on their vigil, both of them bent forward at the waist and peering into the darkness as though they had spotted what they were looking for. Buchanan was too late to transfer his attention to the water but got ready to make best use of the next opportunity.

He watched the lookouts from the corner of his eye as he concentrated his attention on the featureless backdrop beyond them. The binoculars were useless: they covered only a few square meters of sea at a time and the chances of their being focused on the correct area during the next lightning flash were infinitesimal.

There were few lights to be seen out there and those that winked faintly through the gloom clearly belonged to large vessels: oil tankers headed up river to Bo'ness or container ships for Leith Docks. He stayed focused, his blind eyes probing the darkness, the green-apple smell of Fizz's hair in his nostrils, and when the next split-second day broke across the seascape, he spotted it: a distant, fast moving smudge that could only be a rubber dinghy. It was still some way off but the next flash showed it significantly closer and in only a few minutes they could hear the powerful throb of its engine.

Concentrating hard on the sound of the engine, Buchanan managed to get the binoculars on it. There were several people aboard: one man sitting up on the stern and handling the engine, the others cowering down so far that it was impossible to count them.

'Well, now, there's a thing,' Fizz mumbled, through what appeared to be a mouthful of food. 'Who have we here, I wonder?'

Buchanan couldn't credit it. 'What are you eating?'

'A sandwich. Cream cheese and cashew

nuts. D'you want one? An army travels on its stomach.'

Both of her fellow-combatants recoiled from the offer, a rebuff which she accepted stoically with the comment that there would be all the more for other people. There seemed to be no limit to her capacity for food and Buchanan calculated that she had just about finished the pack of sandwiches before the dinghy skidded to a halt with its engine cut and half its length on dry land.

A series of half-second images, presented against a progressively crushing onslaught of thunder, showed at least ten figures scrambling out of the dinghy onto the pebbles and being hustled up the beach by the waiting men. Those at the stern, either from choice or because they were being chivvied to do so, jumped from the gunwales and waded ashore with unmistakable urgency, some of them slipping on the wet rocks and taking a dive into the knee-deep water.

The depth of the darkness, between flashes, appeared to cause some confusion and they were still milling about on the beach when the dinghy took off again. In seconds its engine had faded to a hum that was barely perceptible above the hiss of the waves and before it disappeared completely it was superseded by a rattle like machine gun fire. Rain.

It fell from the sky in massive drops, any one of which, Buchanan felt, would have soaked him to the skin. He could sense Fizz trying to take some evasive action but he could hold out no hope of her success. There was no place of shelter they could run to and the rock wall behind them became almost instantly a torrent so there was nothing for it but to stand there in misery and drown.

The electrical storm had passed over towards the west but the occasional clatter of rocks indicated that the hindmost incomers were taking time to find their way off the beach. Buchanan was jittery with impatience. If they were going to grasp the opportunity of chasing the van and discovering its destination it was imperative to get a good start. They had a four or five minute climb back to the cars and the van could be back at the junction with the main road in half that time. Even in the dark, however, it was too chancy to start off until the beach was clear.

When the rain eased, as rapidly as it had started, they could see the sky still paling intermittently as the storm rolled east over Edinburgh. Every few seconds the familiar skyline, from the castle to the hump of Arthur's Seat, flashed up like a *son et lumière* show. One particular bolt silhouetted two men moving away from Buchanan's hiding place half-carrying a third who must have fallen and hurt himself. It also showed Fizz, in bra and briefs, drying herself with a sock.

Buchanan was too astonished to comment. His first assumption was that Fizz had flipped at last but this was revoked when she took her T-shirt and jeans out of the plastic bag that had contained the sandwiches and donned them with unselfconscious swiftness. The wet bra was presently removed in a complicated manoeuvre that presented it down one sleeve leaving her apparently dry, warm and comfortable, in contrast to her now shivering playmates.

The question of what had happened to the briefs: whether they were still in situ or whether Buchanan had missed their removal in the darkness between flashes, exercised his mind for several minutes and returned to worry him at intervals throughout the remainder of the night.

He had seen Fizz — once — in a swimming costume, a black, utilitarian affair she'd had since her schooldays, but the sight of her wet skin, so tantalizingly illuminated, was infinitely sexier and well worth getting soaked for. She was on the small side, of course, but not so skinny she'd set your teeth on edge and her shape went deliciously in at the waist and out again over two sweet, tear-drop shaped hips.

Buchanan dragged his eyes back to business and was presently compensated by the sight of the last of the bedraggled seafarers disappearing up the cliff path. In the distance he could hear the purr of an engine but it wasn't coming from the van as he feared at first; it appeared that the dinghy was hanging around offshore in case it had to stage a quick rescue mission.

As he was about to say, 'Let's go,' Fizz said it for him and dug him in the ribs. She always had to be a chief, never an indian.

They scrambled up the cliff as best they could, feet skidding from under them on the mud and gravel. It wasn't exactly precipitous but the rain had loosened stones and turned bare earth into mud and patches of grass into treacherous slides. Fizz led the way with her trusty staff, a testimony to forward planning.

Because of the conditions it took considerably longer to ascend than it had taken to go down which meant that by the time they reached the cars they had no idea whether the van had passed that way or taken off in the other direction.

'We'll have to split up,' Fizz announced, stating the obvious. 'There are only two directions they can head from here so at least one of us should lock on. We can move faster than they can so it shouldn't take us long to catch up with them.'

Buchanan thought it almost certain that the van would be heading back to the garden centre, so he said, 'I'll head west, Hector. That way, if I strike a blank I can go home and wait for you to call me.'

Hector hesitated for a second, obviously suspecting he'd won the booby prize but unable to come up with an instant alternative.

'Okay,' he said, through teeth that were now chattering with cold. 'If I find I'm on the wrong track I'll about turn and catch up with you.'

Buchanan was already behind the wheel.

'If we miss each other, I'll be at my flat.'

They sprang into action like something out of *Z Cars* and much too fast for discretion. It was after two a.m. but the road was by no means empty and Buchanan didn't like taking chances. He had seen police patrols in this area at the most unlikely hours and Larry would go ballistic if his devil was done for speeding. However, if he were going to make sure of overtaking the van before it turned off, he had to put his foot down.

The Saab handled well at speed and the road was a series of long straights so they covered the first few miles at a velocity the van could never have matched. On their right there was nothing but the Firth of Forth, on their left they passed no turnoffs till they reached Aberlady, nonetheless, by the time they hit the built-up area approaching Prestonpans it was fairly obvious that they were on a wild goose chase. Hector had scooped the pool after all.

Fizz was all for turning around and chasing off in the opposite direction but Buchanan had had enough. He was shuddering and miserable in his wet clothes, he had to be at work in a few hours and, even more cogently, he was confident that Hector would not risk losing yet another van so soon after losing the others. Now was definitely the time to delegate.

'It's not as if Hector's going to do anything,' he comforted Fizz. 'He's just going to trail the van to its destination. You're not likely to miss out on any action. Even if all hell is breaking loose when he gets there, what could he do about it — or the three of us, for that matter — against so many? All he can do is observe and report back.'

Muttering grumpily, she removed her boots and positioned her bare feet on the dashboard where the blast from the heater was most concentrated. Buchanan wished he could do the same. She then found a pack of Kleenex in the glove compartment and, oblivious to the fact that his need was infinitely greater than hers, used most of it's contents to blot dry what was left of her hair.

'What were they — those people? Illegal immigrants?'

'Difficult to say.' Buchanan couldn't think of anything likelier, but jumping to conclusions wasn't his style. 'I didn't get a good look at them, did you?'

'Are you kidding? I was hugging that rock like it was my long lost child. They did seem to be carrying stuff, though.'

Buchanan glanced at her. 'Did they? I didn't see that.'

'I think so. Some of them were, at any rate. Small bundles. Didn't you see one of them drop his in the water and dive back in for it?'

'No. I missed that. Did they look heavy — the bundles?'

'Couldn't tell. They looked to me like they could have contained their belongings.' She extracted the last two tissues from the box and held them out. 'Want these?'

Buchanan answered her with a sour face to which she replied, 'Suit yourself,' and put them back in the glove compartment.

Lurking in Buchanan's mind, there was still the worry that Hector too had drawn a blank.

Admittedly, Hector was a fast and confident driver, and it didn't seem likely that the van could have pulled off the road in the few minutes it would have taken him to catch up on it but, the way the convoy had been playing cat and mouse, anything was possible.

Fizz said, 'There was a report in one of the Inverness papers about the body of a foreign sailor being washed up near Achiltiebuie. Makes you wonder, doesn't it? I mean, it could have been an illegal immigrant. Maybe this is a large-scale operation.'

'I have a feeling we may be close to finding out,' Buchanan said. 'We don't have much choice, now, other than to tell the police what we know.'

'What? You're joking! And let McKenzie take his chance with the due processes of the Law?'

He spared her a worried glance. 'You don't trust the courts, Fizz? Are you sure you're in the right job?'

'And you *do* trust them, of course,' she returned rudely. 'There's probably more real evidence against McKenzie than there was against Freddie McAuslan and even Freddie was about to sink without trace till you took on his case.'

'Freddie was a known offender,' Buchanan

started to say but Fizz was having none of it. She said,

'You could tell by the way the way the Inverness-shire police were hunting McKenzie down that they had good evidence against him. Armed robbery doesn't happen every day of the week up there and the CID will be desperate for an arrest. If you hand him over with things as they are now he won't stand a chance.'

'Yes, and if I don't hand him over I could find myself charged as an accessory after the fact!' Buchanan pointed out, through teeth clenched to forestall a grinding attack. 'I'm helping a wanted man to evade arrest and now I've witnessed a probable felony without reporting it.'

'How do you know it was a felony? There's no law against crossing the Firth at night. Not when I last checked. What we just saw could have been some sea angling club arriving home with their catch.'

'What jury's going to swallow that one? I'd need half a dozen expert witnesses to my congenital stupidity before I could claim that that's what I believed.'

'Well, if you're so brainy,' Fizz nagged on, 'you should be able to think up another excuse. The fact is, we don't know what this mob is up to or why they want McKenzie, so you'd be making a big mistake if you blew the gaff right now.' She picked thoughtfully at the mud under her fingernails. 'If you're worried, why don't you have a chat with your pal Fleming.'

Buchanan's breath burst from him in a bitter laugh. The last time he had been at police headquarters DCI Ian Fleming had walked straight past him with only the coolest of greetings. Okay, they had never been bosom buddies but something a little warmer than a nod and an offhand, 'Hi, Tam,' might have been expected.

'I reckon he must have been hauled over the coals after the last help he gave us,' he said. 'He was poking his nose into a case that was properly the business of another department. No doubt he blames us for that.'

That invoked a small snigger. 'Fleming's lot is not an 'appy one, is it? Why is it always our fault, though?' she mused: she who had caused Fleming incalculable trauma more than once. 'He always was a touchy bugger. It was thanks to us that he got his last promotion, but does he remember that when we ask him for a favour? Does he hell.'

'He came through for us last time, Fizz. You can't expect him to keep paying us back for the rest of his life.'

'Tcha!' She swept the matter from the

agenda with a brusque gesture. 'Well, all we can hope for is that this new development rings a few bells with McKenzie.'

Buchanan didn't feel tempted to put money on that possibility. He said,

'He'd have had to be totally unconscious to remember nothing about a trip in an open boat. Even witnessing what we've just witnessed would, you'd think, lodge in the most besotted memory.'

Fizz shook her head. 'But he must be caught up in it one way or another. Whether he witnessed this part of the operation or a different part, he must have seen something he wasn't meant to see. I've been over it and over it and, really, there can't be any other reason for their being so desperate to see him dead.'

Buchanan too had been over it and over it *ad nauseum*. He said, merely throwing the idea at the wall to see if it stuck,

'I wonder if it's possible that 'They' started off wanting to kill him and then decided he might be more use to them alive.'

Fizz glanced at his face and then fell silent while they cruised through sleeping Mussel-burgh and out again.

'It's possible,' she granted eventually, 'but I'm swinging around to the idea that there might be two lots after him. Don't laugh, I know it's hard to credit that even one lot would have a use for him, never mind two, but that's what the facts point to. Think about it.'

Buchanan had already thought about it, long and hard. 'I think you have to be right,' he said. 'In fact, what happened tonight is making me suspect that we may be in the middle of a gang war or something close to it. That could be why Taff goes nowhere without his bodyguards.'

'I reckon there's one gang in Inverness and a different one here in Edinburgh, don't you think so?'

'I think it's a premise we have to consider,' Buchanan said cannily. 'There are certainly indications that one faction wants McKenzie dead while another faction is keen to keep him alive and in their custody.'

'And Hector too?' Fizz asked of the night sky, her face a parody of complete bewilderment. 'What value does Hector have for Them? You couldn't find two people more dissimilar than McKenzie and Hector. They can't both be witnesses, surely? They didn't even know each other before they met in Inverness and if they were both totally unconnected witnesses to the same nefarious deed it must have been either a coincidence — and you know what I think about coincidences — or a singularly ill-planned operation. Neither of which gets my vote. Nope, there has to be something else that makes them valuable.'

This, Buchanan reflected, was one of the things about Fizz that stayed his hand when he was tempted to strangle her. She filled in the gaps in his own pattern of thinking. It had never occurred to him to look at Hector and McKenzie as a pair, yet it was now obvious that the commodity that made them valuable to the opposition was likely to be something they had in common. All they now had to do was to pinpoint what it was.

Yeah. Right.

'Well that dinghy hadn't travelled from Inverness, that's for sure,' Fizz said. 'It might have crossed over from Fife or it could have liaised with a bigger ship out in the roads. The buggers couldn't have asked for a better night for their little games.'

Buchanan looked out across the water and had to agree with her. He could see a couple of red lights moving steadily upriver and a row of white ones heading for the open sea but the vessels themselves were invisible. In another hour or so there would be enough light in the sky to reveal them but by then they'd be well out of sight from this angle.

'What I'd really like to know,' he said, 'is

where the other vans went. They could have been picking up other boat people at different points along the coast, of course, but there are other possibilities. I can't help feeling that the whole manoeuvre had an organised feel to it, like a military operation. The vans all set off around the same time, each to a different destination — maybe to a different task. Ours could have been detailed to pick up reinforcements for the main event, but what were the others up to?'

Fizz was silent for a long time. The short curls that had earlier lain flat to her head were now fluffing up in the warmth from the car heater making her look not so very different from the old familiar Fizz.

'Hector will be able to tell us,' she decided, with an assurance that Buchanan was unable to share. 'If you weren't so paranoiac about using mobile phones he could probably have let us know by now.'

Buchanan was shocked that she had guessed the real reason why he refused to accept a mobile, even as a gift. He had made various excuses in the past, most of them perfectly valid, but he liked to think that he kept his irrational fears a well guarded secret.

'It's a proven fact,' he said, since she knew now anyway, 'that they cause brain damage in mice.'

'Rubbish. How many calls do mice get in a day?' She smiled at her own quip, then frowned again. 'It's all right for you, Buchanan. Hector'll probably phone you tonight but I'll have to wait till I get to the office tomorrow before I know what's happening — or even what's already happened. The whole case could be wrapped up by daylight and I wouldn't even know about it.'

Buchanan had to concede the point. He should have a car phone at least. Not to use, but solely for occasions like the present. Maybe he'd buy one for Fizz at the same time so that she could phone him if she were in trouble.

'If anything exciting happens I'll come and get you,' he promised rashly. There was a faint chance that he and Hector might find themselves in action again before morning but he hoped very sincerely that a dramatic conclusion to the inquiry — if one were indeed imminent — would hold off till he could grab a long hot shower and a few hours sleep.

He dropped Fizz off at her flat and drove home with his clothes steaming and his *joie de vivre* at a low ebb. He had, in fact, little hope of a speedy end to McKenzie's troubles and his confidence in his own abilities was a trifle wilted. One had to ask oneself, just occasionally, if one should be sticking to one's day job.

As he cut the engine he noticed a plastic carrier bag on the floor. It contained Fizz's wet clothes: a pair of socks, a bra, and a pair of bikini briefs.

18

Fizz woke at six as usual, confident in the certain knowledge that the mystery had reached its climax overnight and that she'd missed out on the whole shebang. How much of this specious assumption was due to the dreams that had disturbed her repose she was unsure, but by the time she arrived at the office after an invigorating walk, she was rather less inclined to fell Buchanan on sight than she had been when she set off.

He had obviously been at his desk for some time before her arrival and had already gone through the morning's post and checked his e-mail.

'Heard from Hector?' she greeted him, falling into the creaky old chair he provided for clients.

He looked up from his reading, all bright-eyed and starchy and squeaky clean as though he'd just emerged from ten hours of transcendental meditation.

'Yes. He phoned just after I got home last night, to say he'd caught up with the van, and again this morning with the news that its destination was another garden centre on the outskirts of Manchester.'

'Sheesh!' Fizz commented, unsure whether to be relieved that the game was still afoot or disgusted that so little had emerged after all their effort. 'Another garden centre? What are they up to, for God's sake? Growing their own pot?'

Buchanan opened his bottom drawer and propped his feet on it. 'Beats me,' he said. 'But, when you think about it, garden centres are pretty well ideal as cover for unlawful practices. Like the one we saw, they're often remotely situated, with few neighbours, and the coming and going of vans — and of numerous people of all kinds — wouldn't raise an eyebrow.'

'So that's it? That's all we got?'

'For the moment, yes,' he said with a take-it-or-leave-it look as though he thought she were blaming it on him. 'Unfortunately, it appears that this new garden centre is not so easy to keep under observation — particularly after working hours. It's even bigger than the other one and it has three different entrances. Hector reckons he'd have better luck returning to his stake-out at Bo'ness so I told him to go ahead and do that. He's the best judge of what's feasible and what isn't.'

'Okay,' said Fizz, as if she accepted that. 'In the meantime, we might as well see what

McKenzie has to say about last night's events. I'll give his daughter a ring and let them know that I'll be dropping by later this morning.'

Buchanan looked at his watch. 'Actually, there's something else I thought might be useful: something you'd be better at than me.'

Fizz was intrigued by this admission of her superiority. 'Uh-huh?'

'If those people we saw coming ashore last night had been ferried from a larger vessel out in the roads there's a high probability that it docked at Leith early this morning.' He was busying himself by packing his briefcase but squinting at her emphatically at the same time. 'Okay, you're going to say it could have been heading out, not in, and that's true, but it's still worth looking into. If you latch on to the right source you could save us a lot of time.'

He was quite right: this was something Fizz knew she could achieve much more easily than he could. Furthermore, if it put off having to quiz McKenzie she was all for it.

'I'll try to fit in a few words with McKenzie during my lunch hour,' Buchanan said, slamming drawers shut and standing up. 'I've already got Hector thinking about a possible link between himself and McKenzie but I won't hear from him now till this evening.

He'll check in every hour on the hour with Beatrice, so that we know he's okay, and she can contact me if things start to move.'

'Will you be back in the office today?'

He paused in the doorway. 'Depends how things go. Larry has already shown the prosecution's case to be so damn shaky, I wouldn't be surprised if it's thrown out of court, so there's a chance we might finish early. I'll ring in.'

She heard him exchanging a few words with Beatrice in the outer office and then watched from the window as he loped across the road to where he parked his car. He had his good suit on again today, not because he wanted to cut a dash in court as he'd like her to believe, but because the suits he customarily wore to work were either at the cleaners or becoming less immaculate than he felt befitting to his calling, and he couldn't afford a new one. Served him right for throwing his money around when he had it. It would do him good to learn to count his pennies.

She put in an hour on a divorce settlement and got it ready for Buchanan's approval before setting off for Leith. The weather was not only fresher than yesterday but a bit on the parky side especially as she approached the dock, where there was little to break the stiff breeze.

This was the first time she'd seen the recent development of the area for herself and she was surprised to find much of it quite attractive. Any change would have been an improvement on the dingy tenements and warehouses she remembered from a school trip a hundred years ago, but there were now several waterfront complexes that reminded her forcibly of Amsterdam. She had a quick look round the flashy shopping mall and then headed for the dock gates.

Some parts were open to all comers but those were locks that were not in use by anything other than small craft and the occasional yacht. The place she really wanted to be was surrounded by a high metal fence and the entrance was defended by one of those barriers that can be raised to let cars through, plus a well manned security office. Even approaching the gates was enough to bring one of the security guards out to waylay her.

'Anything I can do for you, miss?'

Fizz swiftly donned her sweet-sixteen face. 'Just looking, thank you.'

He nodded pleasantly, a smiley, kind-looking man in his forties. 'I'm sorry, but you can't go in there. It's strictly private.'

'Oh gosh, I didn't realise that,' Fizz said, wondering if he could be talked around with the right kind of sob story. She really wanted to see the area for herself so that she could suss out the possibilities for smuggling or whatever. She could hardly hit him with something like, 'If I were planning on smuggling drugs or people ashore, what would be the best way to get away with it?' It wasn't likely to be something the security company gave out fact sheets on.

'What a disappointment,' she muttered, looking really gutted. 'I was counting on getting some facts to help me with my Transport project.'

He pressed his lips together sympathetically. 'Doing your Highers, are you? That's too bad. I wish I could help you but we have to stick to the rules I'm afraid. I could certainly help you with any questions you want answered. Was there anything in particular you wanted to know?'

Fizz vacillated with fake uncertainty, still looking utterly devastated and close to tears, but he wasn't buying. Short of a fake suicide attempt, there was clearly no way of melting his heart. Unfortunately, it was too late now to come out with a direct inquiry regarding a vessel that had docked in the wee small hours, so she had to curve it like Beckham, pretending an interest in what he felt like telling her about the trafficking in the harbour: motors and diesels for the North Sea oil business, supply vessels, deliveries from Valetta, Amsterdam and Limasol. She made conspicuous notes about cargoes of fertilizer, cement and gravel and asked intelligent questions about the few vessels visible from where she stood. Then she slipped in the decider.

'I suppose the ships start coming in as soon as it's light in the morning?'

'Oh no,' he said. 'The Seafield gate's open twenty-four hours a day. The pipe vessels are coming and going all the time.'

'Pipe vessels?' Fizz asked, looking up with her pencil poised over her notebook. Pipe vessels? Pipes? Who was it — McKenzie? — who had said that someone was 'on the pipes?' No, it was Buchanan, quoting McKenzie's daughter — who'd been quoting McKenzie. That's right — one of McKenzie's drinking buddies had been 'on the pipes'. Same pipes? Maybe.

'The BTC vessels.' He pointed to a long low building that lined a distant dock.

Fizz couldn't see any ships from where she stood. She said, 'What sort of pipes?'

'Underwater pipes. For the oil industry. They come here to BTC from all over the world to be treated with an anti-rust coating and then they're shipped out to most places where there's oil extraction: Mexico, Canada, Guatemala. Lots of destinations.'

'And they come and go all through the night?'

'Every day except Saturday.'

Fizz had never thought about underwater pipelines. 'I suppose the pipes are quite big,' she hazarded.

'About that size.' His hands sketched a circle of air approximately eighteen inches across: just big enough to accommodate a small adult in luxury or a large one in only a minimum of discomfort.

A warm glow, not dissimilar to that produced by a large slug of Buchanan's Glenmorangie, suffused Fizz's being. What a sweet set-up for people-laundering. You could ship them in overnight — from Albania, or wherever — either land them on the way up the Forth or store them here, still in the pipes, till a suitable vessel headed out.

How many refugees to a pipe? How many pipes to a ship? How many pesos, zloty, quetzales, lek, or whatever, per item of cargo? Lots. Maybe even more than that. Lots and lots, probably. Wait till Buchanan heard about this.

'You've given me some really interesting

facts,' she said, brimming with genuine gratification. 'I'm very grateful to you.'

He took a business card out of his pocket and handed it to her. 'If you get stuck with anything just give me a ring.'

'That's very kind of you, Mr, uh, Boslem. Thank you so much.'

You win some, you lose some, she thought as she headed back to the bus stop. One day crabby Mrs Mulvey: the next, nice Dave Boslem. *Vive la difference.*

It was nearly eleven o'clock when she got back to the office and as soon as she went in the Wonderful Beatrice collared her.

'Fizz! Come into my office, will you? I need to talk to you.'

Fizz followed her into the cubby hole Beatie had laid claim to — largely to spite her rival, Margaret, secretary to the other partner, who had to share space in the outer office.

'What's up, doc?'

'Mr Buchanan told me that Hector McSween would be checking in every hour on the hour, but there was no call from him at ten o'clock.'

'Oh shite,' Fizz muttered, before she remembered that she wasn't going to swear in the office ever again. 'Buchanan spoke to him at nine o'clock, right? And he was fine then, presumably.' She sat down on Beatrice's desk and thought about it. 'You've told Buchanan, I suppose?'

Beatrice resumed her seat and ostentatiously shifted her keyboard, mouse and reading glasses to a place of safety. 'I have, but he's in court and you know Larry Grassick won't allow his juniors to be paged during a sitting. I left a message for Mr Buchanan just after ten but I've had no reply. I dare say I could tell them it's an emergency but that might embarrass Mr Buchanan unnecessarily. We all know what a bully Grassick is, but I don't know what else I can do.'

Neither did Fizz. No way could she fool herself that Hector's mobile had conked out, or that he'd maybe lost it, or that last night's lightning storm had done something detrimental to the phone lines. The guy was in big trouble, otherwise he'd have contacted the office somehow.

'You're right, Beatie, you can't push it any further. Grassick would have a fit if Buchanan let his private affairs interfere with business. What time is it?'

'Just gone eleven.'

'Okay. We'll give it another few minutes to see if Hector phones and then, if he doesn't, I'll hop on a bus and check things out.'

Beatrice picked up her specs and started to put them on, then changed her mind and slid them up over her curly perm so that she could give Fizz a hard look.

'You know what Mr Buchanan will say if you do that, Fizz? He won't like it, will he?'

'Beatie, if I worried about what Buchanan liked I wouldn't even be in this job, would I?'

Beatie almost smiled, a rare occurrence at the best of times and a concession normally reserved for Buchanan.

'Considering he has already sacked you at least three times by my reckoning, no, I suppose you wouldn't. All the same . . . '

'Yeah, okay, Beatie, I hear what you're saying. I'm not likely to do anything daft.'

Beatie raised exaggeratedly incredulous eyebrows at that claim but Fizz wasn't going to debate the issue. Somebody had to find out what had happened to Hector and it was pointless to wait for Buchanan to turn up. Even if he were here now there was nothing he could do except go and look for Hector, as she herself was about to do. There was nothing at all dangerous about the mission because, if Hector had indeed disappeared, they'd have to confer before taking the matter any further.

'Tell him I'm going to check out the situation and come straight back. And that's a promise, okay? I'll just grab a quick coffee while I'm waiting.'

'Oh, there's another thing I should maybe mention.' Beatrice reached for her scribble pad. 'There was a call for Mr Buchanan about half an hour ago from a young lady called Celia. I'm not sure if it's connected with the same case . . . ?'

'Yes, it is,' Fizz nodded. 'You can tell me about it.'

'Well, really, there's nothing to tell. She just sounded anxious to contact him.'

'Did she leave a number?'

'No, that's what was unusual about the call.' Beatrice leaned back in her chair and doubled the front of her cardigan tightly across her chest. 'I offered to ask Mr Buchanan to return her call but she said she didn't want that. She sounded . . . furtive, I suppose you'd call it. Sort of . . . not whispering, exactly, but mumbling a bit, you know? Anyway, she said to tell Mr Buchanan to phone her but to hang up after one ring and she'd phone him back at this number.'

'Oh great. And nobody but Buchanan knows her number, right?'

No doubt the number of the brothel, sauna, massage parlour or whatever sobriquet it employed, could be found in the Yellow Pages but it was unlikely that Celia would be

342

using the reception number. It was worth a try, of course, so she tried it and hung up after one ring, but with predictable results. After waiting for five more minutes for either Celia or Hector to call, she penned a brief note for Buchanan and left it with Beatrice.

'I shouldn't be more than a couple of hours,' she said, 'but if I decide there's anything to be gained by hanging around for longer than that I'll find a phone and let you know what's happening.'

Beatrice put on her flintiest face, which was pretty damn flinty. 'If you're so set on going, Fizz, for goodness sake take my mobile. At least I'll be able to tell Mr Buchanan that he can contact you.'

Fizz took the phone to please her. 'Buchanan won't phone me for the same reason he won't phone Hector: because if a person is trying to keep a low profile the last thing she wants is for her mobile to ring. Never mind, I dare say it'll save me hunting for a call box. I'll give you a buzz to let you know when I'll be back.'

'Well, see you do that, Fizz, okay? Just keep in contact. And promise me again that you'll do nothing but *look* — and from a safe distance.'

Fizz blew out her cheeks with exasperation. It was bad enough having to go through all this with Buchanan every time she crossed the road without holding his hand without having Beatie turning into her mother as well. She said,

'Beatie, you know I can refuse you nothing. I promise. There. Happy now?' She waggled her head impertinently and added, for pure devilment, 'If you don't hear from me by one o'clock I'll be dead.'

Beatrice compressed her already tight lips and her reproachful glare followed Fizz around till she sallied forth to catch a bus to Bo'ness.

It was one of those buses that took forever: looping in and out of every hamlet and pausing to allow the driver to exchange pleasantries with every acquaintance he spotted along the way. There were only three other passengers on the bus, a sleepy-looking teenager and two middle-aged ladies loaded with shopping, none of whom appeared in any rush to reach their destination. Fizz spent the time worrying about what had happened to Hector and cursing Buchanan for choosing a time like this to maintain radio silence.

The bus route, although it was the only option on offer, actually passed nowhere near the garden centre. When she got off at the closest point she still had about two and a half miles to walk before she spotted the greenhouses. However, the poor bus service had not deterred the swarm of customers which she could see milling about among the plants. Evidently, the business was not just a cover for less savoury enterprises but a healthy little earner in its own right.

She kept her eyes open as she walked past the gates, in the hope of spotting Hector among the shoppers or lurking around outside the perimeter. Somehow, she doubted that he would be inside the centre in broad daylight. He could do that once, maybe, without being sussed but the proprietors would soon get suspicious of a lone male who turned up every day and snooped around without buying anything.

If he were still on the job she reckoned he would be up there on the wooded hill where he had a good view of the rear of the enclosure: the storage area, the poly-tunnels and the long huts where McKenzie had been held prisoner. That's where the action was likely to be, if there was any, and it could be overlooked only from one narrowly restricted area of woodland.

It was cool under the trees but the ascent was so steep that she was glad of that before she had climbed halfway. There were no tracks through the thick undergrowth, which made the going slow and aggravating, and she saw no trampled bracken or broken branches to indicate that Hector or anyone else had been here before her in the recent past.

Just short of the crown of the hill, however, Hector had left his mark: a temporary shelter, constructed from larch boughs and nicely thatched with leafy branches and moss. Fizz felt she could have done better with the materials at hand — a good lashing with spruce roots would have made it a lot more stable — but considering Hector had only needed something to keep the wind and rain off for a few hours, it was perfectly adequate. Of Hector himself, however, there was no sign.

She sat there for a minute or two, on the dry branches beneath the shelter, and watched the activity below. None of the workers appeared to be doing anything nefarious and she could see no movement at all around the outbuildings other than a youth hosing mud off a path. How Hector could suffer such boredom day after day was a mystery to her, but no doubt the job would hold more interest for someone whose life was at stake, as his was.

He had obviously not been sleeping in the shelter, it was too small to stretch out in, so that meant he must be using the Rover for overnight accommodation. She hadn't noticed it in the culvert as she passed but that meant nothing as most of the trough was invisible from the road and, in any case, it was so overgrown with trees that a car could have been hidden at any point along its length.

She went back down the hill and made sure she was unobserved before she cut down into the culvert. It was full of rosebay willow herb and muddy underfoot from last night's storm but luckily she didn't have to go far before she found the car.

It was easy to find because the vegetation around it was well trodden, the willow herb mashed into the mud by more than one pair of feet, judging by the footprints. Fizz was already uneasy before she came close to it and it didn't cheer her up much to discover that the doors were not locked. Inside she could see Hector's shaving kit, a travelling rug, a packet of oatcakes and a wide stain on the headrest that was unmistakably blood.

Fizz leaned against the bonnet, wracked by a despondency that was beyond the power of her stockpile of expletives to alleviate. This was bad news. If Hector had been nabbed by the opposition — and that was the most optimistic view she could take — they'd make him talk. Buchanan hadn't told him where McKenzie had taken refuge but he certainly knew where Buchanan lived and might also have a pretty good idea where she herself could be found.

What would they do to him? These were the people who had refrained from killing McKenzie — at least temporarily — so maybe Hector would be lucky too. And, if he were being held captive somewhere, the chances were that it would be in the garden centre.

Fizz took her time thinking that over. She had been accused, once or twice in the past — well, several times, actually — of dashing off like a bull at a gate, and she didn't want any come-backs this time. Not that this could be termed a dangerous situation. None of this bunch had seen her before so she'd have no difficulty in melting into the body of shoppers. Even if some of The Persevere gang happened to be staking out the place, as they well might be, it was unlikely they'd recognise her with her new hairstyle and in her business clothes.

Nonetheless, she kept her wits about her as she started back to the garden centre and waited till she could slip through the gates under cover of a couple of cars. Once inside it was easy enough to move from display to display, many of which were roofed over and thick with potted vegetation. She was in no hurry and, although her objective was the long hut at the back of the complex, there was plenty to look at en route.

The assistants, identifiable by their green aprons, all appeared pretty genuine and were getting on with their various jobs as though they knew what they were doing. One of them, an older man with a beat-up face and a surly expression, did look a bit iffy, but his reply to a customer's inquiry regarding the correct soil acidity for *Ceanothus* established his bona fides to Fizz's satisfaction.

Step by patient step, she worked her way from Annuals to Perennials, through Shrubs and Ornamental Trees, and skirted the central Indoor Plants and Checkout area on the ground floor of the ex-farmhouse. The beds that surrounded the building were laid out as various display gardens, possibly with the double intention of inspiring the punters and providing a pleasant aspect for the occupants of the upper flat. She skirted a huge ornamental pool starry with water lilies and slipped down the side of the building towards a walled and cobbled courtyard at the rear.

There were no signs around to indicate that the area was private so she was not immediately disconcerted to find, as she rounded the corner, that there were people there: three men, apparently crossing from a car to the rear door of the farmhouse. Although only a few steps away from her, they had their backs to her, and paid her no heed whatsoever for the split second it took her to register their presence.

What did attract their attention was the gasp that exploded from her as she realised that, leading the group — and with an air of brisk authority — was McKenzie.

Three heads snapped round to stare at her as she heard herself say,

'What are you doing, McKenzie, for G-G-G-G-'

The words withered on her lips as she perceived that McKenzie was not wearing his own face but that of a frightening, ugly, and very *very* interested stranger.

19

Buchanan's morning was a bit of a parson's egg. Bits of it were terrible, largely because Larry had one of his recurrent migraines. Even on a good day he was a foul tempered old bastard but on a bad day he could make his colleagues, the judge, the accused, the prosecution, the jury and people passing him in the street wish they'd never been born.

He had, several times, driven Buchanan to the point of walking out but that was something Larry was able to do without in the least diminishing his devil's profound admiration for his legal acumen. As far as Buchanan was concerned, the man was a genius and you had to cut a genius some slack, especially on those days when the poor sod's head felt, as he had once remarked, like it was about to give birth to a cannonball.

Larry aside, however, other parts of the morning were excellent, not least the part where the judge lost his patience with the prosecution, whose case was, at best, shaky and whose witnesses had failed to materialise, and threw the action out of court. It was not yet eleven-thirty but Larry had had enough.

'The hell with this, I'm going home,' he muttered as the judge rose. The guy was in so much pain he could hardly enunciate the words and his eyes were closed to mere slits. He might not be an easy man to live with but it was pitiful to see him suffer so much.

'You shouldn't be driving,' Buchanan said. 'You'd better let me take you home.'

'No. I'll take a taxi. The car will be safe enough where it is.'

Buchanan held the door for him. 'Actually, I could use a couple of hours off,' he said. 'One or two things I ought to attend to.'

Larry groaned, holding his head together with tightly clamped fingers. 'Take the whole bloody afternoon off if you want to.'

This unexpected bonus recharged Buchanan's batteries instantly. Now he could have a long, relaxed and hopefully productive lunch with Kerry and still have time to drop in at the office and make sure everything was ticking over. Time off was, of course, a figment of the imagination since he should be spending every spare minute reading in the Advocate's Library, but having Larry's blessing eased his conscience. The sun was shining, he was wearing his good suit and the prospects looked encouraging.

It was second nature to him to check the

devils' tray for messages on the way out and there he found two from Beatrice. One told him to dial Celia's number and wait till she called him back, and the other announced that Fizz had gone to Bo'ness to find out why Hector had twice omitted to call in.

A sudden, chill breeze blew across Buchanan's paradise. Bloody Fizz! Why couldn't she have waited to speak to him? The chances were that Hector's phone had simply gone phutt or he was engaged in some surveillance that precluded making a noise. And even if he was in trouble, dammit, there was no immediate need for Fizz to go galloping off to the rescue like the third cavalry.

He discovered that his legs had carried him out into Parliament Square and were hurrying him along the arcade towards some unknown and utterly pointless destination. Obviously, what he should be doing was phoning Beatrice to find out what, precisely, was going on. He went back into the court building and made the call.

'I told her,' Beatrice claimed. 'I knew you wouldn't like it but you know Fizz, there's no arguing with her.'

Beatrice knew only what she needed to know about the case but she had never been slow at putting two and two together.

'How long has she been gone?' he asked her.

A pause. Beatrice was no doubt checking her watch: she liked to get things right.

'Nearly forty-five minutes. She'll scarcely be there yet.'

Buchanan ground his teeth. Too late to beat her to it.

'If it's any comfort to you,' Beatrice said, 'she did give me her word that she would do nothing but look around. Also, I made her take my mobile with her and she said she'd phone if she was going to be more than a couple of hours.'

'Well, thank you for thinking of that, Beatrice,' Buchanan said, breathing a little easier, and determining once and for all that he would buy Fizz, and himself, a mobile before the week was out. Brain damage would be infinitely preferable to the worry of not knowing what was happening to her. 'Okay, I'll see you shortly, but if Fizz phones before I get there would you tell her to expect a call from me within the hour?'

As he hung up he caught sight of a colleague grinning at him from across the room and he realised that he was probably wearing a cartoon expression of utter dismay. He grinned back, and nodded, and rolled his eyes, but all the time he was thinking, *what to do next?* He had a couple of hours free before his date with Kerry but pursuing Fizz to Bo'ness might warrant a charge of hysteria. She got really stroppy when he underestimated her judgment. Maybe he should bite the bullet, at least till one o'clock, and let her get on with it.

He looked at the pieces of paper in his hand and suddenly remembered the message from Celia. That, at least, looked promising. He dialled the number and hung up after one ring and, a minute later, the phone buzzed under his hand.

'William?'

Buchanan had been about to answer with his own name, as usual, but was able to turn it into a mumble before she picked up on it. 'Er . . . yes. Are you all right, Celia?'

'Yes, I'm fine. I can only talk for a minute.' She sounded indistinct and breathless and her words were running into each other with haste. 'Listen. Taff was here last night. He came in to pick me up and take me back to the garden centre.'

'Did he hit you again?' Buchanan had to ask.

'No . . . well . . . never mind that, just listen. When we went out to the car Sharon was with us. He told me to get in the car and then stood talking to Sharon for a minute.'

She stopped suddenly and then went on in a louder voice, 'Yes, it hurts when I drink something hot or very cold, so if you could fit me in quite soon I'd be really grateful.'

Buchanan got the picture and waited patiently till she felt safe enough to say, 'Sorry, someone was passing. Anyway, I didn't get in the car. He had parked round at the side so I waited behind the hedge and I heard him say to Sharon something like 'Don't you worry about that. He may think he's got me over a barrel but I've dealt with his kind before and I can do it again.' I couldn't make out what he was talking about but I think someone is trying to damage his business. Sharon said something about trouble at the garden centre the other night and she seemed afraid that the same would happen here at our place.'

'She doesn't need to be,' Buchanan said. 'I know about that incident and I don't think you'll have any trouble from the same source.'

'Right.' Celia paused, her breath fluttering in Buchanan's ear. 'But I think Taff's really angry about what's happening. I couldn't make out what he was saying most of the time but I could tell from his tone of voice, y'know? And then, a bit later, I heard him say, 'If the worst comes to the worst I'll send the boys over to Ratho and sort him out for good.' He sounded really vicious, William, y'know? Like he was talking about having the guy killed, or something. I had to get in the car then, in case he caught me listening. I know it's not much but I thought you'd want me to let you know.'

Buchanan was astonished at her bravery. He said, 'Celia, you're a star. This is valuable information. I'll check up on it right away and with a bit of luck it might give me some evidence I can take to the police. I want you out of that hellhole as soon as possible.'

'Oh, William . . . ' Her voice wobbled and failed, then she hauled in a gusty breath and went on, 'Also I'm sure they had a big job on last night. Somebody phoned Taff about three o'clock in the morning to tell him it had gone off okay. I don't know what it was but — '

'That's okay, Celia. I know what it was, but it's good to have it confirmed that Taff was involved. If that's all you have to tell me just now you'd better get off the phone.'

'Yes,' she said and added in a whisper, 'Thank you for caring, William.'

Buchanan put the phone down and sat staring at it for a moment. It was barely twenty past eleven. He had the choice of going back to the office and biting his knuckles for two hours till Fizz phoned in or zapping over to Ratho and looking for a place that might be the headquarters of Taff's rival gang. No contest, really.

Ratho was one of those neighbourhoods that was neither one thing nor the other. It had once been a small rural community on the edge of the city but, first, new residential development had robbed it of much of its character and then old farm buildings had been taken over by haulage and demolition firms, which caused a bit of an eyesore.

Buchanan drove around the industrial sites but found them unmanned and used exclusively for storage. On the edge of the community, however, he found a motor spares yard which was not only operational but apparently required a high density of staff. In a matter of minutes he counted eleven workers, brawny types in hard hats and gauntlets, plus an indeterminate number whose presence he suspected in a series of Portacabins parked among piles of rusting vehicles.

There was no angle from which he could eyeball the place without being seen but he parked the car as inconspicuously as he could and spread a road map over the steering wheel in the hope he might be taken for a tourist who had lost his way. The binoculars were still lying on the back seat so he got them focused on the closest batch of workers

358

and started looking for a familiar face. It wasn't an entirely relaxing operation, since one could never be certain that someone in one of those Portacabins wasn't focusing in on him, and the realisation that Fizz might currently be taking the same sort of risk didn't help any.

With that thought nagging him, he couldn't settle to the surveillance. He wanted to be at the office in case she phoned in — admit it, he wanted to be *with* her — but at the same time, he knew he was over-reacting. Fizz was no fool and she was no longer the tearaway she'd been when they first met. She'd be fine.

He stuck it for only ten minutes and was ready to pack in when, astoundingly, a familiar face appeared behind the wheel of a dumper truck. Beyond any shadow of doubt, it was one of the pseudo-coppers he had spoken to after Fizz had rescued McKenzie from a watery grave.

The discovery was a real shot in the arm. Buchanan had been sure, the minute he saw the yard, that this was the place he was looking for, but now he had evidence to prove it. This was the bunch who had been operating around Inverness but clearly they had more than one iron in the fire and, if Taff had his facts right, this yard was where the head honcho was to be found.

None of which, he reflected as he headed back to the city centre, brought him one step nearer to getting McKenzie and Hector off the hook. Simply drawing the attention of the CID to the two gangs was extremely unlikely to have the desired effect. Operations of such large caliber seldom went entirely unsuspected by the authorities and such information as Buchanan was able to give them at this point would merely be added to the dossier. Proof was what was needed: proof that would make the police get their fingers out, proof that would clear McKenzie of deliberate involvement and protect him from further threat.

He stopped at the first telephone box he came to and phoned the office. It was only twenty past twelve and there was no reason why he should expect to hear anything of Fizz for another half hour at least but he was tense with hope as he waited to be put through to Beatrice.

'Buchanan here, Beatrice. Have you heard from Fizz?'

'Not yet, Mr Buchanan, no,' she said, adopting the motherly tone she used when she suspected he was about to hit the panic button. 'I don't really expect to hear from her till one o'clock at the earliest. She said — '

'Yes, I know. I just wondered if she had

phoned. No joy from Hector either, I suppose?'

'I'm afraid not.'

Buchanan looked at his watch. Three quarters of an hour before he could hope to see or hear from Fizz. Three quarters of an hour before he had to meet Kerry. What the hell. He wouldn't enjoy his lunch anyway.

'Right, Beatrice. I'm coming in to the office. See you in about ten minutes.'

He hung up and dialled Kerry's number but there was no reply. Obviously, she and her father had left early for the meeting and it was unlikely that they would already have arrived at the hotel. All he could do was leave a message for them at the reception desk and, frankly, his excuses sounded a little lame, even to his own ears. So, Fizz had gone to look for Hector? Yes? So? And that was his only reason for standing her up?

There were other questions that followed on from that but they were questions Buchanan preferred not to dwell on. If Kerry couldn't understand a guy's natural concern for his staff, well that was just too bad. When he thought about it, he wasn't all that bothered one way or another. Kerry might be fantastic to look at but she was never going to mean anything to him. The magic simply wasn't there.

Beatrice made it obvious from the minute he rushed into the office that she knew he was in a fragile state. This was profoundly irritating because Buchanan felt he hid it very well. He abhorred being spoken to in a calm voice, being offered a nice cup of tea instead of his customary coffee, and having to listen to progress reports which were nothing but blatant attempts to take his mind off the passage of time. Having to pretend — without even the comfort of drumming his fingers on the desk — that he was listening to her verbal sedation only made matters worse.

All too soon it became obvious that Fizz was not going to call. Buchanan gave it till nearly quarter past one, just to prove to himself and Beatrice that he could do it, and then said,

'She told you she'd keep you informed of what was happening, right Beatrice? Okay. She's now fifteen minutes overdue and she hasn't phoned so I'll have to do something about it. Just give me a few minutes to make a phone call and I'll let you know my plans.'

Beatrice had nothing bright and optimistic left to say. She shut her mouth like a trap and left the room with her cardigan doubled tight across her chest, always a sign that she was worried.

Now that he had peace to think, Buchanan

took a minute to review his options. It was about fifty-five seconds longer than he needed. Barging in to the garden centre swinging a fence stob had worked once — miraculously — but it wouldn't work again. For one thing, there was no certainty that Fizz was there and, for that reason, even a police raid might have the wrong effect. The last thing one wanted was to put her in a hostage position. Furthermore, although this consideration now mattered scarcely at all, involving the police would drop McKenzie straight into the shit.

The problem was that whatever course he decided on, whatever action he set in motion, he had to bear in mind that both Fizz and Hector could swan into the office at any moment, bright-eyed and bushy-tailed and asking what all the fuss was about.

In a situation like this, Fizz's advice was invariably: do *something* even if it's anything. It wasn't often that a sane man would listen to her advice on any subject whatsoever but it happened, in this one instance, to accord well with his own feelings re the matter in hand.

He pulled the phone towards him and dialled the number of police headquarters. Ian Fleming would tell him to go to hell, he knew that for sure, but every man had his price and Buchanan didn't care what it was.

'DCI Fleming.'

'Ian? Tam Buchanan.'

'Tam? What do you want? No — don't answer that. I don't want to know.'

'I've got to talk to you,' Buchanan said tersely. 'It's an emergency.'

'Not another emergency! For chrissake, life's just one long emergency for you. Do me a favour and take your emergencies to somebody else for a change.'

'Listen, Ian. I wouldn't hit on you again if it weren't really serious. I know you came off rather badly last time and I know I promised I'd never ask another favour of you but I don't know where else to turn. Fizz is in trouble — '

'You can stop right there, Tam.' Fleming's voice cracked like a bullwhip. 'That woman is poison ivy. If I want to flush my career down the jaxie I can do it without Fizz's help. If she's involved — even peripherally — you can count me out.'

Buchanan closed his eyes and breathed deeply. 'I'm coming round to see you right now, Ian,' he said. 'You've got to help me. I need what information you can lay your hands on about two organisations operating around the Edinburgh area. They're into illegal immigration, prostitution, and I don't know what else. One is based out at Ratho and the other at a garden centre near Bo'ness.'

That produced a short silence, then Fleming said,

'You know that's not my scene any more. I don't — '

'You can get the information I need, right? So I'll see you in twenty minutes.'

Buchanan hung up and pushed back his chair.

No more Mr Nice Guy.

20

In the space of a single heartbeat several things became clear to Fizz. The first thing was that McKenzie was not McKenzie but someone she'd never seen before in her life; the second thing was that the two other strangers were acting like bodyguards; and the sixteen or so other things added up to the fact that this was a flight-or-flannel situation.

Flight would not have been her first choice since she was wearing the silly shoes forced on her by public opinion which decreed that solicitors do not wear Doc's in the office. However, the sudden lunge forward of the two heavies quickly persuaded her that the other option would require enough flannel to gift-wrap greater London.

She whipped round and fled down the side of the building with her legs threatening to outrun her body and the footfalls of the guards pounding behind her like the echo of her own pulse. The first stretch offered her no problem, being the lawn that circled the lily pond, but as she rounded the front of the building she found herself in a maze of high shelf units filled with bedding plants. The aisles between the units were dotted with browsing customers who stared at her in astonishment as she hurtled past. One big fat guy with a red face stood gawping in her path till she was almost on top of him and bethought himself to budge only when she yelled, 'Move your ass, thicko!'

Beyond the bedding plants was a thicket of fruit trees and for a moment, as she slalomed rapidly through it, she began to hope she could throw off the pursuit. But, in the same second as she registered the silence behind her, the pounding feet caught up with her again, slightly to her right but no further away than they had been. The footfalls held to a slower beat than did her own feet but, given the length of her legs, that wasn't as comforting as it might have been.

She went straight through an ornamental Chinese garden like Hitler through the Sudetenland, sending bamboo furniture flying into a water feature and disfiguring the neatly raked gravel. To her left she spotted a paved area covered with tall stacks of plastic plant pots and swerved into it with her legs pumping like steel pistons. The towers of pots were not dense enough to hide her but they were light enough to topple over as she passed, which slowed up the guards and gave her a second to dive, unobserved, into the conifer section.

Once again, the sounds of pursuit faded. She heard a shout from way back among the pots but she didn't pause to listen. If she could gain a two minute respite she could make it to the gates and lose herself in the woods where it would take more than two muscle-bound morons to catch her.

Dodging from tree to tree, she sprinted downhill and came to two long rows of garden sheds and greenhouses that slanted in the right direction. Choosing speed over caution, she high-tailed it down the middle of the centre path, hurdling wheelbarrows and bags of compost, swerving around shopping trolleys, and yelling a warning to everyone in her way. The scene ahead of her looked like a still from a movie, all the extras frozen in attitudes of dismay and alarm.

A third of the way along, the sudden appearance of one of the guards at the far end of the aisle brought her skidding to a halt. She spun round to head the other way but — shit! — the other guard was charging down on her barely twenty feet away. All she had time to do was dive through a two foot gap between two sheds, which brought her out into a propagation area.

A poly-tunnel loomed up ahead of her and she shot in one end and out the other, her progress blocked only momentarily by a long trolley piled high with potted orchids. Already one of the guards was visible through the polythene but she forced herself to brace her back against the door post and use a well-placed foot to heave the trolley and its contents into his path. As she ran out into the full sunlight she heard him go down in a burst of curses and knew she had gained herself the few spare seconds she needed to lose him — and his much slower partner — by doubling back to the sheds.

Okay, she was thinking, let's go, kid, when two fat arms encircled her from behind and she was lifted off her feet against a spongy gut. Frantic thrashing and biting only increased the constriction but did afford her a momentary glimpse of a face she recognised as the guy she'd called Thicko.

A salutory lesson in the advisability of not being nasty to people, even those for whom you had no immediate use.

There seemed, however, to be no reason why she should not be nasty now, so she was very nasty indeed, so nasty, in fact, that she had almost fought her way clear before the guards arrived. One of them had a deeply cut cheek and bits of orchids in his hair, the other was holding his torn trousers closed over his arse and, clearly, neither of them was in a mood to clap hands for Tinkerbell.

'Thank you very much, sir,' wheezed Guard #1, accepting custody of Fizz and twisting her arm up her back in a professional manner. 'Very public spirited of you.'

Thicko had his eyes screwed tight and both hands hanging on to his balls as if he thought they too were trying to escape detention. 'Bloody shoplifters,' he ground out. 'They put the prices up for the rest of us.'

'Too true, sir,' said Guard #2, who was in better shape than his mate but just as short of breath. He picked up a potted orchid that had escaped the devastation and held it out. 'Have this for your trouble.'

Thicko couldn't spare a hand to accept his prize so the guard set it on the ground beside him and, half-nelsoning Fizz's other arm, started trundling her back towards the farmhouse.

'Let's get her to Taff before she causes any more trouble,' Guard #1 ground out through gritted teeth.

Fizz could barely move without dislocating her shoulders but she twisted her head round and shouted,

'Listen — !'

Her idea had been to tell Thicko to phone

the police but Guard #2 dealt her a covert punch in the mouth that stunned her sufficiently to prevent any repeat performance.

By the time they neared the farmhouse Fizz knew what it felt like to be famous: all that was lacking was the flashbulbs. Her chase and subsequent capture had apparently escaped the attention of only a handful of customers and the others lined the route of her parade as though they hadn't seen anything so interesting in years.

Embarrassment was a foreign concept to Fizz. How other people perceived her was not something that kept her awake at night and indeed, on this occasion, she was more than happy to have so many people witness her arrest. It was now well after one o'clock, probably nearly two, and Buchanan would already have been informed that she had reneged on her promise to phone. That meant — if Fizz knew her Buchanan, and she was pretty sure she did — that he would currently be going apeshit and phoning everybody from the Boy Scouts to the United Nations. He knew where she was, and she now had a couple of dozen witnesses to prove it, so this Taff would have to be mad to mistreat her any further . . . wouldn't he?

Inside the back door of the house there was

a flight of stairs that rose sharply from a cramped little hallway and she was half pushed, half carried up these to a space that didn't look like any farmhouse she'd ever seen.

Most of the interior walls had been removed to create a vast living area with windows on three walls and an open doorway on the fourth. Beyond the doorway Fizz could see a passageway and a further doorway, this one also ajar and showing a patch of turquoise blue tiles beyond. From behind this second door a voice inquired,

'What took you so long?'

Her two captors looked at each other and licked their lips in a preparatory sort of way but neither of them spoke immediately so Fizz said,

'They had a little trouble keeping up.'

Guard #2 rewarded her with a spiteful little jerk that made her shoulder scream but she wouldn't give him the satisfaction of knowing he'd hurt her and added, 'Wouldn't do either of them any harm to lose a few stone.'

She was tensed to resist another jerk but as she finished speaking the pseudo-McKenzie appeared in the open doorway, drying his hands on a towel. He had removed his jacket and tie and his hair was ruffled, making him, from some angles at least, look even more like

McKenzie. His head was every bit as round, his frame and the way he carried himself were virtually identical, even the shape and arrangement of his features were not all that dissimilar. It was mainly his eyes that made it easy to tell them apart. Taff's were not the innocent orbs that McKenzie sported, they were as cold and glittering as the nameplate on a coffin.

He moved slowly into the room, folding down his shirt cuffs over a familiar-looking tatoo, and regarding Fizz with a brooding expression that boded her no good.

'Well,' he said, in a silky Home Counties accent, 'aren't you the lippy little bitch? We'll have to teach you to speak when you're spoken to, I think.'

'That wouldn't be very clever,' Fizz told him, hoping her expression looked as perky as she was trying to make it. 'My colleagues know where I am and plenty of people saw me come in here. Believe me, you don't want anything nasty to happen to me.'

He tipped his head back and laughed with convincing amusement. 'She's a real cutie-pie, isn't she lads? Park her over there.'

Fizz was hoisted across the room and catapulted onto a fancy sofa which bounced her about a bit before accepting her weight. She was scared, sure, but she'd been more scared, and she knew better than to let a bully spot any sign of weakness. This was a guy who got his jollies by terrorising women but, by hell, he'd have to work hard for it with this cookie!

Taff picked up an Omega watch and slipped it on, while his eyes swung from Fizz to the two goons and back again in a contemplation that appeared to leave him in a sort of furious amazement. The guards watched him warily, following his thoughts as easily as did Fizz, and both of them twitched as he said,

'I don't believe this. Ten minutes alone with Miss Muffet here and you come back like you've crossed the Wolfman of Krakow. What are you? Ballet dancers?'

Guard #2 parted his lips to say something but the blast of savage violence beamed at him from his boss made him reconsider. Taff held his towel out to one side, level with his shoulder, and Guard #1 moved forward hastily to take it from him and return it to the bathroom.

'Get yourselves cleaned up,' he spat at them. 'And make sure there's somebody on the door. I don't want any interruptions.'

Fizz made sure they both caught her sympathetic smile as they departed, and then curled her muddy shoes up onto the couch and composed herself to look as relaxed as she could.

'Nice place you've got here,' she remarked. 'What is it? A pied à terre or a little nest you wouldn't like your wife to know about?'

Taff smiled: not in amusement but with the voracity of a gourmet choosing from an excellent menu. He pulled an armchair closer to the couch and sat down, stretching out long narrow legs so like McKenzie's it wasn't true.

He said, 'Okay, missy. You're very amusing but that's enough of the cheeky chat. If you're not scared shitless, I promise you — you ought to be, so just shut your pretty little face and keep it shut unless you're answering my questions. Do you understand me?'

'Oh, sure, I understand you.' Fizz nodded obligingly. 'But I have to tell you, I think you're labouring under a misconception.'

'Yes? What misconception's that?'

'You think you've got me over a barrel when, in fact, it's you who's in deep shit. Plenty of people saw me dragged in here and if I don't come out again, radiant in health and spirit, there will be questions asked.'

'Wrong,' said Taff, the single word reverberating like the toll of a funeral bell. 'They saw you come in and they'll see you go out but they won't see you committing

375

suicide, later today, rather than face prosecution. Sad occurrences like that happen all the time, I'm afraid, but we honest traders can't be held responsible for the actions of drug addicts who steal to feed their habit, can we?'

Fizz felt sick. She kept her chin up and her eyes level but an icy little rush of panic ran through her veins. Buchanan knew where she was but, as far as Taff was concerned, so did a lot of people so the knowledge wasn't going to stay his hand. She could claim that the police would be here at any minute but that would only result in getting her whisked off to some other location where the hope of rescue would be even less likely.

As far as she could determine, her only option was to play for time and hope like hell that the opportunity to escape would present itself before things got too hairy. There was only one possible way out of the flat, other than the downstairs door which Taff had told his goons to cover, and that was the tall window behind her. It was firmly closed and besides, it was indisputably too high to drop from without breaking something, but if push came to shove it could be the lesser of two evils.

'However,' Taff was lying blandly, 'if I get your full cooperation I see no reason why you shouldn't walk out of here on your own feet.'

'Oh sure,' said Fizz, and again he pretended to smile.

'Your name is?'

'My own affair.'

The smile vanished. 'As you please. It's of no interest to me anyway. What I'd really like to know — what you'll tell me before you leave — is what you know about Scott McKenzie.'

Fizz sighed and looked out of the window as though she couldn't see the point of the question. 'McKenzie? What's to know about McKenzie? He's a boring old fart who lives down our road. Drinks like a fish. Looks a bit like you. So what?'

Taff's hand shot out and made a grab for her wrist but she was too fast for him and he missed, which made his face go red.

'Don't get me rattled, you little brat, or I'll take the back of my hand to you and push that cute little button nose out the back of your head. You got that? Now what do you know about McKenzie?'

'I just told you.'

'So why did you take a runner?' he snarled. 'Remembered a previous engagement, did you?'

'Of course I ran — who wouldn't with those two ugly goons coming at me like — '

Taff moved like a cobra, showing more

respect for the speed of her reactions this time, and walloped her across the side of the head, knocking her over and making her bite her already swollen lip.

'Okay now. Let's start again. What d'you know about McKenzie?'

Fizz took her time about sitting up and made sure she got plenty of blood on his silk cushions before she did so.

'Well,' she said, 'since you ask me so nicely: I know somebody wants him dead. I don't know who and I don't know why — though, now that I've seen you I could probably make a damn good guess.'

'Go ahead. Guess.' Taff smiled happily, leaning back in his chair.

'As to *who* wants him dead,' Fizz said slowly, dabbing at her lips to draw out every micro-second as long as she could stretch it, 'I reckon it's not you. To a crook in your position a double — even an almost-double like McKenzie — would be worth his weight in gold. A ready-made alibi for whatever you might choose to get up to for the rest of your criminal life. A handy corpse — suitably mutilated, of course — to leave behind should you wish to close your CID file for good. No, you'd want him alive and on ice, wouldn't you? So it would have to be the other lot who are trying to eliminate him.'

Taff lifted his head, his eyes hard and infinitely depressing. 'What other lot?'

'You know — the lot who set up the building society robbery, shot the security guard, and framed you for both jobs. Nice one, eh? The police think they've got you on the security footage. They've certainly got Hector filmed — even if they don't have his corpse, which must have been what was intended — and they know him for one of your little helpers, so it's an open and shut case. You're up to your neck in it, possum.'

'I'll let my lawyer worry about that,' Taff muttered. 'It's an obvious frame-up.'

'That's right, always look on the bright side of life,' Fizz nodded, smiling with her eyes because her lips demurred. 'However, I doubt very much if the police will mind whether its a frame-up or not. I'll bet they've had their eye on you for years and are just waiting for an excuse to put you away for good.'

Taff thought — quite visibly — about clouting her again and then changed his mind about it, probably saving that pleasure for later. He got up and walked across the room to a cocktail cabinet and poured himself a large whisky. Fizz wasn't offered one but it would probably have stung anyway.

'McKenzie was removed from my custody last Monday evening,' he said in his silky accent. 'Who was responsible for that?'

Fizz dabbed her lips as though absorbed by the task but watched his reaction carefully as she said, 'Didn't Hector tell you about that?'

'Hector? Ah, yes, you mentioned a Hector earlier. One of my little helpers, you called him.' He resumed his seat and fed himself a gulp of whisky. 'Not someone I know, I'm afraid. Possibly a junior employee. That's all taken care of by the recruitment and training department.'

'Oh you must remember Hector,' Fizz insisted.

'Must I? Why?'

'He's the guy your goons discovered camping out in his car this morning. The one they duffed up over there in the culvert, right?'

A faint shimmer of amusement passed across his face. 'Oh, *that* Hector.'

'Right. Hector McSween.' Fizz held his eye. 'He's no harm to you, you know. He's just trying to find out whether it's you or the other bunch who're trying to kill him. He must realise by now that his only function in the robbery was as a corpse to be left behind to incriminate you, so there's no need for you to hold him.'

'Thank you for explaining that to me.' He ducked his head insultingly. 'But I'm waiting for an answer to my question. Who got McKenzie away last Monday night?'

'As far as I know it was the other bunch. The guys who are trying to frame you.'

Taff sat glaring at her for a minute and then started to go red in the face again. A distended vein bisected his forehead and a pulse began to beat visibly under the skin of his temples. 'Don't give me that shit. Somebody helped that ugly little runt to get McKenzie out the window. You'd better tell me fucking fast who it was and where they took him.'

Fizz knew a blow was coming and she got ready for it as she said, 'All I know is what Hector told me. As far as I'm con — '

He didn't strike out at her, he threw the glass of whisky which caught her on the cheekbone, and dived after it grabbing her by the arms and lifting her bodily into the air till her eyes were level with his. It wasn't just painful, it was bloody scary.

'I fucking warned you, you c — '

A buzzer sounded, loud and sudden, behind him making him pause with his head drawn back ready to butt her. Cursing, he threw her back on the sofa and strode across to shout down the stairwell.

'Yes, what?'

He was answered by a rumble of words

which the buzzing in Fizz's head made indistinct.

'Okay. Bring him up.'

Shit, Fizz thought bitterly. What next? She steeled herself for an unpleasant surprise, maybe a bloody and beaten Hector, maybe another psychopathic bully. It was way too early to be optimistic about the arrival of reinforcements so she was completely stunned and disoriented when Buchanan walked into the room, bracketed by guards #1 and #2.

A huge surge of mixed emotions surged through her: alarm, of course, at the sight of him there, in the same situation as herself, but also an overriding gladness to have him with her.

It became immediately clear, however, that, whatever had brought him here, he was not a victim. From the second he stepped into the room the atmosphere changed; Taff ceased to dominate, the two bodyguards became tense and uneasy. Still in his good suit, with his binoculars slung round his neck, Buchanan looked totally relaxed and in charge.

'You okay, Fizz?' he said, stepping past Taff without glancing at him and leaning over her for a closer look.

Fizz laid the tip of one finger to her temple. 'A slight headache. Must be the weather.'

His eyes had never looked so blue or so full of tenderness. 'Don't worry. You'll be out of here in no time.'

He straightened and turned to look at Taff. 'Mr Powell? I'm Tam Buchanan. Forgive me if I don't shake hands.'

Taff took his time looking him over, saying nothing but holding himself tight as a bow string, his expression a strange cross between caution and smugness. He flicked a glance along his shoulder at the two goons but didn't tell them to leave.

Buchanan waited a moment for his reply and then said impatiently, 'I believe I have something you want.'

'Really?' said Taff, still intent, still moving nothing but his lips. 'Now what could that be, I wonder.'

'Scott McKenzie.'

'I see. Well, well. And I, apparently, have something you want. Correct?'

'You have two things I want, Mr Powell. I want Hector McSween and I want this young lady here.'

'Two for the price of one, eh?'

'One in good condition,' said Buchanan in a steely voice Fizz had never heard from him before, 'for two who are, no doubt, somewhat the worse for wear.'

Fizz couldn't believe she was interpreting

this conversation correctly. Either Taff's blows had addled her brain or Buchanan — Buchanan, of all people — was offering to swop McKenzie for herself and Hector.

She said, 'You can't do this, Buchanan!'

His head snapped round. 'You bet I can!' he said venomously, shocking her into silence. 'The sooner I get shot of that obnoxious old cretin the better I'll like it. He's been nothing but trouble since the word go!'

Taff moved stiffly back to his seat but didn't sit down, just stood beside it with his fingers rub-rubbing the back.

'And what if I'm not interested in taking him off your hands, Mr Buchanan?'

Buchanan looked a little bored. 'I don't think that's an eventuality we need waste time in discussing, do you? Of course you're interested. Without producing McKenzie, how are you going to prove your non-involvement in the murder and robbery with violence charges you're currently dodging? If you don't need McKenzie, why have you spent all week trying to get your hands on him?'

Fizz couldn't get her head round the composure with which this conversation was being conducted. It was bogus composure, of course. You could feel Taff's tension singing in the air like static electricity but Buchanan's

384

calm assurance was clearly disconcerting him and keeping a lid on his temper. There was a short silence, then Taff said,

'Granted that McKenzie may prove to be of some value to me, perhaps you'll explain to me why I should buy him from you at the price of parting with two equally valuable witnesses.'

'Because that's the only way you're going to get him,' said this new Buchanan in a voice that would have cut glass.

Taff's eyes darted, for a split second, towards his two heavies who were standing at the head of the staircase with their hands clasped in front of them as though they were waiting for a goal kick. It was the tiniest of eye movements but, to Fizz's mind, it marked him as a coward just like every other bully she'd ever come across. She watched him swagger across the room, ostensibly to look out the window, a movement which placed the two guards between himself and Buchanan.

He motioned at Guard #2 to pour him a drink and, with a gesture, extended an invitation to Buchanan to join him. It was refused. Buchanan turned his back on him, walked over to the window behind the couch and stared down, for a moment, at the model gardens. Then, as Taff waited for his whisky, he moved round and sat down on the couch beside Fizz. He put his arm round her shoulders and looked closely at her face.

'Don't start,' she said.

He pressed his lips together over the recriminations and laments but he couldn't hide the sudden reddening of his eyes. Fizz hated it when he did that because it always made her feel so bloody sorry for herself that she wanted to blubber all over him and blubbering was something she positively did not do. Not ever. Once you started down that road there was no telling where it would end.

She pushed him away. 'I can't believe you just did that,' she said. 'You promised Marianne you'd look after McKenzie.'

'Not for the rest of his life,' Buchanan said, looking at her with an odd fixedness. 'McKenzie knows the score. Taff can protect him from the Inverness bunch better than I ever could and you can be sure he'll take very good care of him. He's a valuable asset.'

He was lying, of course, as she would have realised right away had she been thinking rationally. There was no way Buchanan would use McKenzie as currency, which meant that he was going to try to get her away from Taff by some other means. The thought was not one that brought her a great deal of reassurance.

'I'll say this for you, Mr Buchanan,' Taff said. 'You've got balls. Either that or you're too thick to appreciate the trouble you're in. What makes you think I'd have any difficulty in making you tell me where McKenzie is? Always assuming that you actually know his whereabouts.'

Buchanan got up and loitered across the room towards him. If he was faking his self-confidence he was doing it hellish well.

'Oh, I know his whereabouts, Mr Powell. I won't ask you to take my word about that.' He handed Taff his binoculars. 'Take a look across the car park. See the white Porsche just beside the entrance?'

Taff twiddled the focus ring impatiently for a few seconds, opened the window to get a clearer view, then froze in an attitude of close attention. When he turned round he was smiling.

'A sight to gladden the heart, Mr Buchanan,' he crooned, his confidence burgeoning again like the desert after a rain shower. 'I'm most grateful to you for delivering him to me.'

Buchanan gestured to him to hang on to the binoculars. 'Don't count your chickens. He's not delivered to you yet. Observe the chap in the driving seat. If I don't walk out of here within another five minutes — clearly unescorted and accompanied by both Hector and Fizz — he will deliver McKenzie to your friends out at Ratho.'

Ratho? Fizz shot an accusing glare at Buchanan, a glare that demanded: *Ratho? Where the hell does Ratho come in? Have you been hiding things from me, you bastard?*

But he wasn't looking her way as he said, 'The Ratho bunch obviously believe that you still have McKenzie in your custody, you know. Otherwise they'd have told the CID where to find you. So let's not play silly buggers, Mr Powell. McKenzie is your only safeguard against spending the rest of your life in jail.'

Taff's composure fell from him like a stripper's bra. His face became so contorted that he looked barely human. Spinning around to swing an arm at the bodyguards he yelled,

'What are you fucking waiting for, you daisies? See if you can do something right for a change! Or are an old man and a biker too much for you to handle? And get rid of this fucker while you're about it.'

'Permanently?' enquired Guard #1.

'Permanently.'

The suddenness with which the situation had deteriorated caught Fizz by surprise. One minute she had been within minutes of freedom and, the next, her deliverer was thrashing in the practiced grip of the two heavies. There was nothing she could do to assist his struggles but, seeing the whole shooting match going fast down the john, she shouted the first thing that came into her head.

'Let him go, you fools! The whole place is surrounded by armed police!'

The uproar subsided instantly and Fizz found herself the focus of four pairs of shocked eyes. Then,

'She's lying,' said Guard #1. 'Baz and me chased all over the place after the bitch. If there'd been anything funny we'd've seen it.'

Fizz lifted bored brows. 'Please yourself.'

There was a short silence while Taff communed with himself and then he jerked his head at Guard #1.

'It's been half an hour since then. You'd better make sure. Take Walsh and Benny and for God's sake don't be all day about it.'

He looked carefully at Fizz as Guard #1 hurried down the stairs. 'You're a lying little bastard. Don't think that crap fools me for a minute. It just makes me look forward all the more to teaching you your manners. You're going to wish — '

Through the open window behind him a

voice blasted into the room, rasping with urgency.

'Boss! The place is fuckin' deserted! Something's — '

The abrupt truncation of the sentence spurred both Taff and Guard #2 to lightning speed. They were at the window on the instant but, just as quickly, Buchanan was at Fizz's side, plucking her from the couch and whisking her around it. She had just time to see that the long window was partly ajar before she was through it and plunging, head first, into space.

21

Buchanan hit the water an instant after Fizz and surfaced with a mouth full of water lilies and his best suit gone for a Burton.

A bullhorn was informing somebody that this was a police raid and that they'd better come out with their hands up if they had any plans for the future, or words to that effect, the details being inaudible to Buchanan under the barrage of choking and imprecation close to his left ear.

'You might at least give a girl a second to hold her nose, dammit!'

'Sorry. Are you okay? Did it hurt?' He pulled her up and held her till she got her balance. Her face was violently discoloured but she was able to deepen her scowl without obvious pain as she spluttered,

'Stop fussing over me. You're like my grannie.'

She fought clear of his grasp and was headed for shore when the pool exploded into a zillion droplets, the shock wave knocking them both off balance. It took Buchanan several seconds to cough up two lungfuls of mud and register what had happened and by that time Taff had staggered to his feet and was getting the hell out of it.

He was a game 'un, no doubt about it. He must have hit something on the way down because blood was streaming from his cheek in a wide, diluted fan that covered his whole jaw. As he lurched from leg to leg through the clinging water lilies, arms thrashing, head thrown back with the effort, he looked like Frankenstein on acid.

Buchanan let him go. He wouldn't get far with half of Lothian and Borders police in the surrounding bushes and gagging to get their hands on him. Fizz, however, was not aware that she had been speaking the truth when she claimed the place was surrounded. She was up and running before Buchanan could stop her, her feet clear of the water at every bound, her injuries — if not her beating — forgotten.

She hit Taff behind the knees like a pocket-sized full back and they went down in a tidal wave that half emptied the pool. Before Buchanan could reach them they were up again, Taff struggling blindly forward to reach the edge of the pool, Fizz determined he was going nowhere. She had one fistful of hair and another of ear, and she was wrenching them apart to such effect that they were liable to come off in her hands.

Buchanan made a grab for her but missed as both combatants plunged again beneath the lilies. The water boiled for a couple of seconds with heaving bodies and when Fizz came up she was clutching a perforated flowerpot full of mud and bits of lily roots. As Taff's torso broke through the foam, the pot connected with his skull with a force that snapped his head back and sank him in a fountain of spray. Without waiting for him to surface Fizz, howling like a banshee, hauled him up again.

'That was for *me*, you pig turd, and this is for Celia!'

Buchanan could have stopped her. Easily. He had plenty of time to see what she was about and her strength was at its last ebb. He could have held her hand with two fingers, but he didn't.

She let him have it, full in the face, with a smack that could have been heard in Inverness, and as he went under, the water clouded with a red haze.

That, as far as Buchanan was concerned, was enough. He grabbed Fizz around the waist and lifted her bodily away from the sunken Taff.

'Stop it, Fizz! You've done enough! You don't want to kill the guy.'

Apparently she did, and had a bunch of

coppers in flak jackets not arrived at that moment she'd have had a damn good try. It was only the shock of seeing them there — after herself predicting their arrival — that overcame her resistance.

'This way, miss, fast as you like.'

Somebody took the back of Fizz's jacket in one hand and Buchanan's sleeve in the other and precipitated them, at a run, across the lawn to the back of the farmhouse.

There were coppers all around the courtyard, some carrying weapons, some jabbering into radios, some packing hand-cuffed heavies into a police van.

'My God! It *is* a police raid!' Fizz, on the point of being hustled into a minibus, dug her heels in and craned to see over her shoulder. 'What's going on?'

'You'll hear all about it later, miss,' said the attendant copper and, without bothering to argue with her, picked her up like a child and popped her into the bus. Buchanan dived in behind her, intent only on getting her away before she got into any more trouble.

'Is there . . . ' He spat out a bit of leaf and indicated Fizz's wet clothes. 'Is there a couple of blankets? A towel?'

'Oh . . . right sir.' The copper's eyes scanned the pool of water around their feet. 'I'll see what I can find.'

He went off to pass the buck to a WPC and Buchanan sat down on the step to let the water drain from his Boss suit. By God, somebody was going to cough up for a new one. The CID owed him that at the very least for giving them the goods on two of their Ten Most Wanted.

'There he goes,' said Fizz, coming to sit beside him, the better to see Taff being led round the corner of the building. She stood up to give him a cheery wave, with two fingers. 'I'll tell you this, amigo, it was worth all the hassle just to get a swing at that bastard. If anyone deserved to be kicked a new asshole, that's the chappie.'

Buchanan wasn't going to disagree with her. Taff looked a mess, and was obviously in great pain from what looked like a broken nose, but the sight caused Buchanan no distress whatsoever. Profound depression, yes; angst, no.

Fizz wasn't slow to note his reaction.

'What's wrong?'

'Huh? Nothing.'

'So what are you looking so down in the mouth about? Look at me when I'm talking to you. We're not in trouble are we?'

Buchanan tried to lighten up. 'No, no. We're flavour of the month. It's just . . . oh, reaction, I suppose.'

'Reaction? Don't make me laugh, Buchanan, I've got sore lips.'

'It's been a long day.'

Her eyes bored into his. There was no chance she was going to let up. 'What the hell is wrong with you? Aren't you glad that streak of snot got his comeuppance?'

'Glad?' Buchanan snapped, driven into a corner by her nag, nag, nagging. 'Of course I'm bloody glad. I wanted him mutilated — castrated — just as much as you did! But I stood by and let *you* do it, didn't I? Didn't even have the bottle to — Oh, *bugger*!'

Her head went back and, sore lips or not, she laughed till her face was red. Buchanan clenched his teeth and tried to ignore her, sinking deeper into his shame and misery.

'Buchanan,' she said finally, amidst a series of gradually fading gasps like a spin drier slowing down, 'you are something else, you really are. Age cannot wither you, muchacho, nor custom fade your infinite variety. Oh, boy!'

She went off again into another fit of the giggles, then noticed that Buchanan was not amused and sobered up.

'Listen,' she said, laying an arm across his shoulders. 'It takes all kinds to make a world and a lot of people — *most* people — would say that you're right and I'm wrong. We're different, that's all, and maybe if I had your imagination I'd throw up at the thought of what I just did. Right now, I believe that if you try to reason with animals they'll just nod and nod and laugh behind their hand but thank God for squeamish types like you. In my book, you don't have to be violent to be a hero.'

Buchanan stared at her face in utter stupefaction. Fizz simply did not say things like that. It was a revelation to discover that she could even *think* like that. And, what was that about a hero? Was she implying —

'There y'go, folks. That's the best we could do.'

A PCW swam into focus, her arms draped with clothing. She leaned past them and tossed it onto the seats behind them. 'There's bin bags full of the stuff down in the basement. Looks like they were taking good care to make their customers blend in as soon as they arrived.'

'And Ratho?' Buchanan asked quickly as she turned away. 'Any word yet about how that went?'

'Not yet.' She smiled, a hint of excitement breaking through the professional coolness. 'But if it went half as well as this operation we'll have enough to put both firms out of business. The immigrants who were waiting to be dispersed from the Manchester base have been taken into custody so we have all the proof we need.'

Fizz halted her on the turn again.

'What about Hector? Is he okay?'

'He's fine. Gone on ahead to headquarters. You'll see him when you get there.'

Buchanan needed time to think. He was in no particular hurry to see Hector, or indeed, anyone else, least of all the pack of coppers who filled up the van for the return trip to the city centre. Fizz made the best of her time, ingratiating herself to such an extent that, by the time they arrived at HQ, every one of them was convinced he had seen Taff break his nose on the edge of the pool as he dived in. She looked like a little Victorian ragamuffin in her bare feet and too-large jacket so it was no strain on her to wind them around her finger.

The cache of clothing had provided Buchanan with a Fair Isle sweater, apparently knitted for an orang-outan, and a pair of rather short cords with a decided flare which was scarcely the fashion statement he'd have chosen to make, especially when he saw the audience awaiting their arrival.

Kerry and her father detached themselves from the police escort which was hustling them towards the lift and made a rush for

Buchanan but Ian Fleming was waiting to grab him by the elbow and draw him aside.

'It went as planned, then, Tam?'

Buchanan shrugged. 'Up to the point where Fizz announced that the place was surrounded by coppers, yes.'

'She *what*? How did she — ?'

'She didn't know, she just said it.' Buchanan flapped a cuff. 'Never mind. I'll clue you in later. And, listen mate, thanks for getting them to go to red alert like that. It was brilliant. That's one I owe you.'

'More than one, I reckon, but who's counting?' Fleming slapped him on the shoulder and grinned. 'It didn't take much persuading to make them get their fingers out, I can tell you. God knows we've been trying to get the goods on those two firms for long enough. It hasn't done me any harm, either, being involved in the final showdown. The boss is over the moon. The least you can expect is a get-out-of-jail-free card — something Fizz will be needing one of those days, I don't doubt.'

'Yeah, well,' Buchanan nodded, aware that a copper was hanging about, waiting to escort him to wherever it was they wanted him to be. 'I'll talk to you later, Ian. We'll have a beer.'

'Roger.'

As he made his escape, Buchanan found his elbow caught in a firm grip and Kerry ducked round to face him.

'Oh, Tam! I'm so relieved to see you back here in one piece!' She moved in fast and stood on tiptoe to press a kiss on his cheek. 'It's all so unbelievably exciting! The policewoman told me they've arrested ever so many people from a place at Ratho — some of them very high on the 'Wanted List' — and it's all down to you and Fizz.'

'Well, hardly — '

'And it's just such a relief to know that Daddy's off the hook altogether. I just can't begin to tell you how grateful I am — '

'No, please, Kerry — '

'But, yes! You've got to let me thank you! I've never seen anything so brave! To walk into — '

Buchanan laughed uncomfortably and waved his hands to stem the rush of words. 'Stop! Stop, Kerry! It wasn't all that heroic. I had half the Lothian and Borders police force at my back. Anyway, I have to go now. They're waiting for me upstairs.'

She clung on to his arm, hugging it close to a soft curve of breast. 'But I want to show my gratitude, Tam. We owe you so much, Daddy and I. You know, it scared the life out of him — just seeing how

400

vulnerable he is when he's been drinking — and I really do think he may consent to seek help now. That would be a dream come true — not just for me but for all the family — and we have you to thank for it.'

'Well, I don't know about that — '

'But, of course we do! How could Daddy have even thought about kicking his habit with all that worry hanging over him? He feels born again! I can't begin to tell you how grateful I am. Promise me you'll come over for dinner really soon.'

Twenty-four hours ago Buchanan would have loved this. The mere possibility of cornering Kerry for an hour or two would have made his day, never mind having her twist his arm, staring longingly into his eyes, and invading his personal space with such determination. Where had it all gone: all that excitement and anticipation — all that sexual buzz?

He said, 'That would be nice, Kerry. Let's check with Fizz and arrange something soon.'

Her smile stayed firmly in place but she fell away from him and let him follow the bobby to the lift.

And there was Fizz, leaning against the wall beside the lift doors, watching him closely with her one good eye.

'Well, my-oh-my!' she said brightly. 'Isn't

life full of surprises? That, I take it, was the invisible Kerry?'

'Uh-huh,' Buchanan returned, aware of a certain coolness. He thought of querying the 'invisible' but held his tongue. In situations such as this the less one said, the better.

'I don't know why,' Fizz remarked, 'but I had pictured her older. Considerably older. I wonder what gave me that idea.'

Buchanan murmured something non-committal.

'And dishy too,' went on Fizz at her most relentless. 'Tall, leggy, elegant, and from where I'm standing, hot to trot. Right? You're on to a good thing there, compadre.'

He followed Kerry's retreating figure with his eyes and muttered, 'Not my type.'

Fizz sniggered rudely, but Buchanan had a horrible feeling it was true. He had a horrible feeling that his type was small, cherub-faced and virtually intolerable.

And that was a notion that would make any sane man wake screaming in the night.